SHADOWS
IN THE
WOODS

EVI JAMES

ISBN: 979-8-9911988-3-7 (Paperback)

ISBN: 979-8-9911988-2-0 (e-book)

Library of Congress Control Number: 2025905598

Cover Art by Miblart

Editing by Mandi Andrejka, Inky Pen Editorial Services

Visit www.evijamesauthor.com for more information.

AUTHOR'S NOTE

Shadows in the Woods contains adult themes that may be difficult for some readers.

Please read the content warnings on this website for more information.

www.evijamesauthor.com

To those who are chronically curious.
May you never stop exploring.

1

EVERETT

I HAD FAILED HER—FAILED MY MATE.

I had failed to protect her from my father.

The one promise male shifters made to their mates—to protect—and I'd already broken it.

I'd fallen unconscious after my wolf had taken over and leaped to attack the True Alpha, my father, but it hadn't been enough. I'd acted too late. I'd left Elise in his hold, at his mercy while I lay in the woods lifeless.

As my vision cleared, all I saw was her—being held upside down, limp in my father's arms while he bled her out. He'd made quick work of it; I hadn't been out for long. He was lethal, with no conscious, draining his son's mate at the slightest allusion of a threat.

He would never hurt anyone again. I'd make sure of it.

I'd felt her anguish through the thread of the mating bond earlier as I'd prepared to leave for the last weekend of the tournament. Tearing through the woods, I'd gotten there just in time to see her friend, Leo, dead in a puddle of blood and my father touching my mate, holding what was *mine*, like she was

"

his. I hadn't fully claimed her as my mate yet, but he knew what she was to me. He would've known it the minute he saw her in our tent during the tournament, her scent all over me from when she'd healed the deep cut on my arm. Hell, Wilder probably told him too—the traitor that he was.

After Wilder had run away, I couldn't control my wolf as we'd looked at Elise. Her face had been red from exertion—tear streaks and snot had covered her face. She'd looked helpless, her eyes hollow.

My father had taunted me, held her in front of me like bait, trying to prove that he was more powerful than me. He'd enjoyed having that control, enjoyed listening to Elise whimper in his grasp. It would be harder for me to attack while he was holding her—yet he knew I'd attack. He knew I'd do anything to rescue my mate from his claws.

At the sight of Elise in trouble, my wolf had taken over. We'd leaped to attack the True Alpha, mouth open, teeth ready to latch onto his side. His free hand had reached over the top of my wolf's head, grabbing onto the scruff of skin along the back of my spine. He threw me—and I could do nothing but helplessly tumble through the air, watching Elise become farther and farther away. It all had gone black the moment my head had hit the tree—the scent of her fear still in my nose.

Now my head was pounding from where it had hit the raised tree root. I pushed the feeling aside and zeroed in on my father and Elise standing next to the giant oak tree. Everything he'd said about the Lifestone and the forest would have to wait. My priority was my mate. Her eyes fluttered closed, unable to focus on anything as the blood left her body. The scent of her fear was palpable in the surrounding air. I snarled. The True Alpha had already written off his son and was busy crooning words against Elise's ear as she slipped away.

I stood up quietly, making sure not to rustle any leaves that would cause him to look in my direction. My wolf came to the forefront of my mind. He was ready to attack. We were ready to protect our mate—this time we wouldn't fail. We couldn't fail. I let him take control, and I shifted back into the large black wolf with golden-yellow eyes.

My wolf was stealthy and clever. Even with giant black paws, he knew how to walk across the forest floor soundlessly. My wolf and I, as an enforcer in my father's pack and the alpha of the Cedar Moon Pack, had honed our skills in the art of hunting, and that was what we were doing—hunting our prey.

Only this time, our prey was my father.

He'd become uncontrollable in the last few decades, letting the power that came with being the True Alpha get to his head. Some of his advisors worried that after my mother died he'd lost his reason. Insanity could happen when one lost their mate. But what he was doing now went beyond just losing his reason.

Many packs feared him. The fear they felt was logical—he had a reputation for taking female wolves from the weaker packs who couldn't fight back. Rumor had it he used those wolves as his private courtesans until he grew tired of them, tossing their abused bodies aside. The women he discarded were shells of their normal selves. Some were returned to their families, while others wandered aimlessly around his pack house like ghosts.

I'd confronted him one evening—once I'd become old enough to realize what he was doing. I'd told him to end his torment of women, told him I knew what he was doing and how wrong it was. He'd laughed at me. I'd then told him my mother would've never approved of his behavior. At the mention of my mother, his eyes had narrowed, his face growing red. We'd both shifted, our wolves battling, destroying his office until Gavrill had intervened—pulling my neck from my father's jaws. I'd known that night my only option was to leave.

My father would never change—his own son couldn't convince him to.

As my four paws stalked closer to my father, I could hear the whispers he fed Elise. "There you go, little wolf."

His words made my stomach roll. *Wolf.* He'd claimed Elise was part wolf. I'd never smelled wolf in her, even when I'd been intimate with her earlier this morning. All the pheromones between us really threw off my senses. Her genetics were something we would have to explore in the future. Right now, my focus was on getting my father away from her. He was still in his human form, holding Elise over the trunk of the tree, draining her blood.

As the True Alpha, he was stronger than me in his wolf form. I'd have to take him down in his human form if I had a chance of defeating him. Crouched down, my wolf dug its back paws into the dirt and raised his haunches, ready to spring forward to attack. My eye line focused on the back of my father. We'd have to jump at him from behind and hope he would drop Elise in surprise. She was already so close to the ground; the fall wouldn't hurt her.

An acorn fell from a tree behind me, making a loud cracking sound as it hit the hard ground. My father's concentration on draining Elise's blood broke, and his head turned around quickly to find my wolf poised to attack.

It had to happen now.

I didn't hold my wolf back as he leaped forward, claws extended and fangs foaming with saliva. The crunch of my father's neck between my wolf's jaws vibrated through my head and echoed across the forest. My wolf's giant black paws held down his shoulders as sharp teeth went to work, shaking his neck and removing his head from his body.

It was almost too easy. His skin and muscle split like putty between my teeth, and his spine cracked like the wishbone from a turkey. Once his head rolled to the ground and his body slumped over unnaturally, I shifted back to my human form.

It was done.

I hadn't been as strong as I was now when I'd confronted him all those years ago. Ending this standoff with *his* neck in *my* jaws had been years in the making—years of me growing stronger—strong enough to defeat him. My only regret was that I hadn't killed him sooner. I could've saved a lot of shifters from a lot of misery. I'd have to carry that guilt on my shoulders for the rest of my life. I hoped his death would bring some comfort to his victims and protect those who'd become targets in the future.

I wiped my forearm across my mouth, quickly trying to remove as much blood from my lips as possible before turning my attention to my mate, lying in a puddle of her own blood beneath the large oak tree that dominated the space. I scrambled over to her and tugged her into my arms.

This time, I'd really screwed up. I should've had one of my pack members tail her the moment my father had noticed her in the tent last weekend. I should've known he'd been up to something.

Hunching down over her, I put my nose between her shoulder and neck. I breathed in deeply, letting her sweet scent fill my nose. Her usual smell of cucumber and melon was now mixed with the tangy smell of iron—of blood. I turned her head to look at the other side of her neck. My father had sliced her open, precisely over the major artery in her neck. Her weak pulse continued to push out small gushes of blood that dripped down into the puddle below her. This wasn't good.

"Lyka! Lyka!" I shouted. "Don't you leave me. I fucking need you, Elise!" My voice sounded foreign, echoing through the woods as I yelled. It didn't take a doctor to tell me she'd lost too much blood. Even her natural medicinal remedies couldn't help her now. Not that I knew how to make any of them. I looked around the forest for an answer. Leo's body lay twenty feet away from us, and my father's decapitated body lay next to me, blood still draining from his neck.

Elise looked awful lying in my arms. Bile rose in the back of my throat as I my eyes darted around her facial features. Her skin was void of her usual pink-dusted cheeks and her rose-colored lips. Small tendrils of hair fell out of her bun and stuck to the sweat on her forehead. I couldn't see her green eyes through her closed eyelids, but I knew she could hear me. She was barely there, barely hanging on.

She didn't have time left.

"Open your eyes. Come on, mate," I urged. "Open those eyes for me."

Her eyelashes fluttered as I shook her body in my arms—trying to do something, anything to get her to wake up. Her arm lifted from the dirt, her hand reaching toward me. Part of me relaxed, just a little. She was still alive.

"You've still got some fight left in you." I traced her cheek with my finger, feeling that her skin was chilled. "Don't waste your energy."

Elise's eyes widened as her pupils contracted, taking in my face.

I looked down at my chest, at the blood splatters that spotted my skin. "Not my blood. My father's."

Elise's hand fell back down to the dirt, her body collapsing further. It was his blood that I'd spilled for her. To save her from certain death by his hands. Now I wasn't sure I'd be able to save her from the injuries she'd sustained. I might've been too late.

If I didn't want her to turn into the third dead body in the woods, I'd have to do something I'd never done before. Something that was frowned upon.

I stroked her cheek, feeling her skin continue to chill beneath my fingertips. "I didn't want to have to do it this way."

No one would be happy with my decision, especially not Elise. Maybe I was being selfish. Maybe it was my natural instincts to save my mate. I'd make it work with Elise. She wouldn't be happy with me at first, but she'd see that it was for the best. We'd be happy together. My lyka would be my luna. Luna to my entire pack. I knew she'd be good at it, a natural.

The fangs in my mouth tensed as I opened my mouth, preparing to use them. This would be the first time I'd used them to pierce something other than wolf flesh. The bite had to be gentle but also deep enough to inflict the change. The saliva that dripped from my fangs would have to get deep into her bloodstream to save her. I'd only heard of a wolf inflicting the change on a human in stories. I didn't know how she'd react if she made it through the transition. My hope was that the supposed small amount of wolf blood she had inside of her would make the transition less painful, less intense.

There wasn't any choice as I watched the blood slow its exit from her body. She didn't have much left. I looked at her face. Her eyes were closed; she looked peaceful. I brushed some hair from her cheeks and kissed her lips softly.

With her head in my hand, I turned it to reveal the side of her neck that was unharmed. My finger trailed her soft skin from the hollow under her earlobe to the spot between her shoulder and collarbone that would soon have my mark.

"This will hurt. I'll try to make it as quick as possible." This wasn't the way I wanted to place my mark upon her skin. I didn't want it to be forced, marking was supposed to be a tender moment between mates. Not to mention, I wasn't sure she was ready. Maybe no one was really ready to be claimed in this way. Soon Elise and I would be bound so tightly, it would pain us to be away from each other. My pain would be hers and hers would be mine.

"I'm sorry, Elise," I whispered. "I can't lose you."

Her heartbeat was nothing more than a flicker when my lips touched her neck. It had to be now.

I opened my mouth and placed my fangs against her skin. My eyes closed as I mentally apologized to Elise for any pain that she would experience because of me. Bracing her body beneath me, I pushed my fangs through her skin, deep enough that her pale skin reached my gums. I let my fangs sit inside of her body, letting what blood remained inside of her mix with the toxin in my saliva.

Her body tensed against me, all her muscles contracting at once—she'd absorbed enough of my toxin. I slowly removed my fangs from her body, licking them with my tongue, tasting her.

Sitting in the dirt, I held her body against mine, preparing for what was coming. She let me know the transition was beginning when a scream left her lips. The sound was full of pain and agony. My heart clenched at the sound, and I held her tight against me. I was ready to ride the waves of pain with her.

2

────────

EVERETT

THE FOREST WAS DARK WHEN ELISE'S BODY FINALLY finished shaking. I'd held her through all the tremors that had racked her body, my own muscles fatiguing from holding her against me for so long. She was still unconscious. Her head fell back over the crook of my arm, her long hair spilling like a waterfall to the ground. The small hairs that surrounded her face stuck to her sweaty skin. She'd continue to be in a deep sleep for at least the next day as her body recovered from the transition.

"You're strong, Lyka." I whispered into her ear. I didn't know if she could hear me, but if she could, I wanted to be the voice in her ear supporting her, letting her know she wasn't alone, that I hadn't made the decision to change her lightly. I hoped that when she woke, she'd forgive me.

This was entirely my fault. Gavrill had warned me about getting too close to her the first time I'd seen her at No Bars all those weeks ago. I'd taken the advice of my beta—Gavrill had always given me good guidance. Being older than me, he'd experienced more and had seen the way Lycans lost themselves

9

when they found their mate. I'd watched Wilder touch and kiss my mate. Watched as he'd walked her out of the bar holding her hand. Sat at the bar knowing exactly where Wilder had been taking her and what they'd do late at night all alone.

What Gavrill hadn't known was that his warning had come too late—I'd already been consumed by her and her scent. Watching her leave with Wilder and the montage of scenes that had looped in my head of them together had had my hand bringing drink after drink to my lips.

When I'd gotten completely intoxicated, Gavrill and Kostas had carried me out and returned me back to the pack house. The snippets of memory from that night involved me destroying my bedroom. Throwing vases at the wall to see the glass shatter. Flipping tables to hear the crack of the wood against the stone floor. Tearing into the bedding to feel my muscles tense at the effort. Anything to get the image of Elise leaving with Wilder out of my head. Get her scent out of my nose. Get the feeling I'd just made a serious mistake out of my heart.

Gavrill had just stood in the doorway of my room and watched me as I'd destroyed everything in it. He'd known the crazed state I'd been in. Keeping a Lycan from their mate was harmful to their sanity.

I had scented my mate. My instincts had driven me to be with her, to claim her. And I had let her go home with another man.

Now she was mine. She was coming home with me.

My head fell to the mark on her pale skin in the tender spot where her neck met her shoulder. The bite had been clean. The skin around it was red, but that was to be expected with a newly placed mark. I dragged my tongue over the holes I'd created—it was important to keep them clean as they healed. Some of the dried blood on her skin stuck to my tongue. She tasted sweet. I could feel my cock twitch beneath her. I pushed aside any thoughts of claiming her with my fangs embedded into her skin aside. She needed to heal. There would be time for all my own needs soon enough.

Elise's cheeks regained some color as her breathing deepened.

I'd never marked someone before. I'd taken my aunt's advice to save my mark for my mate. Things between shifters could get messy otherwise. There was always drama at the pack house over mating and marking. It was smart to wait. To make sure you found your *fated* mate before marking them and connecting them to you. It'd been hard all those years without my mate. Plenty of she-wolves had warmed my bed while I waited to find her—all of them pining for my fangs to pierce their skin. It was natural to want that bond. Especially with an alpha. But I'd waited. Waited for my lyka. My luna.

Now that I'd marked Elise, she was mine. Her body would instinctively recognize me as her mate, overpowering any resistance from her mind and drawing her toward me. It would cause us pain to be apart from one another. Of course, it would get better with time, as the bond solidified between us, but in the beginning, our bodies would crave each other. I could already feel my body gravitate toward hers, needing the physical contact. Her body had warmed from the cold state I'd found her in. She'd run warmer in general now that she'd transitioned. I looked forward to feeling that heat in my bed.

I stood up with her body limp, hanging from the crooks of my elbows. Her backpack lay in a heap next to a tree. I maneuvered it onto my back while trying to keep Elise as still as possible. It was time to go to the pack house. With my father dead beside me, the tournament was over. The wards he'd put around the tournament were down. The leftover rogues wandering the forest would have to be dealt with—but my priority right now was Elise. She needed a bed and rest.

It wasn't far to the pack house if you ran in your wolf form. I didn't have that ability as I walked through the forest carrying Elise in my arms. She wasn't heavy, but she was unconscious. Unable to grip the back of my wolf with her thighs and hold my black fur between her fingers as she rode me, I had to carry her in my human form. It took an hour of walking through under-brush—making sure the long brown hair on her head dangling from the crook of my arm didn't snag on any bushes before I saw the glow of the pack house in front of me.

Tension left my body as I saw the familiar house. I had it built when I'd left my father's pack at twenty years old, knowing it would have to be big enough for my new pack to grow—I'd seen over the building plans myself. Those who wanted to join the Cedar Moon Pack were invited to live there. The pack house was full of apartments for the families and individuals of Cedar Moon. Those pack members who didn't live here lived in homes scattered around our lands. It was important we were all together. We were stronger as a pack.

It reminded me of a ski lodge with its wood-and-stone elements. A wide front porch with thick wooden pillars that held up the sloping roof welcomed us home. Our home.

I looked down at Elise, still sleeping in my arms, unaware of how much her life had changed. This would be her new home. I hadn't thought I'd bring her here so soon—there was a lot that needed to be done to make sure she felt welcomed. I'd do anything to make sure she was happy here. This was where we'd lead our pack, where we'd celebrate our achievements and lick our wounds at our losses. Where our pups would run someday.

On the porch, I saw my inner circle waiting for me. Gavrill and Kostas stood watching me, hands gripping the porch railing, their faces tense. Kleio and Jack stood together, holding each other. I'd left them without an explanation when I'd felt Elise's cries for help earlier, and I'd also involuntarily blocked their voices out of my head. The concern for my mate had taken all my attention. I was sure I'd get an earful about the lack of communication later.

"Are you harmed, Alpha?" Gavrill asked, and judging by his tone it was clear he was irritated with me. I trusted him as my beta to not hold anything back. More than once, he'd helped keep me in line when the path got a little fuzzy.

"I'm fine. There was an incident with my father...he's dead." I watched their eyes widen. "Elise needs a bed. I'll explain what happened after I tend to her."

Gavrill nodded at me and headed into the house to ready my chambers. Kostas came down the steps of the porch and approached me with his arms extended, ready to take Elise from me. I growled at him, showing him my teeth. In my mind, my wolf lunged at Kostas, attempting to keep any other males far from her. There was no way I'd let anyone touch my mate.

Kostas lifted his arms up in a surrender position. He knelt on one knee, his head tilting to the left, exposing the right side of his neck in submission. "I mean your mate no harm, True Alpha."

His words shook me. The thought hadn't crossed my mind during all the conflict this afternoon. I'd killed my father. As his only heir, I'd inherited the title of True Alpha. The weight of the responsibility fell on my shoulders, a weight much heavier than the woman I carried in my arms.

My inner wolf calmed when he saw Kostas in the submissive position. Kostas was old enough that he would know how possessive newly mated Lycans could be. I looked back up at the porch. Kleio and Jack were in similar submissive positions, on their knees with their heads tilted to the side. I proceeded forward to the porch, nodding, accepting their submission. Jack and Kostas stood, turned, and disappeared into the house to alert the rest of the pack of my father's death.

"Is Elise okay?" Kleio stood up from kneeling and ran over to the top of the porch stairs I'd just climbed. She reached out to brush a piece of hair off Elise's face. I twisted my body, keeping Elise away from her touch. My lips curled up at her, showing my teeth.

"Jeez, Everett! I'm just trying to see my friend," Kleio said. Elise's head had shifted in my arms when I'd twisted. Kleio's eyes grew wide when she saw the new mark on her neck. "You didn't."

"I had to, Kleio," I snarled. "She was dying." The pain my mate was experiencing was already causing me agitation. I didn't need her judgment too.

"It was supposed to be her choice," Kleio whispered. "You've changed the entire course of her life with a single bite."

"My father stole away her choice the minute he drained all the blood from her body." I turned to look Kleio in the eyes. "There wasn't a choice. I had to save her."

Kleio glanced back at Elise's face. "Let's hope she sees it that way."

I carried her into the pack house, intent on getting her to my bedroom. The pack members who were in the house stopped to stare at me before falling to their knees in submission. I heard whispers of *"True Alpha"* floating around the pack's mind-link. That title would take some getting used to.

I covered Elise with my body the best I could—it was important not to let the rest of the pack see my mate in such a weak and vulnerable moment. As quickly as possible, I headed for the large main staircase. The stair treads had been made from thick logs cut in half lengthwise to make a flat surface to step on. The underside of the treads was still rounded, keeping the character of the log. When Kleio had moved in, she'd installed an expensive red kilim rug that covered the middle of the treads.

My bedroom was at the end of the long hallway on the third floor. We passed Gavrill's and Kostas's rooms on the way to the thick wood door that blocked the entrance to my room. I opened the door, letting the familiar smell enter my nose. My foot kicked the door closed behind me. Gavrill, Kostas, Jack, and Kleio stood outside the door in the hallway. They wouldn't get another look at my mate while she was injured. If I had it my way, I'd keep her locked up here, only for my eyes to feast on. But that wouldn't be healthy for Elise. She needed to have a purpose within the pack, and the pack needed her to be their luna. I'd eventually have to let her find her way into the new life I was giving her.

That wouldn't stop me from keeping her to myself for as long as possible. Keeping her next to me for however long it took for her to accept what I'd turned her into. To accept me as her mate.

This room was my sanctuary, my home, one that I'd share with Elise. I nuzzled her neck, letting her scent mingle with the scent of my room in my nose. The two smells mixed well together. It felt right.

Soon she'd wake up and have questions.

Questions about what had happened in the woods. I needed to be there for her when she woke. This was going to be new to both of us. I'd never brought a woman into my chambers before. I always met them in their beds—it was easier to leave and separate myself from them when I'd finished. There'd be no leaving Elise—the separation would weaken both of us.

I laid her down on my bed. It was much bigger than the one in her cabin. It wouldn't fold up and break after sex. The memory of Elise stuck in between the fold of the mattress brought a smile to my lips—seeing her there naked, vulnerable, and mine.

I took off her backpack before I lay next to her, pulling her body against my own. We fit together perfectly. It felt so right having her here in my bed, tucked in next to me, underneath my arm splayed possessively over her unconscious body. She was safe now—there was no need for the lingering panic I was still feeling. What we'd just gone through hadn't left my blood-stream—the adrenaline was still pumping through my body. I needed to be closer. The skin beneath my clothes ached for the touch of her skin.

Standing up, I stripped off my clothing, throwing it onto the ground. I got to work ridding Elise of her clothing. She couldn't tell me, but as new mates, I knew her body craved the skin contact as much as mine did.

I unlaced her shoes and removed her socks, setting them gently on the floor next to the bed. Hooking the waistband of her leggings with my thumbs, I peeled them off her. My father had destroyed the sweatshirt she wore, and I easily removed it. Not wanting to injure her further, I extended a single black claw from my index finger and sliced her sports bra down her sternum.

Once I'd removed everything from her body, I pulled up the blankets and pulled her form closer to mine. The instant our skin touched, I felt my body deflate, relaxing in a way that I'd never experienced. It felt like I was home. I didn't think it was my imagination, but I swore I could feel Elise's body relax against me. I hoped she felt like she was home too.

3

____

DAFNI, AGE TWELVE

The wind blew my hair around, pulling it in front of my eyes. I pushed it aside, gathering the bright red strands in the rubber band I kept on my wrist.

Croak.

Maybe I should chop it off. That would shock them. My grandmother's face would be limp with surprise. In my mind, I could see her jaw open when she noticed my long hair was gone. All the nights she'd spent brushing it growing up. All the attention she gave to my hair. *It's part of your beauty. Beauty is power,* she'd whisper while she dragged the brush across my scalp over and over again. It took a lot of time to detangle all the knots I got out in the woods playing. It became a point of pride for her, keeping my hair smooth and long.

Croak.

I tucked a strand of hair that fluttered out of the rubber band behind my ear. I could never do something like that. I was too much of a fraidy-cat to rebel against my grandmother. But it would feel nice to do something extreme. Something unexpected.

Croak.

I looked over at the pond next to me. Extending my index and middle fingers together, I pointed them toward the water, where I assumed the irritating frog was croaking at me. I came here to escape my chores. A quiet break. The water around the edge of the pond turned an opaque white as it froze solid. I waited a moment. Silence. I smirked to myself, retracting my fingers back into my hand.

"Dafni!" My grandmother's voice traveled across the field of long grass where I had hidden myself.

Frogfeet.

That break hadn't been nearly long enough. I stood up, gathering the braided grass crown I'd absentmindedly made to busy my fingers while I hid. I'd woven in twelve flowers I had found growing between the blades.

Placing the crown on my head, I looked around the field. I was barely taller than the green grasses that grew around me. The tips brushed across my cheeks, tickling me affectionately. The grass enjoyed me tending to it. Picking out the old blades of grass to make way for the fresh shoots to grow. I wore the old grasses on my head, and that made me their queen. Pretending they were my loyal subjects, like out of the stories Grandmother spun, they bowed away as I walked toward my grandmother's cottage. I let my hands dance along the soft blades in thanks as my bare feet followed the path the grasses made. Her Royal Highness, Queen Dafni. Maybe my king would be at the end of the path?

The long grasses parted, opening to the shorter grass surrounding the cottage. The fairytale bubble I was in popped. My grandmother stood on the porch waiting for me, leaning against a broom. When she saw me, she began sweeping the porch, brushing off the leaves that fell on the worn wood planks last night. It was a chore she did daily. There were always leaves in the morning and she was always there to brush them away. It was another boring task to fill the time.

Time moved slowly here at the cottage. We were isolated here, my grandmother and me. She liked it that way—but I didn't. Whenever I asked why we couldn't leave, why we couldn't have adventures like the ones the characters did in the books that stood in tall stacks in our living room, she'd sigh and say, *Maybe when you're older,* or *It's not safe out there.* I never understood what could be so dangerous. My mother came and went from the cottage now and then to check in on me, and she seemed fine. Always in a terrible mood—but fine.

So, we stayed. Grandmother swept the porch each morning and tended to her potions. I spent time outside the cottage and made my way through the books in the living room. Some of the books were new, with crisp white pages, and others had already been read, their pages dog-eared and wrinkled.

Their pages with black print comforted me. I was able to get lost in the pages of the books at night under the glow of the single lamp we had in the cottage. It was a silver lamp with a white shade. My favorite part was the tiny chain that hung from the lightbulb, on its end a tiny black glass oval with the letters *BTC* etched in gold. With one pull of the chain, the entire cottage illuminated with light.

Grandmother let me plug the lamp into the single outlet we had, the wiring for it strung outside the cottage between wooden poles making a pattern that reminded me of waves on the pond. The waves of the wire got smaller the farther away they got from the cottage, the poles growing shorter. I wanted to follow them, see where our electricity came from, but Grandmother had forbidden me. So, I had to imagine where the wire waves led, making up stories in my mind about faraway places —places where girls weren't stuck inside cottages and got to go on adventures.

I'd read those books over and over. They were like old friends to me, calming and stable. Grandmother had taught me to read when I'd been younger. It'd been hard at first—she'd patiently helped me sound out each word, correcting me when I'd made a mistake. But I'd learned quickly. The stories were my only escape. My favorites were the fairytales. Especially *Rapunzel*. I was trapped, just like her—although there was no handsome prince in sight. Maybe he'd show up one day. Maybe I shouldn't cut my hair...just in case I needed it like Rapunzel did.

"Did you finish your morning chores?" she asked.

I didn't know why she was asking. She already knew the answer.

"Not yet, Grandmother."

"Best you finish them before you disappear next." She noted my grass crown before she continued sweeping. "When did the wind start answering to you?" She kept her eyes down, as if she was uninterested in the question she was asking. I knew better. My emerging powers were of the utmost interest to her.

"Just today," I lied. The wind had been answering to me for the last couple of days. It had surprised me at first, when the breeze would follow my fingers, blowing my hair or the grasses out of my way as I walked through it. But she didn't need to know that.

I picked up my skirt and walked toward my unfinished chores. The chickens were hungry. Clucking and scratching at the dirt in their coop, their noises only got louder as they saw me approach. I scattered feed and scratch among their feet. They rushed to eat the feed before the chicken next to them could eat it. Greedy little devils.

A loud *moo* caught my attention. Our large dairy cow bellowed for her own breakfast. I scooped her grain into one of the clean metal pails and hooked it on the wall of her stall. Grabbing another clean pail, I walked along her length, trailing my hand along her black and white hide, letting her know where I was. My nimble hands squeezed the white milk from her. She adjusted herself, rocking her hips as the pressure from her udders was relieved.

I let the milk slosh over the sides of the pail as I carried it back to the cottage. Spirals of smoke floated out of the stone chimney. Grandmother must've already been cooking. She never used the outlet in the house, preferring the fire for cooking food and brewing potions. When I'd mentioned an electric stove, like one I'd read about, she'd shushed me, telling me she preferred the fire. That she knew the flames, where they'd reach, how hot they'd get. Grandmother didn't trust the electricity that came through the wires.

The sound of my black boots climbing the steps of the porch alerted the screen door of my approach. It creaked open, welcoming me into the warm cottage.

"Where do you want the milk, Grandmother?" I asked. The pail was full and heavy. My arms ached from carrying it.

"Come over here. Let me see what you know," Grandmother said. Every day it was the same. I didn't know why I expected anything different. Grandmother cleaned. She cooked, took time to test my magic. Each day flowed into the next without interruption.

I carried the pail of milk over to the hearth where Grandmother stirred the cauldron that hung over the fire. The bubbling liquid was purple today. Maybe that was the only thing that changed—the brew she cooked daily.

"Let me see." It was a command, not a question. I set the pail down on the floorboards between us. Her eyes met mine, waiting for me, watching me. I looked down at the milk in the pail. This might've been difficult for me last year. Milk was slightly thicker than water, but she and I both knew that this was easy for me now.

I extended my index and middle fingers, pointing them at the pail, as I had earlier at the pond. The top of the liquid frosted over. The metal pail creaked as the milk froze and expanded. A crack appeared at the surface, then opened wider, and the liquid expanded under the frozen pressure I put on it. Tiny ice crystals formed around the edges of the pail, making tiny frozen designs.

"Too much." Grandmother's voice broke my concentration. "You went too far. It's frost burned now." Her disappointed eyes met mine before they flicked back to her brew.

I sighed, looking down at my frozen-milk creation. Was there such a thing as the perfect frozen consistency? Frozen was frozen. I'd already achieved that. What else did she want from me?

I picked up the milky ice I'd created and brought it to the back door. I looked back at my grandmother, bent over the hearth, carefully stirring. She'd been up since dawn cooking.

My fingers froze from holding the frosty pail. I set it down at my feet and extended my two fingers, pointing them at the boiling caldron. The wooden spoon she was stirring with went still. My lips curled upward ever so slightly at my success.

Long gray hair spun in the air as Grandmother turned around quickly to look at me. I went through the back door as fast as I could, hoping to be where she couldn't see me.

"You little harpy!" Her angry tone found my ears as I kept my back pressed against the outside wall of the cottage. "Now I'll have to start all over again."

I reached for the pail. The outer edges had started to melt, and the frozen milk had turned into a large ice cube, spinning around when I lifted the pail. I swung it back to launch the ice cube out onto the lawn to melt in the sun.

"Your mother will not be happy about that when she gets here!"

The milk ice cube flew out of the pail in a perfect arch and landed with a thud on the green grass. It was already melting in the morning sun.

I, however, stood there, perfectly frozen at my grandmother's words.

4

―――――

ELISE

"Who's the new luna?"

"I can't believe the True Alpha's dead."

"Stop doing that! You're going to hurt yourself!"

"What's for lunch?"

"When will Alpha be back?"

"Is he going to stay in his room forever?"

The pounding in my head was worse than any hangover I'd ever experienced. There were voices in my head that wouldn't shut up. It was like I could hear everyone's thoughts around me.

"Shut up!" I yelled. My voice sounded scratchy, like I hadn't used it in weeks. I wanted silence. I wanted to stay in this warm cocoon I was in and fall back into unconsciousness. It was comfortable here. I just needed the voices in my head to cease the constant chatter. Maybe if I kept my eyes closed, I could drop back into the deep sleep I'd been in.

"Lyka, open your eyes for me." The voice sounded warm and familiar. A firm hand turned my face toward the sound. The same hand traced a path from my face down my neck and

25

along my shoulder. It continued down my arm, brushing my naked breast...

"What the fuck!" My eyes shot open, and I sat up, pulling up the blanket that covered the bottom half of my body to cover my exposed chest.

"Come back to me, Elise. We need each other right now." The man lying next to me was just as naked as I was. When I'd pulled on the blanket to cover myself, I had inadvertently pulled the shared blanket off him. He lay there with his hands behind his head, completely exposed. My eyes went directly to his hard length that lay against his stomach. I could hear his smirk.

"Come here, Lyka," he said. "Your body needs to be touching mine."

Letting my eyes leave the sight of his strained length, my vision traveled up his body to his face. The moment I looked into his golden-yellow eyes, hundreds of memories slammed into my brain at once. I yelped and grabbed my forehead, closing my eyes, trying to brace myself for their impact.

I'd been in the woods. With Leo. Meeting Mr. Daniels. The rot—it'd spread.

Keep squirming, little wolf. Everett's father?

No.

The tree. It'd been a huge oak. The rot seemed to have spread from it, infecting the forest.

Let him go, Wilder! My own voice echoed through my head. It sounded muffled, as if I was listening to myself through a cup pressed against a door.

Everett. The True Alpha. Wilder. Leo.

My fingers tangled in my hair, pulling it at the roots. I wanted it to stop, these memories. No, not memories. Delusions. I'd spent so much time researching this past month, and I was tired. Too tired. I was starting to imagine things, see things that weren't real. Making up things that hadn't happened. I needed sleep. Maybe a meeting with the university's psychologist.

I felt strong hands unfurl my fingers from my hair, the sting of my scalp dissipating as they stopped pulling. "Relax, Lyka."

My eyes popped open. I looked down to where my hands were encased in Everett's. Dried red blood covered my wrists, streaks smearing up my forearms. "Whose blood is on me?" No, it wasn't blood. I'd probably gotten into some berries in the woods. They stained your skin for days.

"Mostly yours, maybe a bit of Leo's."

Leo's?

"*No!*" I yelled, pulling my hands from his grasp. I rubbed them together, using my nails to scrape the red stain from my skin.

"Don't hurt yourself," Everett whispered before grabbing ahold of my hands again.

I pressed my eyes closed. "Tell me this isn't real. Tell me Leo's back at the cabin." What I remembered was foggy. As if it'd happened in a dream. This wasn't real. It couldn't be.

Everett cleared his throat. "I can't tell you either of those things, Elise."

"He's...he's dead, isn't he? It's his blood on my hands." Both of my hands came together as Everett wrapped one of his around them. I felt his thumb brush against one of my closed eyelids. They fluttered open as if he'd cast a spell upon them with his fingers.

"Yes, Leo's dead. His blood is on your hands, but not his death. That was Wilder's doing."

I pulled back, Everett's hand keeping me from tangling my fingers back into my hair. "And Leo? His body. He's still out there, lying in the forest, alone?" I asked.

Everett shook his head. "One of the pack members dropped

his body outside a hospital about fifty miles away. He'll get back to his family."

So much blood. There'd been so much of it. So much of it had been mine. My hand went to the side of my neck where the True Alpha had sliced me open. I pulled my hand away from my neck and looked at my fingers for the blood that should have been there. My fingers were clean. I'd already healed. "And your father...he tried to kill me."

Everett closed his eyes for a moment before opening them and nodding.

I winced, my teeth clenching as the memories continued to bombard me. Pain. Popping. My body on fire. My hand flew to the other side of my neck, breaking free from his hold. Everett caught my wrist, kissing the palm of my hand before lowering it back down to the bed. He had bitten me—right after his father had tried to drain me.

Warmth flooded me with the memories of him holding me in the woods. I'd been cold—so cold. His body had felt like paradise. Then there'd been pain...and then darkness...until now. Now I was lucid, but everything was still unclear.

"What about all my research? The university?" I asked. "And Jenny? Where's Jenny? She has to be worried that Leo and I never came back. She probably called the university on the sat phone. And my mother...she must be worried. She'll drive up here—she'll go to the cabin and check on me. How am I going to explain this?" I gestured to the bite mark pulsing on my neck.

I flinched at the pain in my neck where Everett had bitten me. It was stinging again. I reached up to touch it.

Everett's hand grabbed my wrist and pulled my hand away again. "It's a lot right now—I know." His thumb rubbed in circles on the inside of my wrist. "Everything has been taken care of. I'll answer your questions later. Right now, you need to heal, to get stronger."

My body involuntarily relaxed as Everett now rubbed the insides of both my wrists with his thumbs. Maybe it was a pressure point I wasn't aware of.

"Let me take care of you," he said. Everett pulled my body down on the bed so I was lying beside him. I melted into the soft mattress, the blanket shifting with me, still covering me. He lifted his body above mine, placing one hand on either side of my head. "It's my job to take care of you."

His head dipped down to my neck. I could feel his tongue brush gently along the angry skin he'd created when he'd bit me. His tongue lapped the sore spot. The sensation of his tongue against my newly sensitive skin went quickly from odd to pleasurable. I braced myself for each swipe of his tongue. Every time his wet tongue dragged over the broken skin, my body pulsed slightly. The feeling traveling from my neck down between my legs. My thighs squeezed together, trying to lessen the feeling.

Everett had never lied to me—and the way his tongue felt against my skin made him all the more convincing.

I believed him.

Everything had been taken care of. Jenny was probably enjoying having the cabin to herself. Leo, Jenny, and I had all been so busy with our research that not running into each other for days at a time had become the norm. It was possible she didn't know we were missing. Maybe my mom would be so engrossed in a sculpture that she'd forget I existed for a couple days. My research was fine, sitting in the cabin.

"Mmm, my beautiful lyka. Already so responsive to me." Everett finished licking me and pulled his head away from my neck. He looked thoughtfully down at the bite, satisfied with the care he'd given it.

Bite. He'd sunk his teeth into me.

"Can I?" I asked. My hand traveled up to my neck to investigate.

Everett's hand grabbed my wrist once again and brought my hand to his chest. "Don't touch it yet. It needs to heal."

"So, I can't touch it, but you can lick it?" I asked.

"I'm your mate; it's my responsibility to tend to you." His eyes traveled down to the blankets that currently covered my center. "I didn't hear any complaints when I was licking you." I squeezed my thighs together again, this time tighter. "It felt nice, didn't it? Kleio had told me it would feel...good."

"You talked about me with Kleio?" I asked.

"Of course," he said. "She's been in here to check on you many times during the last few days."

Few days. Had I been asleep for days?

I laid my head back on my pillow and squeezed my eyes shut. Kleio's bouncy strawberry blonde hair and smiling face filled my mind.

"Elise? Do you need something?"

I shot up in my bed, headbutting Everett in the face.

"Fuck!" He stood on his knees, holding his nose in his hand.

"Did you hear something? Is Kleio in here?"

I looked around the massive bedroom for the first time. The room was dark. Heavy green velvet curtains covered the windows from floor to ceiling. Only a small amount of sunlight peeked around the sides. In front of the bed, a stone fireplace centered the room. A small couch in front of the fireplace had fur blankets draped over the back of it. The side of the wall behind the bed had a wooden door that was open only a crack. I could see the reflection of a mirror inside and figured it must be a bathroom.

"No one is here but us. I thought you'd want some privacy," said Everett.

"Weird. I swear I heard her ask if I was okay."

"Ah, you're experiencing the mind-link part of being a Lycan."

"Lycan?"

I stood up on the bed, holding the blanket against my body. My feet took several steps back from the man kneeling in bed next to me. I reached up, snaking my hand around the side of my body, wincing before I felt the bite on my neck with my fingers. It stung when I touched it. It wasn't just a bite. There were holes in my neck. Two rounded, healing holes. It couldn't be a *mark*. I couldn't be...one of them. Taking stock, I wiggled my toes and evaluated my muscles as I worked my way up my body. I didn't feel any different.

"You lost too much blood, Elise. I was going to lose you," Everett said.

More flashbacks of his father draining my blood into the ground raced through my mind. My heart started racing, my skin sweating.

"You promised you'd wait until I was ready for you to mark me!" I looked around the room for an escape. He'd told me he wouldn't put a mark on my skin until I was ready. I'd thought he'd just bitten me, like a love bite in a moment of passion. A hickey. Marking was supposed to be on my timeline, my choice.

My breathing increased. I felt myself taking more inhales than exhales. I backed up on the bed further, my foot finding the edge of the bed. The heel of my foot dropped over the side of the mattress and pulled the rest of my body with it. Tumbling off the bed, wrapped in a blanket, I fell hard onto the stone floor, my hip taking the brunt of the fall. I sucked air between my teeth as I rolled onto my back. The floor was cold beneath my skin.

Two hands gripped under my arms and lifted me into a standing position. My hands never left the blanket I held to cover my body.

"Please don't be scared," Everett said, holding my upper arms in his hands. "I'm sorry I took the choice away from you. I just couldn't lose you." His yellow eyes met mine. I could see pain in his eyes as he looked at me.

"Don't touch me!" I pushed his chest away from me, and he immediately let go of my arms. A look of hurt flashed across his face. I didn't want any more of his touch, no matter how platonic.

"Let's go for a run."

"When will we meet the new luna?"

"Mom, I'm hungry."

"We have all those rogues in the Vault."

The voices were back in my brain. It felt like everyone was yelling at me at once. I crumpled down to my knees, my hands coming up to squeeze my head, trying to make them stop. The blanket covering me fell to the floor. I was too bothered by the voices in my brain to realize I'd lost it.

"It's happening again!" I yelled at Everett, trying to speak louder than the sounds in my head.

I heard the door to his room open. A couple of squeals of surprise entered the room from the hallway. Whoever was out there hadn't been expecting to see a naked shifter standing in the doorway.

"Everybody, shut up!" Everett roared into the hallway. He slammed the door before walking over to my folded body.

Slowly, the voices quieted in my head. I lifted my neck to see Everett crouching next to me, his hand reaching to stroke my back. I shifted out of his reach.

"I'll teach you how to control the mind-linking," he said. "I know it can be overwhelming at first."

I probably looked like a feral kitten, crouched naked in a ball on the floor. I was practically hissing at Everett, trying to keep him away from me. He read my body language and backed away, knowing I needed some space.

"I'll be on the bed when you're ready to join me." Everett grabbed the blanket next to me and climbed into the bed and sat leaning against the headboard. He pulled the blanket up around his waist and folded his hands together. Patiently waiting. As if he didn't expect to be waiting long.

"Will it go away?" I asked.

"Will what go away, Lyka?"

"The voices in my head."

"No, Elise. It's part of being a shifter. Part of being a member of a pack. You'll learn to control who can mind-link you. Your mind can be as quiet as you wish."

"Come here, my lyka." Everett's smooth voice entered my mind. I grimaced, clenching my teeth.

"That's not quiet enough."

He chuckled in the bed. "You'll get used to it. I think eventually you'll find it very useful."

"You look cold over there all by yourself."

I'd forgotten that I was naked. There wasn't anything around me to cover myself with. I refused to let it get to me. If he could strut around with all his bits hanging out there, so could I.

But that didn't stop my body from shivering against the stone floor. I crossed my arms and hunched over, folding myself in a ball, trying to keep warm. Everett sat comfortably on the bed with his head leaned back against the headboard with his eyes closed. I crouched there, jealous of Everett's comfort, but I was stubborn enough that I refused to give in and join him on the bed.

The mark on my neck felt like someone had pinched it. I

brushed my hair away from it, exposing the damaged skin to the air. The pain went away.

"Ah!" I yelled in surprise when pain reentered the mark. This time it felt like someone had stuck a needle inside and twisted it. My hand flew up to cover the mark. I pulled my hand away to check if there was blood. It felt like there should be.

"Come here Elise, I don't want to see you in pain," Everett said, opening his eyes to look at me. He patted the spot on the bed next to him. I shook my head at him as the pain in my neck subsided once again.

The absence of pain only lasted a few seconds before the piercing pain in my neck brought me to the ground. I rolled to my side as the pain radiated down my arm and into my stomach. My stomach lurched at the feeling, and I gagged, trying to keep the contents of my stomach inside my body. Sweat bubbled up through my skin, making me feel as though I just got out of a bath. A drop trickled down my forehead and into my eye. It stung, but not as bad as the mark on my neck hurt.

"What's wrong with me?" I begged Everett for an answer. I sat up as the pain receded.

"You need me, Elise. Come here—I can make all the pain go away."

"I don't want anything to..." My words stopped as the stabbing sensation returned to my neck. If there wasn't a knife sticking out of my jugular, I couldn't imagine what caused this pain. I fell against the hard floor, trying to claw my way away from the pain. I screamed loud enough that I made my own ears ring.

The door to the room opened. The pain stopped long enough for me to lift my head to see who entered. Kleio stopped in the doorway to scan the room. She glanced over at

Everett before she made eye contact with me and rushed to my side.

"Oh my god, Elise. What's wrong? I could hear you from downstairs. And after you mind-linked me earlier..." Kleio held my face up while another lightning bolt of pain racked my body. "I know exactly what's going on." She lifted me up under my arms and walked me toward the bed.

I dug in my heels once I figured out where she was guiding me. "No, I don't want him," I said.

"Oh yes, you do. You need him." Kleio pulled me toward Everett.

"That's what I've been telling her," Everett said, as relaxed as ever.

"Did you tell her *why* she needs to touch you?" she asked. Everett sat there without an answer. Kleio shook her head at him as she used her shifter strength to pull me forward. "It's the mating bond. You and Everett need skin contact to satisfy the bond. The pain will go away once you start touching."

I was close enough to Everett that when the next wave of pain hit me, Kleio put my palm on top of Everett's chest. Like flipping a light switch, the pain lessened. I could breathe again. My body felt like jelly from the waves of pain. The muscles in my body ached from all the tension. I let Kleio guide me into bed beside Everett. The more places our body touched, the less pain I felt in my neck. A sigh left my lips as I settled into the curve of Everett's body.

"There you go. That feels better, doesn't it?" she asked.

I closed my eyes in response. Being against his body felt like heaven after being on the stone floor. My arms wrapped around Everett's chest and my legs straddled his thigh. I couldn't get enough contact with his body.

"These mating bonds are finicky in the beginning. You

need to stay close to Everett until they grow stronger," Kleio explained.

Everett grunted his approval, wrapping his own arms around my torso. I tucked my nose between his ear and shoulder, inhaling his scent.

"Have you told her yet?" she asked.

Told me what?

"Not the time," Everett growled. He squeezed me against him tighter, my body and mind relaxing further into mush.

Kleio took a blanket from the foot of the bed and covered us up. My eyes shot open as I realized I had been naked in front of her this whole time. She winked at me. "Nothing I haven't seen before."

She tiptoed out of the room, quietly closing the door. Leaving me with the shifter who had taken away my freedom yet kept me captive to his touch.

5

ELISE

EVERETT'S BODY AGAINST MINE FELT SO GOOD. IT WAS LIKE drinking a cup of hot chocolate after being outside in a snowstorm. The warmth flowed throughout my body, relaxing my muscles and soothing my nerves. His arm that wound around my body pulled me closer to him. I couldn't help but meld right into him.

"This is better, isn't it, Elise?" Everett asked. I was hesitant to tell him he was right. It felt strange to need someone else to make me feel good. I was used to managing my feelings on my own. To have to rely on someone else to make me feel complete was uncomfortable. It felt like I was giving some of my control away. I didn't like it.

"Am I allowed to use the bathroom?" I asked. I pushed away from Everett. Cool air flowed where our bodies separated, sending goose bumps across my skin.

"Of course you can," he said. "Just don't take too long, or I'll have to join you." He grabbed my face with his hands and planted a kiss on my forehead. I tried to ignore how good that felt.

My feet hit the cold stone floor, and I quickly tiptoed over to what I had guessed was the bathroom. The wooden door creaked as it opened, revealing a large washroom. Lights automatically switched on as I crossed the threshold. The light was dim but enough that I could see. Two stone sinks were directly to my right. Next to them was a toilet. The back wall of the bathroom was a large shower with a rain shower head hanging from the ceiling. As I walked over to the toilet, the heated stone floors pleasantly surprised me.

After I quickly relieved myself, I stood at one of the sinks and looked at myself in the mirror above it. I looked the same: Long brown hair and green eyes. A few freckles dotted my nose from the time I'd spent in the sun.

I lifted my hand in front of my face and rotated it, examining my fingernails and skin. There wasn't any fur. No claws that I could see. My nails were the same short unpolished ones I always had. I turned around, looking at my back. My ribs were more pronounced than they usually were. I hadn't been eating while I'd been unconscious—my body was eating itself.

Getting close to the mirror, I leaned over the stone counter, trying to ignore my sunken cheeks and looked closely at my irises. I expected to see a different color or swirls like I saw in Everett's eyes. They were the same jade green as they always were.

I backed up, smoothing my hair that desperately needed to be washed. My fingers slipped through the strands and brushed over the two red circles on my neck. It was the first time I could see them for myself. Two pink marks about an inch apart branded my skin. It made me nauseous to look at them. They were larger than the marks I saw on Kleio's neck, but mine were new. Maybe they'd shrink down as they healed.

I felt a tiny pinch on the skin around my mark. At first, I thought I'd accidentally scraped it with my fingernail when I was touching it, but the pinching feeling happened again. This time, a little stronger. Shit. Not again. I gripped the counter and looked around the bathroom for a remedy, but if Everett was right, the only solution was his touch. I groaned as a stronger pulse of pain hit my body. I leaned over the counter, resting my head on the cool stone.

The door to the bathroom opened slowly. The footsteps behind me were quiet, like the person knew how to distribute their weight for maximum stealth. My eyes were closed as I recovered from the wave of pain that had just exhausted my body. Stooping over the counter, limp and naked, I couldn't find it in me to care who was walking up behind me. The firm hands that palmed my hips did not surprise me, bringing my backside against muscular thighs. The small amount of skin contact brought relief to my body. My knees buckled at the warm feeling that flooded me from head to toe. Everett wrapped an arm under my breasts and lifted the top half of my body to his. My head leaned back against his chest as I let out a sigh, relaxing against him.

"Please don't fight me, Elise. I only want to help you," Everett whispered.

"We can't be naked, touching each other every day for the rest of our lives," I said. My eyes were still closed. His skin felt so good against mine. I took a moment to enjoy the feeling.

"If I had it my way, that's what we'd be doing every day for the rest of our lives." Everett nipped at my ear.

I pulled away from his teeth and tilted my head up to look at his face. "That's not realistic."

He looked at me, his face changing from silly to serious. His cheeks were rosy with the amount of heat we were creating between our bodies. "Of course it's not. It'll get better every day." The corded muscles in his arms beneath my breasts rolled against my ribs as he pulled me tighter against his chest. "We'll slowly be able to separate, to be apart from each other for longer amounts of time. We need to feed the bond in the beginning. Building a solid bond helps us each become stronger." I let the back of my head fall against his chest. He nuzzled his face between my shoulder and ear, his beard scratching the already sensitive skin on my neck. "Makes our relationship stronger. Our wolves also need time to get to know each other."

"Wolf? I have a wolf?" I turned, pushing away from Everett. *That* aspect of being a Lycan hadn't crossed my mind—another being running around in my head. It was enough to make me dizzy.

Everett grabbed back onto me, pulling me close. This time my breasts pushed into his chest, his arms wrapped around my back, his hand rubbing the sore muscles between my shoulder blades. Disuse had made my entire body tender. I reluctantly leaned into him, relishing the warmth.

"You'll meet her eventually. She's going to get restless soon and want to go for a run," Everett said.

I scrunched my nose up. "Does that mean I'm going to shift?" Thinking back to the Deca Tournament, I'd seen the stretching, cracking, and bone elongating that came with shifting. It grossed me out. I couldn't imagine how it would feel. The sounds I'd heard come from the shifter's bodies were enough to make me fear the shift.

"Eventually you will." Everett's hand fell lower on my back, his hand tracing figure eights along my spine, dipping lower and lower with each bottom curve of the eight. "I can tell you're getting anxious just thinking about it all," he said.

Of course I was anxious. Who wouldn't be? This change had been thrown at me before I was ready and before I'd agreed. It was all new to me and all scary. Now I had to affix myself to Everett or endure severe pain. Pain that was now gone because I was in his arms.

I couldn't ignore how good it felt, how we fit together. It didn't feel any different than our time together in the cabin. That night had given me the answers to everything I'd questioned. There was no denying that magical pull—the mating bond. Even in this bathroom there was still that thread pulling us together—tightening, tying a knot around us that would be impossible to unravel.

This need to touch, to be touching to avoid pain from consuming my body...Everett had said it was temporary, it would lesson with time.

Part of me wondered if I ever wanted it to stop.

I laid my cheek against his warm chest, breathing in his scent through my nose. My muscles relaxed further. The bottom of the current figure eight dipped low enough that his hand swept beneath my backside, slowing for a moment before continuing its gentle caress back up my spine. I pushed my hips against his body, relishing in the warmth of his body as well as the heat building between my legs.

"You need to trust me. I'll help you with everything," he said. "You're my mate. You're now my life." Everett brushed the hair away from my face, tucking it gently behind my ear. What he said was sweet. He seemed genuine.

It was easy for him to say, to ask that I trust him. He said I was *his* life now, but this was a whole new life for *me*. A new life complete with mystical creatures and the ability to shift into a wolf.

Still, I *knew* him. Even in the short amount of time we'd had together, I knew deep down who he was. I trusted him— even to a fault.

"Let's not live in the future." Everett lifted my chin and planted a kiss on my lips. "Let's live right here." He followed his words with a kiss that melted my insides.

He was right: I needed to forget it all and be present with him. I'd live in the now.

My arms snaked around the back of his neck, pulling his lips harder against my own. It felt good to touch him, for him to touch me. The mating bond might have been part of it, but it wasn't all of it. I wanted Everett's hands on my body. I wanted him to touch me in all the places that pulsed with need. My body became demanding as our kiss deepened, our mouths opening, and our tongues playfully touching one another. We were already bare, and that made everything move faster. There were no clothes to remove, no barriers in our way. Just our hands and our mouths like pioneers, ready to explore each other's bodies.

"Come here," Everett said against my cheek. He pulled me across the bathroom to the shower. The tiled shower was large, with a glass door that reached the ceiling. With a twist, he turned on the water and let it run over his hand, testing the temperature.

Once it was to his liking, he stepped under the flow of water and let it fall down his body. I watched the rivers of water make tributaries along his chest, meandering through all the ridges of his frame. Still holding my hand, he pulled me into the shower with him. The water was warm enough that it initially felt hot against my skin. After a couple of seconds getting used to the temperature, I folded myself in next to Everett, enjoying the waterfall above us. I hadn't realized how dirty I was until I looked down at the shower floor. The water that ran off our bodies was a muddy brown color.

Never letting go of my hand, Everett made quick work of pumping shampoo into his free one. He turned my body so that my back faced him, keeping me under the warm water of the shower. One handed, he used his fingernails to massage the shampoo into my hair. His touch was gentle. He took his time to rinse the suds out of my hair, threading his fingers between the strands.

Next, he pumped a squirt of soap into his hands from the shower niche next to us. This time he used the pads of his fingers to rub the cedar-smelling soap along my skin, gently working his way around the curves of my body. The water rinsed the soap away, and I turned around, keeping his hand in mine. Everett looked down at me. The water had darkened his hair, and it almost looked black. I pushed back the long hair that had fallen over his eyes to the side of his head. My eyes glanced down from his forehead to his eyes. His gold irises locked into my own. He broke eye contact to briefly glance down at my neck.

"Missed a spot," Everett said. He bent his head down to the space between my neck and shoulder. I shuddered at the feeling of his breath on my skin. Everett took his time running his tongue over the mark on my neck. Unlike before, the sensation of his tongue against the mark on my neck wasn't at all odd. It was erotic.

"Everett," I moaned against his wet hair. I could feel liquid pool between my legs. It wasn't normal to be turned on this quickly, to be ready for him so immediately. Was it? Maybe it was the Lycan blood running through my veins.

His lips covered my mark and lightly sucked the skin into his mouth. I jumped at the sensation, causing his teeth to hit the sensitive mark.

"Ohh!" I cried out. Jolts of pleasure flowed from the mark on my neck down my spine to the throbbing spot between my legs. Everett ran his tongue back over the mark, soothing the injured skin. His face lifted to meet my own, a smirk plastered on his face.

"Your mark—I think you'll find it to be quite pleasurable," he said. "If I remember right, the mark is a direct line to your…"

He reached between my legs and pushed his fingers through my folds. "Yep, my memory didn't disappoint me."

I could only imagine what he felt. I could feel the wetness between my legs without using my fingers.

"So ready for me, my lyka." Everett took his fingers and rubbed my liquid across his chest, like war paint. "I'm not the big bad wolf now, am I?" His fingers weaved down my body again, tracing every curve until they found the sensitive nub at the top of my mound. "I was worried I'd lost you when you first woke up," he said quietly.

My arms wrapped around his neck as he applied pressure. I writhed against him, his fingers rubbing small, tight circles against me.

"I was scared," I whispered against his chest, unable to make eye contact. His fingers stopped abruptly, and my body went limp with disappointment.

"Lyka." Everett tipped my chin up with his fingers, so my eyes met his yellow ones. "This is new for you—different. Different isn't the same as bad. Please, don't ever be scared. Especially when you're with me." I blinked before nodding my head, the movement pushing his fingers away from my chin. "You're safe here, with me. It's just us."

I nodded again, snaking my arms around his torso, bringing our bodies together again. Everett's hand snaked between my legs, feeling for and finding that spot so easily. His hand splayed against my cheek, keeping my head pressed against his chest as he wound his fingers around in tight circles, chasing my pleasure. My stomach muscles tensed as I became closer to climaxing. I matched the movements of his fingers, finding my rhythm to ride against his hand. I was there. So close. Almost—

His fingers paused, his hand pulling out from between my legs. I didn't have time to protest before he turned me around and placed my palms on the shower wall above my head.

"Stay," Everett commanded, using his alpha voice. My body froze, complying. It only made me wetter. My body felt extra sensitive to the sensations in the shower: the warm water running down my skin, Everett's body pressed against mine, the cold tile against my hands and face. He was shaking, his body vibrating against me. He was holding himself back.

"I know you're still recovering from your transition," he said, "but I can't wait. My wolf needs to claim you."

That was the only warning I received before Everett impaled me with his cock. I cried out at the sudden stretch, careful to keep my hands where he had commanded me to. My cheek rubbed up and down along the cool tile of the shower as he pumped in and out of me, slightly lifting my body up with every thrust. I felt his chest vibrating against my back, a growl from deep within him making its way to the surface. The sound left his lips, meeting my ear as his lips pressed against my neck. His hand pushed between my stomach and the shower wall, making its way between my legs.

The man knew what he was doing. He quickly found the spot between my legs that brought me to the point of no return. There was no escaping the roller coaster I was riding. There was nowhere to go but to free-fall from the peak he had built me up to.

I didn't recognize the sounds that left my mouth. They didn't sound like me. Had my voice changed too? The sounds that left my lips were inhibited. All control had left my body. I let the waves of pleasure crash through me.

Opening my eyes, I came back down to reality, my exhales fogging the tile my cheek rested against. Everett had found his release sometime between my cries. I could feel it leaking down my leg.

"I love the sight of me dripping out of you," Everett said.

He pulled me off the wall and back under the flow of the

shower, using his hands to wipe away the mess he made on me. His lips trailed kisses from my shoulder to my neck, stopping to lick my mark. I shuddered against his tongue, even though I had just climaxed. Were all female Lycans this insatiable? I wouldn't say no to another round.

Everett squashed my hopes of another shower session when he turned off the water. Goose bumps puckered my skin as the cool air touched it. Keeping me next to his body, he reached out of the shower and grabbed a fluffy white towel. He let go of me long enough to wrap it around my shoulders. Grabbing a towel for himself, he wrapped it around his waist, tucking in the end so it hung casually along his hip bones. Water droplets dripped off the hair that gathered in front of Everett's face. He brushed it back with one of his hands before he wrapped his arm around my back and the other under my knees.

Picking me up, he carried me out of the bathroom and back into the bedroom, setting me gently down on the giant bed. I didn't protest. I was both limp from the shower activities and my arms were busy trying to keep the towel covering my body. My wet hair made a dark halo on the sheets behind my head as I lay there, wrapped in a towel, staring at Everett. He was beautiful. His skin, tanned from the sun, covered all the muscles in his body. You could tell that long days in the gym hadn't built his muscles. They were lean and powerful from actual use in the world. Running, sparring, fighting.

His hands met the fold in his towel, and it fell from his body onto the floor by his feet. I quickly glanced at his face. He was smirking at me. I had been too busy ogling his body to notice he had been staring at me too. Like a predator, he climbed onto the bed and crawled over to me, staring at me hungrily. Apparently his appetite hadn't been sated either.

He pulled the towel off my body with a flick of his hand and threw it off the bed into a pile next to his own used towel.

The moment the cold air hit my skin again, I tensed up, any sense of calm I'd just felt leaving me immediately. Everett made quick work of catching me, pulling my body under his and nuzzling me against the mark on my neck. That mark was like an *on* button. I instantly relaxed when he touched it.

I also felt the ache between my legs return. Okay, apparently I both relaxed and got turned on when he touched me there. It was so easy to melt into his body.

My arms reached around his back and pulled him closer to me. We'd just had sex in the shower less than five minutes ago. How was I already so ready for him? I suddenly felt as hungry as Everett.

A growl vibrated my chest as I lifted my hips to meet his. He was erect and ready for me. Our bodies knew what the other needed. He brought the tip between my folds and pushed inside of me slowly, taking his time to feel every muscle that gripped him. I moaned when he hit the back of me, arching, to lessen the pressure. Everett wrapped his arm around the back of my neck, holding the tops of my shoulders, pulling me closer to him. He kept his erection pushed deep inside of me as I squirmed beneath him, trying to find a position that would lessen the pressure pulsing through me.

"Please forgive me, Lyka," Everett whispered into my ear. His breath was warm against my cool, wet skin. He bent his head lower and went to work, lapping at my mark, and his tongue sent shivers down my spine. My tailbone twitched, moving my pelvis up and down.

"For—for what?" I stammered, trying to form cohesive words as his tongue licked me.

"For changing you into one of us...before you were ready," he said, licking his lips as he looked down at me, his yellow eyes searching my face for forgiveness.

"I just need time to adjust," I said, panting at the sudden

lack of movement between us. My hips pushed up, bringing him deeper inside of me.

"Let me help you adjust," he groaned before dipping his head back down to my neck. His tongue dragged across my mark again, this time with more pressure. I could feel the edges of the mark catch on his taste buds, opening them further.

My muscles flinched at the sensation before I felt Everett's fangs reenter my skin, quick and precise. I didn't feel any skin tearing or hear a popping noise as his teeth reentered the mark. It was like the mark had been made to fit his fangs perfectly—of course, it had been. He'd been the one to make them. The muscles in my body locked up, tense under the feeling of being entered into two different areas of my body. I expected pain and lay there frozen, waiting for waves of pain to rack my body, but the pain never came. Everett's shaft was deep inside of my body, his fangs deep inside of my neck, and he moaned against my skin.

The muscles in my neck relaxed slowly. I could feel my jaw relax and the muscles release until my mouth hung open. The rest of my body followed slowly. Breath returned to my lungs, fast at first, then slowing to calm deep breaths. Muscles deep inside of me relaxed, muscles I hadn't even known I was tensing. I heard Everett groan as I unclenched, releasing my hold on his shaft inside of me. He started slowly moving himself in and out of me, all while holding me still with his teeth still in my neck.

I was pinned to the bed, unable to move, but my body was relaxing. My body wanted Everett, enjoyed being submissive to him. From where he had his fangs embedded in my neck, a tingling sensation began. The relaxed muscles opened pathways throughout my body for the tingles to travel. The tingles traveled slowly at first, then faster as Everett pumped in and out of me. The feeling mimicked the building of an orgasm, one that grew throughout my body, not just between my legs.

My entire body was wired, tensed ready to explode. It was like nothing I'd ever experienced before. I now had two points of pulsing pleasure. Two places on my body that made me writhe with need. All Everett had to do was touch one, and I was at the mercy of his desire. With one hand, Everett snaked between our bodies and found the other button between my legs. I could feel the smile on his lips against my neck as my moans became echoes in my head.

6

EVERETT

It didn't take me long to find my release following Elise's. Her moans as she climaxed vibrated against my fangs inside her neck, making my head tremble. It might've been too soon to bite her again, but it'd become a pattern.

I couldn't control myself.

Kleio had told me what it would be like to be with your mate, but I'd only half listened. She liked to exaggerate. This, however, she hadn't twisted.

Carefully, I extracted my fangs from Elise's neck. I'd been quick but careful when I'd bitten her, making sure to enter at the same angle I had the first time. There hopefully hadn't been any more damage done to her neck, and she could continue healing. I licked the mark on her neck. She moaned, wiggling underneath me. I was still inside of her, and although I'd found my release, her movements threatened round three. Elise wasn't ready for that. She needed to heal; her body had been through a lot. I'd been an asshole, too weak to control myself.

I pulled myself out of her, grimacing at the cool air that

touched my cock as it left the warmth of her body. Lying on my side, I pulled her back next to my chest. Her eyes were closed, and she breathed through her nose, calming herself. It wouldn't be surprising if she fell asleep. The transition to a Lycan was difficult on the body. She was doing so well, my lyka.

I didn't know how to communicate what'd happened in the woods just yesterday, while she'd been unconscious, without upsetting her. She needed time to rest, to recover fully. That meant not upsetting her further—but I had to tell her.

Not now. *Later.*

The bond between us was growing stronger. I could feel the "threads," as she called them, pulling us tighter. I knew she felt scared—this was a whole new world for her. She needed to trust me. There was no one else that would take care of her like I would.

Elise was mine.

She was so beautiful. Especially with my mark on her neck. I brushed her brown hair away from her face and looked down at the delicate bite on her neck. Distaste filled my mouth when I saw the purple bruises beginning to form around them. I hadn't been gentle enough. It had been too soon. I should have left her alone, let her mend. I growled at my idiocy.

Elise sighed, waking from the daze, and rolled over, snuggling her nose into my chest, continuing to take deep breaths. It was working. The mating bond between us was pulling her closer to me, helping her realize she needed me. It would take time, time I didn't want to waste, but for Elise, I'd give it to her, let her take what she needed.

"I don't want to be a wolf." Elise spoke with her lips against my chest. I could feel her soft lips move near my heart. The words that left her mouth traveled through my skin and into my beating heart, cracking it a little. I hadn't wanted to change Elise into a shifter without her agreement. It was my selfish needs that had driven me to bite her, to change her. "I don't want to be a dog."

"We're not dogs," I said to the top of her head. "That's an insult to the entire pack."

Elise lifted her face from my chest and looked at me with those jade-green eyes, lost. "I didn't mean it like that. I just want to be human." She looked down at the bed, and my heart cracked again at her words.

The life she'd known was over. She had a new body, new abilities, and a whole new world to adapt to. It was a lot for anyone to handle. But if anyone could handle it, I knew it was her. She was driven and compassionate. It would take time, but soon she would see being a Lycan was much better than being a human. Not that she'd ever been one completely.

"Sorry to say, Lyka, but you've never been a human."

She looked at me, confused. Her forehead scrunched with tiny wrinkles.

"My father lied about many things, but I believed him when he said he smelled wolf in you. Wilder confirmed it too. They had no reason to lie about that."

"Is that why I don't feel any different?"

"It's possible that you had enough Lycan blood inside of you that my bite just put you over the edge, starting the transition."

"Except—oh God..." Elise pulled herself closer to me, panting against my chest. She pressed her pelvis against mine, grinding against me, trying to find friction to rub herself against. "I can't control myself. What's wrong with me?"

I chuckled at her. "It's the breeding instinct between mates. Our bodies want us to make a pup."

It was like a cold bucket of water had dropped onto Elise. Her body froze mid-grind.

"I haven't been taking my birth control. And you—we—

haven't been using condoms." Her face buried into my chest. She was so cute when she regretted her natural instincts.

"I'm not worried about that, Lyka," I said, running my fingers through her hair, letting her hide in my chest. "Lycan pups are rare."

She exhaled. "Good. I've got school to get back to."

"You aren't going back there." My voice was louder than I intended. I had to tell her. She couldn't go back.

Elise pulled completely away from my body; the cold air filled the space where her warm skin had touched. She pulled herself up to her knees, staring at me with a look of surprise across her face. I looked down at her body—she must have forgotten she was naked, becoming more and more wolflike by the minute.

Her eyes followed my line of sight, and she growled at me, grabbing a sheet to cover herself with. "You don't get to tell me what to do, Everett," she said.

She looked so confident kneeling there. It made me smile. Elise had no idea what kind of world she'd ended up in. It was a world where I had many enemies, many of whom would use her in a heartbeat to get to me. They were already after her; she just didn't know it yet. She wasn't going anywhere.

"I think you forget, Lyka…" I said as I made my way over to her. She kneeled there, frozen, trying to anticipate my moves. "You're mine." I rubbed my thumb across the mark on her neck. Maybe if I could distract her, she'd drop the idea of going back to the cabin. She winced at the pressure before her eyes fluttered closed, a moan leaving her lips. "And you can't leave." She leaned her head to the side, giving me more access to her neck. It was amazing what became instinctual between mates.

"Your life is here now." The words slipped from my lips.

"My life is at the research cabin. All my stuff is there."

At my silence, Elise's eyes flicked open.
I had to tell her.
I met her gaze. "The cabin burned down yesterday."

7

EVERETT

"Wʜᴀᴛ ᴅᴏ ʏᴏᴜ ᴍᴇᴀɴ ɪᴛ ʙᴜʀɴᴇᴅ ᴅᴏᴡɴ?" Eʟɪꜱᴇ'ꜱ ꜰᴀᴄᴇ paled. She pulled back from me, her eyes bouncing around my face.

"It's gone, Lyka. Someone burned it down." The pack scouts had told me there was nothing left but a pile of smoldering ashes.

"That doesn't make sense," she said. "Who would do that? It's the university's cabin... *Jenny!*" Elise grabbed onto my forearms, her fingers digging into my skin. "Jenny wasn't in the cabin when it burned down, was she?"

I paused, trying to choose my words carefully—just long enough that Elise pressed her fingernails into my arm awaiting my answer.

"She was there," I said. Elise let out a small gasp. "But she got out." Her body deflated, her knees buckled as she sat back on the bed, nodding her head, her eyes now on the bed sheets.

Lucky for Jenny, a certain member of my inner circle had pulled her from the cabin and had been tending to her in his room.

"All my things...my research...the Subaru..." Elise's forehead and nose scrunched together.

"I know this is hard, Lyka. What matters is that you're safe—that you've been safe here with me."

The skin on her face suddenly lost all the lines she'd created in her confusion. "Wait. How long have you known about the cabin?"

"It burned down last night," I said.

"And you didn't think to tell me about it until now?"

"Lyka, you were unconscious until a few hours ago."

"You could've shaken me—woken me up."

"I wasn't about to jeopardize your recovery," I said. "I didn't think you were ready..."

"Ready for what, Everett?" Elise pulled herself up to her knees, holding the sheet over her body as a barrier between us. "Ready to be stuck in a shifter tournament? I wasn't ready for that, but I did it." Her hand splayed across her chest, her fingers coming close to the mark on her neck. The urge to tend to it again rolled through my body. *This isn't the time.* "Ready to be turned into a Lycan? I wasn't ready for that, but it happened and I'm still here." Her cheeks were beginning to pinken. "You don't get to decide what I'm ready for, Everett."

I dragged my hand across my face, trying to suppress the urge to hold her against me, to comfort her, try to calm her anger. Though the minute I held her against me, my cock would harden—I didn't even have clothes on to hide my desire. She didn't need that right now. She needed empathy, someone to listen. She'd been through so much in the last week.

"You're right, Lyka."

"I'm...what?"

"You're right. I should've told you. I don't know if I'm ready for any of this either." I had a new mate, a pack to lead, and the new position as True Alpha I'd inherited. I wasn't sure I was ready.

"We're ready for you, True Alpha." Gavrill's voice resonated in my head. I had a meeting with my inner circle. They were ready—more ready than I was.

"I have to go," I said. Standing up, I walked to the armoire to find a pair of pants and a shirt.

"Of course you do," Elise said, slumped over on the bed. I tried to catch her eye, but she wouldn't look at me.

"I'll be back soon," I growled, fighting against my instinct to stay.

———

It pained me to leave Elise there in the bed, confused and angry at me. It wasn't what I wanted. My instincts to claim her, prove that she was mine overwhelmed my body. She made me crazy.

That urge opposed the necessity to get out into the pack house—to let myself be seen. We'd spent the last several days holed up together in my bedroom. I had to make my presence known—I needed to meet with my pack's inner circle to plan a path forward.

My father was dead. I'd seen to that after he'd almost killed Elise. When he'd died, I inherited all he had. There was an influx of wolves from his pack wanting to join mine. A wolf without a pack was a dead wolf. It was a full-time job to weed out all the corrupt shifters he'd had following him. His pack was full of deviants and scumbags who preyed on the weak. They had no place here with my pack. But there were still blameless Lycans that he'd trapped and taken advantage of. Those were the ones worth saving. They'd be welcome members of my pack.

In the past days, my inner circle had shouldered the burden

of managing the pack and spreading the word that I'd taken over. I knew they could handle it for a little while, but a pack couldn't survive without an alpha. They needed me.

I threw open the wooden doors of my office, knowing exactly who I would find inside. Kleio, Kostas, and Gavrill turned their heads, looking at me as I walked through the threshold. They stood over my desk, which was littered with pieces of paper. Apparently it took only a couple of days for the organization to go to shit. They all fell to a knee, tilting their necks at me in submission. I shook my head at the sight. Even though I was now the True Alpha, I couldn't stand to see my friends submit to me like that. It was uncomfortable. I'd known most of them since I was a pup.

"Stand up." I motioned to my three friends on their knees. "Never do that again."

"Do what?" Kleio teased. "It's required that we kneel before our True Alpha." Her eyes gave me a taunting look.

"I don't want you kneeling in front of me. It's...weird," I said.

"Good, because I don't like to get on my knees unless there's a good reason," Gavrill said.

"Is the *good reason* in your room right now waiting for you to get on your knees?" Kleio said, turning her toying onto Gavrill. There was that look in her eye.

Gavrill snarled at her, not divulging anything.

"Weird for you? It's weird for me, knowing my best friend is the True Alpha," Kostas said.

True Alpha. I was the True Alpha. All my father's problems were now my own.

I ran my hand down my face, hoping when I uncovered my eyes, my friends would turn into the leaders I needed them to be. We were in a mess, and there were decisions that needed to be made.

"We can all smell her on you," Kleio said, bringing her attention to me.

No such luck. They were still the gossipy bunch they've always been.

I sighed and walked over to my desk, shifting the papers into piles, trying to figure out what they had been looking at when I walked through the door.

"So, she must be feeling better? I just hated seeing her like that, all curled up in a ball, afraid," Kleio said.

Kostas sat up straighter in his chair. "Did you scare her? What happened?"

Why was he suddenly interested in the well-being of my mate? I growled at him, showing my teeth.

"She just needs some time to...adjust. I have it under control," I snarled.

Kostas closed his mouth like he knew he should. What happened between me and my mate was my business.

"Well, it seems like she's adjusting just fine so far." Kleio leaned in close to me and inhaled deeply. Her cheeks flushed pink, and she backed away with a twinkle in her eye. "You know, I have to let Jack know something...that I forgot to tell him this morning," she said, hurrying toward the door.

The sex pheromones were all over me. I should have showered before coming here.

"Stop."

One word in my alpha voice was all I needed to say to stop her. Kleio paused with her arm extended toward the door handle. "You and I both know Jack's busy assessing the rogues. Let him do his job as the healer."

She deflated like a balloon while she turned around and shuffled toward the desk, following my command. The pack had been busy hunting and capturing the loose rogues from the tournament while Elise had been healing. Jack had been busy the last few days evaluating them as they were captured. He'd reported nothing good.

"We all need to talk, and everyone needs to catch me up," I said. "Jack will have to wait."

"Well, you're no fun," Kleio said.

I sighed; it wasn't always fun being a leader. I motioned to Kostas and Gavrill to pull up chairs. This might take a while.

I'd already filled in my inner circle over the last few days as I'd stayed by Elise's side. I'd told them what had happened in the woods with my father and how I had no remorse for what I'd done to him.

It was a relief to everyone that he was gone. We could all breathe a little lighter. But now the Lifestone was still missing, and so was Wilder.

Ultimately, our goal was to find both.

We needed to find and return the Lifestone to the forest. The pack land was dying, and we now knew what to do to stop the decay.

We had no leads and a missing pack member who had mentally fallen off the rails. I knew Gavrill was worried about his brother. I wouldn't put it past him to go off looking for him himself. But I didn't want that. I needed him here with me. He was my right-hand man. The one who took charge when I was absent. And with Elise here now, I had a feeling I would often find myself indisposed.

"Is there any truth to what Wilder said in the forest about the witches?" I asked my circle. It'd been easy to refute the promises my father had made Wilder, how he'd promised him a meeting with the witches. As far as I knew, we hadn't heard from the witches in one hundred years. But I knew my father had kept secrets from me.

"There haven't been any reports of witch activities in the area," Gavrill said.

"I don't think it's a coincidence," Kostas added, "that your father has been hosting the Deca Tournament for one hundred years and we haven't seen the witches in one hundred years. The two timelines must match up somehow. There must be a reason." He was the logical thinker in the group. My strategist.

"He told Everett he'd been hosting the tournaments so he could have an excuse to hunt other pack lands for the Lifestone," Kleio said. "He must've thought it was hidden somewhere."

My father was manipulative and calculating. I wondered how close he had gotten to finding the stone, what clues he had uncovered that I would never find.

"And now we're stuck with all his damn rogues. They've been a real problem." Gavrill sighed as he ran his hand through his black hair. "We got them locked up in the Vault, but they're a pain to keep. I have to pull straws every night to decide which one of my men will feed them. There've been a lot of injuries. A couple of my men are still in the pack hospital recovering."

"Ugh, I heard about Raven. His arm was left dangling by one tendon? That poor guy," Kleio said. That wasn't surprising —she found out everything that happened in this house.

I brushed the visual of Raven out of my head. "Keep them where they are for now. At least we know they're contained. Pay who ever feeds them each night a bonus." Gavrill nodded appreciatively. "I know Jack's trying to figure out how to heal them, but I'll have to think about what to do with them if he can't. It might end up being a mass disposal."

Kleio gasped at my proposal, her hand covering her mouth in horror. They might have been Lycans at one point, but now they were completely unrecognizable. Mad with anger, hunger, rabies...who knew? They were dangerous and unpredictable. Something I couldn't have in my pack.

"You wouldn't." She looked at me in disbelief.

"I would. I'll do whatever it takes to keep my pack safe."

"But they were like us once. Shifters. They've lost their way," Kleio tried to reason with me.

"They've lost more than their way, Kleio. They're gone. Nothing can bring them back."

"Maybe we can find a way. Give us more time." I looked at her as she begged me with doe eyes. I was a sucker for women with big eyes. She had too much hope. I wouldn't be holding her hand when she lost it.

"Fine," I said. "A week. If they don't cause problems. If any of them are especially violent, take them out." I directed that command at Gavrill. He nodded his head again in agreement.

"Thank you, True Alpha," Kleio said, smiling widely, knowing I hated the title. At least Jack wouldn't come hunt me down later tonight because I made his mate upset.

I dismissed my inner circle, leaving them to their pack tasks.

"Oh, Kleio." I called to her as she was walking through the door. She paused, turning around to look at me. "The Deca Party. I want it to happen this weekend."

Elise needed the distraction. We both did. She needed to be introduced to the pack so we could move forward—me as True Alpha and her as luna.

"Already on it, boss man," Kleio said. She flipped her hair as she left the room.

Boss, True Alpha. Everything I was, but nothing I wanted to be.

8

ELISE

Everett had left me in his room. That was fine with me. The farther away from me he was, the better. Things were moving fast between us, and I needed space to breathe. So much had happened in the last few days—I had a lot to process.

I felt the mark on my neck. It didn't hurt, even though he'd been away from me for the last hour. He'd said something before about our bond growing stronger and being able to separate from one another for longer periods of time. We'd more than fed our bond in the time since I'd woken up. After the hot, all-consuming, seeing-stars sex, I felt stuffed. I hoped it would be enough to keep him away for a while. I needed time to myself to think without him being there, distracting me. Before the bite, I'd a hard time controlling myself around him. But now it was on another level. It was instinctual.

I looked around the room—his room. It was dark and moody, just like him. A small amount of light peeked through the heavy curtains that covered the window, so I figured it must be daytime. I needed some sunlight on my skin, enough to warm my face and brighten up this dim room. Maybe it would brighten my mood. Sunlight helped a lot of things—not only plants.

Everett's bed was enormous. I crawled across it, making my way to the window. My feet hit the cold stone floor, and I lifted myself onto my tiptoes, walking the few steps to the window. I reached up, grabbing onto the velvet curtains and separated the panels. Warm golden rays immediately hit my face and my body. The window behind the curtain was twice as tall as I was and many times as wide.

I closed my eyes, protecting my corneas from the bright light, and enjoyed the glow beneath my eyelids. This was what I needed—the cleansing sun on my skin after being held up in this room for who knew how long.

A high-pitched whistle met my ears, followed by several short howls. I used my hand as a visor, shielding my eyes from the sun. The window looked over an oval-shaped arena. On either side were racks of weapons and training equipment. Piles of coiled rope and heavy-looking barrels scattered about. Three boys and a girl who appeared to be in their early twenties stood on the outside of the arena, behind the walls, waving in my direction. They stood with shovels in their hands, the dirt upturned around them. I automatically looked behind me to see who they were waving at. Of course, there was no one else in the room with me.

I looked back at the shifters and lifted my hand in a tentative wave. One boy gave me a thumbs-up, his eyes leaving my face and drifting lower. I followed, looking down.

"Shit!" I grabbed the heavy curtains and pulled them closed as fast as I could. I'd forgotten I was naked. I was becoming a little too comfortable in the ways of shifter nudity. I hung onto the curtains, my hands squeezing into fists, resting my forehead against my arms. Those shifters had just gotten a free show. How long had I been standing there sunbathing?

How much had they been able to see? I'd be the talk of the pack house by dinnertime—the girl flashing everyone in the window like it was the red-light district.

"Knock, knock!" A woman's voice interrupted my humiliation. "Can I come in?"

"Sure," I said. *Come on in. Everyone has seen everything already. What's another set of eyes?*

A tiny, round woman with graying hair tied into a knot on top of her head entered the room with a sense of authority. She had big round glasses that made her eyes look larger than they were. Her arms were full of folded clothes, which she set down on the corner of the bed before she fluttered around, tucking in the sheets and fluffing the pillows. The white apron she wore over her blue skirt made her look like a grandmother out of a book of fairytales.

"Oh, don't open those curtains, dear. Those boys down there would love it, but I don't think you want them to see you undressed."

Too late.

"I just heard a bunch of yelling down there," she said. "Everyone must really be working hard today."

If only she knew.

"I brought you some clothing. Alpha—excuse me, True Alpha said you needed some new outfits because all your clothing got burned in a fire." She paused to see if I would say anything. I kept my mouth closed, not knowing who this little old woman was. "Thank goodness you're here and not burned to a crisp like your clothes!"

She muttered to herself as she walked around the room, back to the door. "I also brought you some toiletries. Some soap, toothbrush, razors—just all the bits and bobs, you know." She picked up a basket she must have set down on her way in and made her way to the bathroom, placing it on the counter. "Are you hungry?" she asked. "I can have someone fix something for you. We just ate lunch downstairs."

"No, I'm not hungry." Who was this woman? She'd seen enough of me naked. I walked purposefully over to the bed and picked up a white T-shirt and a pair of black leggings from the pile of clothing she'd brought in. My legs slipped into the soft fabric of the leggings. These were nice. Much nicer than the leggings I had—that is, used to have.

"Don't you want..." She stood next to me, holding out a pair of underwear. I didn't grab them as I pulled the leggings up over my hips. "Never mind. Maybe I'm old-fashioned."

I smiled at her as she busied herself picking up cups and plates around the room. Everett must've eaten in here while I'd been unconscious. I pulled on a sports bra on and let a white shirt fall over me. Better.

"Let me help you with your hair," she said from behind me. I turned around sharply, surprised she had snuck up on me. She stood looking up at me with a hairbrush in her hand. She moved fast. I backed up a step, putting some space between us.

"I'm such a silly old lady—I forgot to introduce myself. I've been around for so long; I forget that not everyone knows me." Her feet scurried around me. Once again, I felt her behind me. She didn't ask before I felt the brush pull through my hair. It was one giant rat's nest. I could thank Everett and his non satin sheets for that.

"I'm Bunny Velkan," she said. I turned my head to look at her face. "Forward." My head turned back to the empty room in front of me, and I let Bunny brush my hair like I was eight years old. "I've known Everett since he was a pup," she said. "I used to brush his hair too."

After she got most of the knots out, it started to feel good, someone else caring for me. The scrape of the brush bristles against my scalp made my eyelids heavy as I listened to the sound of the brush run through my hair.

"Done," she said after a few minutes.

It seemed like she had only just started. I lifted my hand to run my fingers through my hair. It was soft and tangle free.

"Everett told me you were quiet, but I didn't think you would be this quiet." Bunny walked over to the window and opened the curtains, letting light flow into the room. I didn't hear any hoots from the boys below. I was sure they were disappointed when they realized it wasn't a naked lady behind the curtains this time.

"I can talk," I answered Bunny.

"Good. You'll need your voice here. Otherwise they'll trot all over you." She grabbed the plates and cups she'd set by the entryway and opened the door, preparing to leave. "Stay strong, Luna. We need you here."

I stood there watching her, not sure what to say. Now my name was Luna?

She smiled as the door closed behind her.

I didn't think I had been locked in this room, but a couple of minutes after Bunny had left, I walked over to the door to check—best to know if I was a prisoner or a guest at this point. I turned the doorknob, feeling the fancy pattern that was pressed into the metal push into my palm. It opened.

I stuck my head far enough outside the door to look at what was around. A long hallway with many doors lining the wall was to my right. To my left was a railing. We were up high, maybe three stories. I didn't get too close, but it seemed like the railing protected people from falling two stories to the first floor. Cheerful voices floated up to the third floor from the open floor two stories below. It sounded like a lot of people. Was there a party going on in the middle of the day? No, thanks. Not today.

I pulled my head back inside the room and closed the door softly, not wanting to alert anyone. So, I wasn't a prisoner. But I wasn't ready to explore the house yet. I needed time.

Everett's room though—that I could investigate. There were side tables on either side of the bed with drawers. I wondered what he kept in there. I padded over to the side he'd been sleeping on, my fingers wrapping around the metal pull.

I heard the door to the room tremble. The doorknob twisted back and forth a few times before the door flew open, a mess of curly blonde hair stumbling through the doorway. I jumped, putting distance between myself and the side table.

"Jenny?" I asked, tilting my head to see the face of who'd just fallen into the room.

"Elise!" She stumbled again toward me, wrapping her arms around me, caging in her arms. "I knew I just saw you in the hallway!"

Jenny released me from her tight grasp, backing away a couple steps. She was walking funny, limping. I looked down at her legs. White bandages were wrapped around her calves, and another bandage was taped to the front of her right thigh.

"What happened to you?" I asked. "Wait, what are you doing here?" I shook my head trying to straighten the jumbled questions in my mind. "Are you okay?"

"I'm okay," Jenny said, limping over to the couch in front of the bed. She sat down, wincing as she bent her legs. I remembered what Everett had told me: She'd been in the cabin fire. But she'd gotten out.

"Are those...burns?" I asked, finding my way over to a seat on the couch next to her.

"Yeah, the freaking cabin burned down." Jenny brushed her hand over the bandages. "When you and Leo didn't come back to the cabin after a day, I went looking for you guys."

I winced. Both of her roommates had left and never came

back. "You must've been worried. I didn't mean to leave you like that."

"When I got back to the cabin," she continued, "it was already in flames. I ran in—stupid, I know—but I wanted to grab my research. A beam fell on me and trapped me beneath it."

My hand covered my open mouth.

"I must've passed out, because I woke up here." My eyebrows raised up. "With *Gavrill*." The last time I'd seen Jenny she'd sitting with Gavrill at No Bars.

"How did he know you were in the cabin?"

"Beats me! We hooked up the night you and Everett left together— "

"Wait, what?" From what I'd remembered, Gavrill hadn't seemed interested in her that night.

"He and I became...friendly...as the night went on."

"Where did you..." She hadn't been at the cabin...I didn't think so at least. Although I'd been busy that night.

"In his car, silly. Those SUV's have lots of room."

"You minx," I said, repeating the words she'd used on me weeks ago.

"I know, right? I've been recovering here. Gavrill has been keeping me in his room. He's so hot—I can't complain." I understood her attraction to the male shifters. They were unfairly good looking, muscular, and intense. "I have a bone to pick with you—a proverbial bone, of course."

I nodded. I knew where this was going.

"They're shifters. The whole lot of them. *Wolf* shifters. Didn't you think you should've filled me in, the wolf expert at the cabin?"

"I felt bad hiding it," I said. "I didn't know if I could share." I'd felt the guilt of keeping what was happening in the woods from Jenny every time I'd returned to the cabin after a weekend away.

"They do seem kind of private. This is the first time I've been out of Gavrill's room." She winced as she rearranged her legs. "He's been gone all day and I've just been sitting there...in his room...alone. I decided to sneak out and do some exploring. His room is just down the hall from here, so it was good timing that I saw you!"

Jenny looked around the room, taking in the grandeur. It seemed there was good reason why Gavrill was keeping her in his room. She was still in the early stages of healing. Knowing the shifters' possessive natures, I wondered if there was another motivation for Gavrill keeping Jenny cooped up.

"When I first got here, I had a lot of questions," she said. "Gavrill communicates by grunting, so I didn't get very many answers out of him. Eventually he brought in Kleio, and she gave me *the talk.*"

"You've met Kleio?" I asked.

"Yes—she barged into Gavrill's room the day after I got here and called herself a 'human concierge.' She told me everything about the shifters."

I nodded. That sounded like Kleio.

"You heard about Leo, didn't you?" Jenny asked, brushing her blonde curls from her face and tucking them behind her ear.

"Yeah... I was there when it happened."

"Jeez. The way Gavrill explained it, it seemed like he got caught up in a bad situation."

"He was in the wrong place, lured there by bad people," I said.

Jenny nodded her head, looking at her feet. I couldn't tell if she was tearing up.

"You seemed close. I'm sorry for your loss."

Jenny's head popped up, her eyes free of tears. "I know what you saw at the cabin, but we never slept together." She wrinkled her nose. "We shared a few kisses, but that's all that happened. We got too focused on our research to do much else."

A knock came from the door. Jenny's eyes bugged out, her breath hitching in her chest. I walked over to open the door, dragging it open to check the identity of my visitor. Strawberry blonde hair filled my vision as Kleio pulled me in for a tight hug.

Jenny let out a loud sigh. "I thought you were Gavrill!"

"I just saw him out stalking the halls..." Kleio said.

"Oh shit." She stood up slowly from the couch. "I'm not supposed to leave his room."

They both rolled their eyes. "*Male shifters...*" Kleio held the door open as she slowly hobbled out of the room and back down the hall toward Gavrill's room. "I'll see you soon! He can't keep me secluded forever!"

"He wishes he could," Kleio said under her breath as she closed the door. She turned around, a bright smile on her face, and joined me on the couch. "Luna! I came here to check on you. This all must be so much for you right now. How's your neck? Are you hurting? Do you need me to call Everett?" She moved and talked so fast I grabbed her cheeks with both of my hands and forced her to focus on my face.

"Don't call Everett. I'm fine." I didn't need him coming up here making my body feel crazier than it already did.

Talking with Jenny had made everything all too real. Jenny had almost died. Leo was dead. The cabin was gone—at least, that was what everyone had been telling me. There were different levels of *gone*. Objects survived fires—if they were hidden in drawers or protected by something metal. There were usually things left, especially if the cabin hadn't completely burned down. Maybe it wasn't a total loss. The researcher in me didn't believe anything I didn't see with my own eyes. I needed to see it for myself. Some of my stuff, my research could still be there.

"Is your neck still feeling okay? No pain?" Kleio asked again, tilting her head to inspect the two puncture wounds. "Your face—it's all scrunched up like you're in pain. Or are you thinking about..."

"It's fine. I'm fine. Everything's fine." My lip wobbled as I pronounced the word *fine* again and again. Fine was a cop-out. I wasn't fine.

Looking at Kleio wrecked me. The way she looked at me with wide eyes, her attention completely on me—I could tell she truly wanted me to be well, and I just wasn't. The tears started to flow out of my eyes in big, fat, warm drops. Once they started, I couldn't stop them.

"Oh, come here!" Kleio pulled me into an all-encompassing hug surrounding my body with hers. "There's no need for tears." She held me as my body shook, all the fear and apprehension trying to leave my body through my eyes. Then she sighed. "Who am I to say that?"

Kleio pulled herself away from me so I could see her face. She had tears rolling down her cheeks, crying along with me. "I can feel what you're feeling, and it's too much," she said. "Everett shouldn't have done that to you. It's unfair to ask you to change your entire life for him. But he didn't have a choice. You were dying. I would've done the same thing if it was Jack." She shuddered at the thought. "We'll figure this out. I'm here. I won't leave your side."

She used her thumbs to brush the tears off my cheeks. "Unless Everett is around—and he gets naked. Then I'll be leaving." I laughed softly.

"I have something to cheer you up!" I waited for her to pull out a kitten or balloons from behind her back. It would take a lot to perk me up. "A party!"

I groaned and fell backward, my back bouncing as it hit the couch. Not a good surprise. "Oh, it'll be so fun. Everett said I could plan it all, so you know it'll be good." She wiggled her eyebrows at me, smiling. "It's only a few days away, and I've been busy, busy. It's the first party that our luna's attending, so I have an unlimited budget. So exciting!"

I felt her bounce on the couch as she sat next to me. "I keep hearing Luna. Who's Luna?" I asked. I stared up at the arched ceiling that had exposed beams spanning its length.

"That's you! Everett is the alpha, and his mate is the luna. It's your new title."

"I like Elise." Or Lyka if Everett was talking—and I was being honest with myself.

"I know you're still Elise, but everyone in the pack house is going to call you Luna. It's a matter of respect. They'll probably kneel and offer you their neck too, in a sign of submission. I should've done that when I came in here." Kleio shifted to get off the couch, getting ready to kneel before me.

"Don't...do that." I sat up to stop her before her knees hit the stone floor. "You're my friend, right? You don't need to... submit to me."

"Oh, I'm so glad you said we're friends, Elise!" Kleio jumped up and tackled me flat on the couch, hugging me. "I'm going to tell you as a friend: It sucks what happened to you, but you need to be brave while we figure everything out," she said. Usually silly and fun, her tone was now serious. "Be strong. People will look for you to falter and to show weakness. You can't let them see that."

Her words struck me. I couldn't let myself be a victim to my current situation. It was time to regroup and figure out how to navigate this new reality I was in. I had her to help me.

"Let me tell you everything I have planned for the party," Kleio said. "It'll cheer us both up."

I sat back and stared at the ceiling while Kleio also leaned back and began prattling off all the vendors and plans she had for the party. I only half heard, nodding or saying one or two words to let her know I was listening.

Inside my head I made other plans. Plans on how I could get to the cabin to see it with my own eyes.

9

———

ELISE

No one was guarding Everett's room.

Their first mistake.

It'd been all too easy to sneak down the stairs and out the large front doors unnoticed. I crouched down behind a tall potted plant on the porch as soon as the door closed behind me, the wood creaking as it latched shut. The two guards standing at the front gate turned around to investigate the noise.

I held my breath until they turned back around, opening the gate for a truck that was coming down the driveway. The truck's brakes squeaked as the vehicle stopped just outside the open gates. The driver parked the truck before getting out of his seat. He shook hands with both guards, one of them patting him on the back as if they were already well acquainted. They all walked around the side of the truck, the driver leaning against the bed with his foot kicked back on the tire behind him. They spent a minute talking before I realized they were all standing there chatting as if they were old buddies catching up. They looked comfortable, like the conversation might take a while. This was my chance.

Staying in a crouched position, I tried to keep my footsteps light as I tiptoed off the porch and onto the gravel drive, then picked up my pace, aiming toward the opposite side of the truck from where they were standing. I'd kept alert to their conversation, any pauses causing my heart to beat faster. Finally I made it to the side of the truck, walking carefully as not to crunch any gravel beneath my feet.

I snuck out of the gate without them noticing, curving tightly around the wall. I leaned against it, taking deep breaths, trying to refill my lungs after having deprived them of oxygen during my escape. I reached up and brushed my fingers against my mark. Everett and I'd been apart for a while now without my mark hurting. I would be okay. Probably. I pushed my worry aside.

The walls surrounding the pack house were made of stone, stacked on top of one another with mortar pushed between the gaps. My hand had brushed along the textured stones as I crept outside the walls, keeping myself low, my footsteps light beneath the crunch of the gravel.

Tall grass tickled my thighs through my leggings as I walked into the woods, my shoes sinking into the dirt, softened from recent rain. That smell, the one that could only be created by the earth, met my nose. I could smell everything—the dew drops hanging from leaves, the rotting bark of a fallen tree. I could taste the smells on my tongue and in the back of my throat. It had to be my new Lycan abilities. I'd never smelled or tasted nature so distinctly before.

Nature was noisy. I'd always heard the birds chirping, the frogs croaking, and the rustling of branches in the breeze, but this was different. I could hear feathers rustling, birds chirping, the wind howling in my ear. I closed my eyes taking a minute to center myself. All the noise couldn't distract me from my errand—the cabin.

I walked aimlessly through the grass, letting it brush against my open hands. It'd been a long time—too long since I'd been out here, in the woods. It'd always relaxed me, making my problems seem as small as I felt surrounded by towering trees.

Everything was green and lush surrounding the pack house. It was beautiful the way branches above me swayed in the breeze, the leaves brushing against each other—some falling like snow around me. I caught one in my hand—a maple leaf, half green, the other half as brown as a paper grocery sack and just as wrinkled. I turned it over in my hand, trying to understand how half could be dead and the other half living. I looked up at the canopy of leaves above me, there was green—a lot of it with some brown color sprinkled within. I dropped the leaf and kept walking.

The woods enveloped me, sucking me in. I'd glanced back a couple of times, only to see the tall grasses rebound from my footsteps, covering my tracks. I couldn't help but notice the farther I walked, the browner the leaves that fell from the trees became.

As I continued, I didn't feel lost. I didn't feel scared. These were my woods. The ones I'd become comfortable in through my research, through the time I'd spent in them with Everett's pack.

Long grasses opened to a gravel trail. Wide enough for an ATV. It had to be one of the trails maintained by the university. Those trails always led to the cabin. I was on the right track.

The foliage became more and more brown as I walked. There was no way rain had somehow missed this area, causing the plants to dry. This was the rot. I bent down along the gravel trail, pinching a brown leaf between my fingers. It instantly disintegrated just like the plants affected by the rot had. It was spreading.

A smoky smell filled my nose as I rounded a bend in the

trail. Surprisingly, the cabin wasn't that far from the pack house. How had Jenny, Leo, and I not run into it? Maybe I'd missed it. I had been thoroughly distracted by shifters throughout my stay, but I also didn't remember such a large compound on the map Robinson had given us. How had our professor missed it after all the time he'd spent out here supervising students?

I stopped in my tracks, taking in the cabin...or what had once been the cabin. It was really gone. The place I had called home this summer, all my notes, my plants. Smoke still rose from the debris, sending curls of tiny particles into the sky. The cabin, being made primarily of wood, had been straight kindling for a flame. There was nothing of the structure left. Only a couple of metal pieces lay in the ashes. The iron weapons that had adorned the walls lay in a pile. They'd probably fallen on top of one another when the cabin had collapsed. The metal inside of the refrigerator remained, the outer plastic shell melted by the hot flames.

I could make out a couple of mattresses from the metal springs and bedframes that had been blackened with soot. At least now I wouldn't get fined for my damaged mattress and window. They were gone. Leo's metal desk was also standing, surprisingly in good shape even after being surrounded by flame. The fire had spread outside the cabin—the body of the Subaru was charred.

My shoulders slumped. Now I didn't even have a car.

Movement caught my eye near where the front porch had been. A man with wrinkled khaki pants bent over the debris, sifting through it with his hands, searching for something. A small animal climbed a tree behind me, rustling the leaves and snapping a branch.

Professor Robinson stood up and turned to face me, his

white mustache lifting into a smile as he saw me. "Sad, isn't it? All the students that stayed here, all the memories made."

I walked closer to the destroyed cabin, watching where my feet fell. What was he doing here? There was still heat coming off the wreckage—I could feel it on my face. And despite his words, he didn't actually seem all that upset. Something about him was off. There weren't any questions about my whereabouts, no sternly delivered warning regarding my behavior with the locals. Robinson didn't even seem surprised to see me here.

"Oh, I have this for you." He opened his jacket, slowly reaching inside his breast pocket. "I figured you'd show up. You never could stay away from trouble."

What?

How could Robinson have known I'd just show up? He pulled out a white piece of paper that was folded into thirds and held it out to me, unmoving.

I walked over to where he was standing and grabbed the paper from his hand. He stood there, watching me while I unfolded the paper. The letterhead from the university was printed on the top of the page. My name was in the subject line —as well as the word *expulsion*. The paper went fuzzy as my eyes lost focus, unable to continue reading the letter.

"It's over, Elise. Your little hunt for the stone is over," Robinson said.

I looked up from the paper to his face. The stone? Everyone was after the damn stone. I didn't have it. I didn't know where it was.

"See what you caused? All your extensive research. You got too close. I had to get rid of it." Robinson motioned to the cabin that no longer existed.

"I don't have the stone," I told him. My neck twinged. All

of me hoped he'd take my word, but no one seemed to believe me about the stone.

"So, you *do* know about the stone. Sneaky, sneaky, Elise," he said. "I should've known. Students with full-ride scholarships are always too ambitious." He walked in a zig-zag path toward me, careful to dodge piles of smoking black debris. I observed his movements, some instinct in me warning me not to let him get too close. "I don't think you have the stone. Otherwise the forest wouldn't be dying, now, would it? You're a good girl. You would've returned the stone to the ground."

Robinson continued to approach. I took a few steps back, trying to keep a distance between us. This wasn't the mumbling professor I had known. He looked more confident, less crusty old professor. "No, the forest will continue to die," he said, "and you and your shifters will have to leave, find a new land that isn't cursed with death."

I shook my head, brushing away his words in favor of my questions. "How do you know about the shifters?" It felt dirty to be talking about the pack without one of them here. Professor Robinson didn't seem like he had anything nice to say. My hand went up to my neck, to the mark on my skin. It was starting to pinch again.

"You think I didn't know? Did I not warn you about the locals? Warn you to stay away?"

"You did..."

"And you didn't listen. The first days you were here, you went gallivanting into the woods and went home with one of them." How did he know about that? He'd gone back to the university after our initial meeting.

My confusion must've shown on my face, because he smirked and said, "I know a lot more than you think I do, Elise. I play a humble professor well, don't I? At least the university thinks so."

Robinson walked over to Leo's desk, pulling a smoking drawer from the metal shell and dumping the charred contents onto the ground. "You're smart, you know. First student in a long time to take an interest in the rot. The samples you took? Textbook. It was impressive. Your technique is perfect. Too bad I had to throw them out the car window on the ride back to my lab."

"You didn't," I whispered. I pictured my samples, collected in glass containers, shattered along a local highway. All that hard work and careful sample taking, labeling, and journaling.

"I did. I had to make sure there wasn't any evidence that made its way back to the university. We can't have noses snooping around where they shouldn't be." He bent down and lifted some of the blackened debris by hand, looking underneath it. "The university would've had a field day with the new matter you collected. It would've made its way into journals and conferences. With strong writing, you probably could've won awards for what you found. No one has discovered anything like that before, and no one ever will."

Robinson continued to walk around the steaming cabin, emptying charred drawers and sifting through piles of soot. "My office at the lab is dusty. I'm not there often. A sweep of a finger along my bookcase was enough to bring to the laboratory to test. After the results, it was easy to convince the university to put you under surveillance." He found a metal safe buried under burned lumber. It was where Jenny's room had been. He lifted it and flipped it over, the door opening wide. It was empty. "And then you didn't follow up. You couldn't, could you? All involved with those dogs."

"What are you still doing here?" I asked, ignoring the insult. He'd admitted to destroying my findings, so it wasn't a stretch to assume he'd also been the one who'd torched the cabin—probably to cover his tracks.

"I'm making sure nothing's left behind," he said.

I did a quick inventory of my belongings in my head. Everything in my room had been destroyed. My desk was wooden and had been burned to a crisp, along with everything inside of it. My backpack. I'd had my backpack at the tree with Everett's father. Had he grabbed it? Or was it still where I had thrown it? I'd put all my research journals in there when I'd left with Leo to get a closer look at the rot. My neck pinched again.

What was Professor Robinson's involvement? He seemed so invested.

"Why do you care? What are you looking for?" I asked. "You could just walk away, pretend none of it happened." I gestured to the smoking cabin. "My research is gone."

"I'm not going to walk away. I have it too good here. They treat me like the man I am."

"The university?"

"Maybe you aren't as smart as I thought. Or maybe your shifter boyfriend isn't as honest as *you* thought." He stopped his searching and straightened his jacket, then traced his upper lip with his index finger and thumb, smoothing his mustache. "I am Arthur Robinson, one of the last two male witches alive." The pride of his position was obvious in his voice and body language. His chest puffed up, and the wrinkles around his eyes deepened as he smiled.

"Am I supposed to be impressed?" I asked with a snarky tone to my voice that I didn't recognize. There was a clawing inside my head, like someone or something was trying to get out. I saw something in my mind—white and fluffy. It had to be my wolf.

Robinson laughed at me. "You'll be impressed when you see what I've created." He walked closer to me again; my body froze in the same spot even though I felt like running. "They treasure me. They appreciate my masculine qualities."

My eyes followed his as they looked down, stopping at the zipper of his pants. Gross. I quickly lifted my eyes.

He looked back up at me with a wicked stare. "The stone has been very useful. Witches aren't fertile; most supernatural beings aren't." Robinson looked at me as if he knew the state of my ovaries. Disgusting. "With the help of the Lifestone, I fertilized ten witches last month. It's amazing the power the stone has."

The images that rushed into my head of Professor Robinson "fertilizing" ten witches was enough to make me nauseous. Even the verbiage he used was repulsive.

"So much life contained in such a small package," he said. "All it takes is the witch holding the stone while I fertilize her to have it be successful."

I gagged, spitting the extra saliva that accumulated in my mouth onto the ground.

"I'm in high demand, appreciated. Even Matilda values me." The look of pride overcame Robinson's face again. "When Matilda found the stone, everything changed for us. Our small numbers grew. Soon, with the help of another male witch who's coming of age, we'll outnumber even the Lycans in this forest."

The Lifestone could create life? I supposed that made sense. It was missing from its rightful place in the tree, causing an unbalance, letting death take over.

"The Coven is developing rapidly," he said. "We need more space. Without the Lifestone in its place, the land will rot completely. You and your shifters will leave, in search of greener pastures, and we can move onto the land, using the Lifestone to create even more witches, Matilda's army."

An army of witches? What was going on in these woods? A lot more than Everett was telling me.

"She promised a spot next to her, you know. Her right-hand man, so to say." Robinson's chest puffed out again.

"No, I didn't know," I said, my voice had a gravelly sound to it.

This wasn't surprising. Throughout our entire relationship, Everett had kept things from me. All under the guise that he was protecting me, trying not to overwhelm me. I wasn't some little girl who needed protection. My life had been great before he'd come into it. Well, maybe not completely great. But him keeping information from me, especially about the other supernatural beings that lived in these woods, had ultimately hurt me. Not only was I physically unprepared to face them, maybe I would've brought some mace or something with me today... but Everett didn't trust me enough to tell me about what was beyond the pack walls—that hurt just as much.

Robinson licked his lips, running the tip of his tongue along the bottom of his mustache. "I don't think you know the Lycans as well as you think you do."

The wolf in my head snarled, pushing to get control of my mind, trying to take over the exchange between Robinson and me.

"That they let you come here all alone speaks volumes about what they think of you." Robinson took a step closer, and I took one back. "They let you come within feet of me—one of the last two male witches." His chest puffed again as he said those words. "Do you know what powers male witches have?"

I shook my head, my wolf growling inside my skull.

"Fire," Robinson said. He pointed his index and middle finger at me, flames instantly shooting toward me.

I yelped, jumping backward. My heart pounded in my chest and my skin felt slick with a glaze of sweat. He really *had* burned down the cabin.

"I could fry you in an instant." His lips upturned in a smile, like he might enjoy using his fire to hurt me. My knees bent, lowering my body closer to the ground. "I never understood what they saw in you anyway. Maybe just a warm body for them to stick their cocks into." Robinson doused the fire in his hand, then pulled at the zipper of his pants. As he adjusted himself, I saw the bulge that had grown his beneath his clothing.

He was getting off on my fear.

"Maybe I should play with you first, see what all the fuss is about." Robinson was too caught up in his sick fantasies to notice my body begin to shake. He stepped closer—close enough that I could see the gray whiskers of his mustache twitch in amusement.

A switch flipped inside my head. My self-control was gone. A shadow overtook my mind dark and consuming. It covered me completely. I was aware of what was happening around me, yet unable to regulate my body.

I no longer had control. My wolf was in charge.

10

———

ELISE

IT WAS UNLIKE ANYTHING I'D EVER EXPERIENCED BEFORE. The bones in my body pushed against my skin, growing longer. My nail beds stung as black claws grew from under my fingernails, their sharp tips pushing through my skin. I watched a snout covered in white fur develop from where my nose sat in the center of my face. My face lifted toward the sky, my neck cracking back at an unnatural angle. A sound left my mouth and vibrated my chest causing goose bumps to pop up along my skin. An echoed howl filled the forest. Birds flew from their perches and small rodents burrowed into the dirt, hiding. I fell into a quadruped position on the ground, my hands protected from the ground by soft pink paw pads.

Paws. I had paws.

The urge to shake took over, and I felt the long fur that covered my body tousle and then lie gently against my skin.

Fur. I had fur.

My eyesight had sharpened in the new form. Tiny drops of dew made tiny iridescent balls of water on top of the snowy white fur of my paws. My sense of smell sharpened too. The scent of the burning building was just as intense as it had been in my human form, but a new, foul-smelling stench entered my nose. A mix of moth balls and butterscotch candies mixed with a bit of body odor.

"What the hell! You're one of them?"

Robinson's voice was loud against my eardrums. My hearing had improved. Every sound was magnified, flooding my senses. My wolf let out a whimper.

"This is your first time shifting, isn't it?" He laughed, the different pitch to his voice surprising me.

I stepped backward slowly, trying to get used to walking with four feet. It was harder than I'd expected, like dancing with two left feet. A couple steps in, my back foot tangled with one of my front feet and my body met the blackened earth, covering the white fur around my body in ash.

"Like a newborn foal, trying to stand on its feet for the first time," Robinson sneered. "It's kind of charming."

I stood back on my paws, flexing my claws into the ground. A snarl left my lips.

"Even your growls are cute. What a nice puppy dog." Robinson took several steps toward me, holding out his hand like he planned on petting my head. "Maybe I'll keep you as a pet for my new offspring. Kids love dogs."

His hand got close to the top of my head before my wolf took control. My sharp teeth snapped at his hand, only air rushing between my teeth. "You bite? Well, we can't have that, can we?"

Robinson picked up a piece of warped, rusted metal from the ground near his feet, holding it in front of him, pointing it at me. In an offensive stance, he got closer to me, stalking me as I did my best to back away and not trip over my new feet.

I looked around the rubble for an escape. My wolf's body was so new to me, I could barely walk without falling over. I was like a toddler waddling around, trying to stay upright. There was no way I could fight Robinson and win.

"Where's your pack now, little wolf? I told you they couldn't care less about their new member." He held the iron weapon outstretched in his hand, getting closer and closer to me.

My backward walk was slow and cumbersome. I did my best to snarl at him, but it only made him laugh and taunt me further.

"Yes, once we break you in, you'll make a nice pet for my little..."

We both stilled at the sound of a low growl coming from the trees. A black wolf burst through the brush behind Professor Robinson, taking him by surprise. Robinson dropped his weapon to the ground, a plume of black ash rising from the impact. The wolf was terrifying, his teeth exposed, dripping with saliva and fur standing up along his back. It was how I'd tried to look to Robinson but failed.

Relief rushed over me. I was no longer alone with the crazed witch professor. Everett had found me as he always did. He was becoming my safety net. But I would deal with how I felt about that later.

Robinson took a step back. I sat on my haunches, my hind feet splayed out in front of me, my tail, blackened with soot, stuck out from between them. Everett stood between Robinson and me, growling and lunging at the professor with his open mouth full of teeth.

"We're here, and we're multiplying." Robinson bent his knees, keeping his hands out in front of him. "Soon your teeth and claws won't be able to stop us." He took another step back.

Everett stayed in front of me—guarding me. Robinson took another step back, watching to see what he would do. "There'll be too many of us and too little of you."

Everett leaped forward, snarling at him again, snapping at the air in his direction. I heard the sound his teeth made when they bit together—his jaw could crush bone.

Robinson yelped, flicking his wrist toward us. A ball of flames shot from his extended fingers, arching up into the air, flying over Everett's wolf and coming down right on top of me. My feet scrambled beneath me as I tried to get out of the way, but the flames fell too fast, sparks raining down upon me.

Almost immediately, I was crushed by Everett's body as he leapt on top of me. The smell of singed fur meeting my nose. The wolf whimpered before pulling himself off me, nudging me into a standing position. I shook out my fur, feeling for any injuries. Everything seemed fine. Just the tips of my fur had burned—thanks to Everett smothering the sparks.

The sound of crunching gravel met our ears. We both turned toward where Robinson had been standing. I could see the soles of his shoes kicking up gravel as he ran down the path that had once led to the front porch and into the woods.

A low growl came from Everett's throat as his back paws dug into the soot. He was getting ready to follow—to chase.

I backed away, tripping over my feet again, a cloud of soot floating up around me as I fell. A whimper left my lips as I tried to stand again. Everett glanced back at me, his yellow eyes assessing if I was injured.

I wasn't hurt, just clumsy in my wolf form, but by the time he'd turned back around, Robinson was gone. Everett's wolf let out another snarl in the direction Robinson had fled before he shook out his fur, shifting back to his human form crouching next to me.

"Are you okay?" he asked, running his hands along the top

of my head, between my ears, and down my neck. The pain in my neck instantly disappeared, and I did my best to give him a nod in response. "This is why you shouldn't be outside the gates without a guard, Lyka. Not until we've trained you more."

He must've read the question in my eyes, wondering how he'd found me in the first place. "I followed your scent here. The smoke from the cabin masked his scent until I got closer..."

We both heard what he left unsaid—before Robinson had managed to do anything else to me.

"Fucking witches," Everett said. "There hasn't been a witch sighting in a long time—and now they're here at your cabin." He glanced around the area, his hands still mindlessly running over my fur. Weight shifted between my back feet as my butt wiggled back and forth. I turned my neck to look behind me, only to see a fluffy white tail wagging at the pleasure of his touch. With Everett, I didn't have control over my wolf's body either.

"You're beautiful in your wolf form, Lyka." Everett spoke quietly, knowing how sensitive my wolf's ears were. "My black fur to your white. A perfect balance." I closed my eyes as he stroked my fur. "You can transition back now."

The dark shadow retreated from my head, letting light in through my closed eyelids. Claws retracted into my skin, settling back inside next to the bones of my fingers. I kept my eyes closed as I listened to the crack of my wolf bones breaking and resetting into smaller, more delicate human ones. The heightened wolf's senses disappeared as my ears slid back into place on the side of my head and my snout shrunk back to the nose I was accustomed to. Nothing about the shift was painful. There was some pressure I wasn't used to, but I kept my mouth closed and breathed slowly through my nose, riding the waves of the new experience.

Sharp debris poked the backs of my thighs, as I was still in a seated position in my human form. Slowly, I opened my eyes. Everett crouched next to me with one hand gripping my upper arm, steadying me.

"How was it?" he asked.

"Wobbly. Loud. Smelly." I looked down at my human body, which, of course, was naked. My clothes hadn't survived the shift.

"The first time is always overwhelming. Especially if there isn't anyone to guide you through it."

"I couldn't control my wolf, Everett," I whispered. "It took over. I didn't know what was happening until I'd already...shifted." The word sounded weird coming from my mouth. Shifting into a wolf had never been on my bingo card.

"Sometimes, if your wolf thinks you're being threatened, they can take over. It happens," he said.

My body started trembling, sitting there naked, surrounded by the smoking rubble of the cabin. I looked around the site of the fire for the first time without the distraction of Professor Robinson. It was all gone. The summer I had planned, the goals I had set for myself had gone up in smoke. The letter Robinson had given me lay trapped between two charred pieces of log from the cabin walls. Tears bubbled up in my eyes, coming dangerously close to spilling down my cheeks.

"You'll be fine, Elise. Sometimes your body can go into shock shifting for the first time," Everett tried to reassure me.

I pulled away from his grasp on my arm. "It's not that!" Disappointment that came out as anger left my mouth. "My future is gone, my hard work is gone, everything I had was burned in a fire set by a witch! Is this my life? Is this what is really happening?"

"It's a lot, Elise. I know. The witches are back and are apparently multiplying." Everett rolled his lips back, showing his teeth.

Tears breached my lower lids, spilling down my cheeks. "You don't understand. Everything I had was here." I stood up on shaky legs and walked over to where my room once stood to the bed we had broken together. "It's gone. Everything is gone." I crouched down among the charred remains of the life I had built this summer. Silky ash ran through my fingers as I sifted through the filth.

"You still have your backpack. I picked it up after I ended things with my father—before I brought you back to the pack house," Everett said.

I looked at him, tears streaking my face. "You had it all this time?" I asked.

"It wasn't like I was hiding it from you. I just didn't know if you were ready to deal with it yet. There's been so much going on."

Part of me was mad he hadn't told me about my backpack. It had a lot of my research in it and my healing supplies. The other part of me understood why he hadn't mentioned it. I had recently transitioned into a Lycan, and I was adjusting to life at the pack house.

"Well, everything else is gone," I said as I looked again at the smoldering cabin.

"You have me. And the life we're going to build together."

"That's not the point, Everett. This was my purpose. I was supposed to get my master's degree, get a job, and live my life." He didn't get it. Everything about me had changed, from my ambitions to the way my body reacted to my emotions.

"Life happens. Things change. We all adapt." I looked at Everett crouched down next to me. His face had softened, a far cry from the terrifying wolf he had burst out of the woods as earlier. "I never wanted to be the True Alpha." He looked away from me like he was ashamed of his confession.

I was surprised. "I know your father wasn't a good man, but

you had to want some of it, some of the power he had," I said. Everett's demeanor had always reeked of alpha tendencies. There wasn't any way the power his position held didn't excite him.

"It has never been about the power or the control. It has always been about the family I wanted to create. The pack is my family, every member a part of it. That's why I left my father when I was younger," he said. "The need to become powerful consumed him. He didn't care about the wolves he led. I had tried to stop him from hurting the others before I left." I looked up, meeting his stare. "He wouldn't listen, refused to change. He almost killed me." Everett had a pained look on his face. "If I'd stayed, I would've become just like him."

I couldn't help but commiserate with him. "I don't think that's true. We don't inevitably turn into our parents." I reached out, touching his arm. The contact sent tingles through my fingertips. "It's a choice we make as we grow, to follow in their footsteps or make our own path. You chose to make your own path—you knew what he was doing was wrong and you left. You're different from your father. I can see it in your eyes."

"What do you see?" Everett locked his eyes with mine. His gold irises were spiraling.

"Your father's eyes were empty, like he was drained. Yours have depth. There's a lot going on in your eyes, a lot of moving parts."

Everett looked away, processing my words. "At least your parents are normal, not power-hungry murderers."

"I wouldn't call them normal." There was nothing normal about having a nude sculptor as a mother.

"I think your mother will like me."

Everett was trying to bait me into reacting. I gave him an

eye roll. My fingers hit a hard object in the ash. I brushed away the dust, my fingers coated in the black powder. It was hard to tell what it was, since everything was covered with black residue, but when I realized what I was holding, I smiled. Made of stone, the small wolf sculpture my mother had made and mailed to me had survived the fire.

"I need a drink. Too much talking." Alpha Everett was back to his broody self. The heart-to-heart was over. "No Bars isn't far from here if we're in our wolf forms. Want to try again?"

If he meant shifting, I wasn't sure I wanted to try again so soon.

"It gets easier each time," he said, but I looked at him with trepidation in my eyes. "Won't it feel good to stretch your legs?"

The wolf inside of me tried to push to the surface, wanting to run. I knew there was no stopping her.

"My clothes." I looked over at scraps of fabric that had earlier been leggings. My clothes were unwearable. "I don't have anything to wear once we get there."

"Lyka," Everett said, brushing his naked body against mine, "do you think I would let anyone else see you like this?" His hand cupped the side of my face, bringing our eyes together. "I've got it covered." He looked down at my exposed skin before looking back up at me with a twinkle in his eye.

"Fine," I conceded. Everett squeezed the side of my face before he backed away, preparing to shift. "Hey, Everett?"

"Hey, Elise?" he quipped back as he made his way through the ashes to the gravel driveway. I followed him, keeping the wolf sculpture tucked in my palm. I'd have to pick it up with my mouth once I shifted.

"Please don't hide things from me anymore. I want to know...everything." I motioned with my arms around our surroundings, but it was more of a euphemism for all the crazy happening around us. If I was going to be his partner, his luna, I needed to know what was going on, not sit in the dark hoping everything would be okay.

Everett stopped walking and looked lost in thought for a moment.

"I'll work on it," he said.

11

EVERETT

WHAT ELISE'S PROFESSOR HAD SAID WAS TROUBLING. THE witches were multiplying. Did they have the Lifestone? Witchlings, like shifter pups, were hard to conceive. If the Coven was growing, they had to have some sort of assistance—but then why did my father and Wilder assume that Elise had the stone? How had they smelled it on her? Elise would have to tell me what else Robinson had told her before I'd appeared.

At another time. This was her first shift, and first shifts were always shocking. Paired with finding her cabin and research up in smoke, it was enough excitement for the day. She needed me now for comfort, not for questioning.

Her eyes had an absent look about them when she turned back to me, standing in the ash of the burned cabin. She had picked up a small trinket from the rubble, which she kept hidden in her hand. I didn't ask, and she didn't tell.

"How do I...shift?" Elise looked at me wide eyed and more confident in her skin, which was all out on display. I kept my eyes above her collarbone, more to keep my wolf under control than a courtesy to her.

"Let your wolf through. She knows what to do."

Elise closed her eyes and raised her eyebrows, causing lines to appear on her forehead. The shift was quick. Within seconds, the beautiful white wolf stood before me again, this time surer on her feet.

Her wolf was striking. The snow-white fur, in contrast to my midnight-black fur, was another piece of evidence that we were the opposite sides of the same coin, meant to complete one another. Even the way she wobbled on her paws, still foreign to her, was intriguing. I could see a look of complete concentration in her jade-green eyes, pushing as she always did to overcome challenges.

It pained me to see her so distraught over the loss of the cabin. She needed a purpose within the pack, so she would know she was contributing. Being my luna wasn't enough for her. I should have expected that it wouldn't be. My lyka was driven. Planning parties and hosting dinners would never be right for her. She was a healer. She thrived at helping others and she was good at it. What Elise had done for my arm during the Deca Tournament was a miracle. Even Jack, our pack healer, had said so. I needed her to see she had value to this pack, value to herself even if she didn't have her research.

The small trinket that she had been holding in her hand lay on the ground next to her. I got a better look and saw it was some sort of stone statue. Elise picked it up with her jaws and held it in her mouth like a dog with a tennis ball. Except she wasn't a dog, she was a wolf. A rare one. White wolves were uncommon. Something about lack of pigment, genetics. I hardly remembered the lessons from my childhood. But I remembered they were rare, something to be protected.

I let my own wolf take over, shifting down to all fours. I shook out my black fur, maybe showing off a bit for Elise's wolf. Starting off in a trot, I glanced around my shoulder to see Elise following, loping along as she got used to using all four of her feet. She was a runner, practiced in distance. I hoped she would enjoy running her wolf. She would be faster than she had ever been and could cover more distance in her wolf form than she could have in her human one.

Once I felt she was keeping up with me, I picked up the pace, letting my feet float above the ground, only touching the gravel when I pushed off for momentum. White fur caught the corner of my eye as I ran. She wasn't only keeping up; she was gaining on me. I ran harder, testing to see if she could match my pace. Her wolf kept up with mine paw for paw. We were yin and yang come together as one. White and black, opposite sides of the spectrum, yet as harmonized as the sounds that our paws made against the earth as we ran. It was beautiful. I had imagined running as a wolf with my mate, but I hadn't expected it to be like this. I didn't want it to end.

The sign for No Bars broke the spell we were under, and we slowed to a trot. I led Elise to the back of the bar, to the small red door the employees used. Shifting back to my human form, I climbed the three wooden steps up to the door and knocked loudly.

The kitchen behind the door was always noisy, but it only took a second for the door to swing open, the cook Dorothy standing there in a dirty apron. She took stock of me, all of me, standing there naked a foot away from her. A low growl came from the white wolf standing below. My innards warmed. So possessive.

She smirked, "What do you want, Everett?"

"Clothes, Dorothy, I want some clothes," I said, like she didn't already know why I was here. Dorothy owned No Bars, one of the few humans who lived permanently in the area. She'd found out about us by accident some years ago and quickly become a friend to the pack. Now she kept her back-room stocked with secondhand clothing for us and we kept her bar stocked with thirsty patrons. It was the only bar we haunted. "Two sets."

She looked around me to Elise, still in her wolf form. "I heard you got hitched. I've had lots of sad girls in here lately, drowning their sorrows with liquor." Another growl emanated from behind me. "It's been good for business."

Dorothy turned away and walked toward the stockroom, letting the door swing shut. She reappeared a minute later with two pairs of sweatpants, two T-shirts, and two pairs of sandals.

"We'll see you inside," I said, turning back toward Elise.

The door slammed shut behind me, and I made my way to the thicker brush we had emerged from. Elise probably wanted some semblance of privacy when she shifted. I heard her soft paws trot behind me, following me. Before I could turn around, she reached around me, grabbing clothing out of my hands.

"You already shifted?" I asked, surprised.

"I'm getting the hang of it." Elise was filthy from the soot around the cabin. Black streaks of ash covered her face from where she'd rubbed it with her hands. Dirt and soot hid the rosy skin on her arms and fingers. She pulled on the pair of gray sweatpants and slipped on the sandals I'd dropped onto the ground. The clothing didn't fit her at all. She had to roll the waistband of the pants several times to keep them from falling to her ankles. The plain black shirt wasn't much better. She was swimming in it, the sleeves falling past her elbows.

"You promised me a drink," she said.

I pulled my clothing on quickly, the outfit fitting my build better. I grabbed her hand, enclosing it in my own. The soot from her hands rubbed onto mine, the grainy texture irritating my skin.

We walked around the bar, toward the front door. I couldn't help but notice all the things about No Bars that weren't visible at night. The foundation was crumbling—the exterior paint bleached by the sun.

I mind-linked Gavrill to pick us up in twenty minutes. Elise would want to rest after her first shift.

Entering the front door like normal patrons, I saw Bill behind the bar, wiping down the counter with a rag. The bar was empty.

He looked up, immediately recognizing me. "Good to see you, Alpha." Elise followed me in and took her place beside me. "We haven't been introduced yet, Luna." Bill was a long-time pack member, managing the bar on the side, keeping all the shifters from causing too much trouble at No Bars.

"This is Bill," I said, gesturing my hand in his direction.

"Nice to meet you, Bill," Elise said.

"It's a pleasure to have you here, Luna. I hope Alpha isn't giving you too much trouble."

We approached the counter, ready for a drink. "Nope, not on my bar." Bill's words made me stop in my tracks. He motioned to our blackened hands. "I just wiped the counter down. Go clean up in the bathroom before you sit."

It felt like we were getting scolded by a parent. Bill had scolded us many times in the past when our drunken antics got out of hand. From experience, I knew it was best to follow his orders, especially if you wanted your drink cold.

I led Elise through the maze of tables to the bathroom, choosing the female side. It was probably cleaner. I let go of her hand, letting her approach the sink while I locked the door behind us.

"Kleio told me this funny story about her and Jack in here, when they first got together." Elise examined the sink before she turned on the water. I knew exactly which story she was talking about; Dorothy had been livid at the state of the bath-room after they'd reemerged, clothing inside out.

Elise let the water run over her hands, turning the water around the drain a dark gray color. I grabbed some paper towels from the dispenser and wet them under the faucet. Standing behind Elise, I used the mirror to guide my hand, carefully wiping the soot off her face. Her eyes closed as I wiped her eyebrows, the hairs instantly lightening with the removal of the ash.

Her body melted into mine, pushing against my chest as she leaned back. A small gasp left her lips as her ass met the hardened cock in my pants. It was impossible not to be hard around her. My body constantly craved hers. It was like it knew when we were in a private setting, that I had her to myself. Instant hard-on. She turned around, looking down. The gray sweatpants hid nothing.

"Running with you in our wolf forms kind of made me... excited," she whispered.

It took a minute for me to compute her words in my brain. This was a different Elise than the one who'd wanted the lights off and felt embarrassed to talk about sex. My wolf jumped to attention.

Elise's eyes narrowed, looking at me, slowly consuming me with her eyes. I knew that look. Her wolf was just as excited as mine. I needed to teach her to control her wolf better eventually, but it was too enjoyable seeing her like this, unrestrained.

Her hands moved to the rolled waistband of her sweatpants. She hooked her thumbs around the band, pulling them down to her ankles and kicking them off. With her lower half bare before me, I stood there like an idiot, too dumbfounded to do anything. Elise took control, hooking her hands around my neck and pulling herself up, wrapping her legs around my core. My trance snapped, and I grabbed her bare ass with my hands, lifting her onto the sink. The ceramic groaned under the weight of her body.

"Careful," she whispered before she grabbed my face in her hands and pulled me to her lips.

This new, more daring Elise made my cock pulse in my sweatpants, pushing against the fleece fabric on the inside. Keeping our lips locked, I pushed down my own pants, kicking them aside as well.

She welcomed me back between her legs, the sink at the perfect height for my cock to drive into her. I couldn't wait, no time for foreplay. Her folds glistened, already ready for me, wanting this as much as I did. My hands met her hips as I lined up my tip. I pushed into her, meeting no resistance as I slid deeper and deeper. Her walls squeezed my cock tightly, trying to milk me before I was ready. I paused when I reached the deepest part of her, my cock completely consumed by her warmth. The moans that left her mouth made me pulse inside of her, stretching her already tight walls.

"I can't be careful with you now. I can't be gentle," I said, rubbing my lips against her mark. Her breath hitched. "You feel so good."

I waited for her response. I was too far gone, no longer in control. A leash made of a single thread held my wolf back.

"Let me have it," she said.

I greedily accepted her answer, pulling myself out of her warmth before I slammed back in, filling her to the hilt. She moaned as my cock battered her pussy. Wet suction sounds finding my ears. It was like music to my ears, giving Elise so much pleasure. Beads of sweat traced down my spine from the exertion, but I was a man possessed, unable to stop.

I felt the weight of Elise in my hands increase before I heard the cracking sound of mortar breaking. I pulled her away before she dropped, keeping myself inside of her. The white ceramic sink fell from the wall, peeling the pink paint off the drywall with it. We stopped for a moment to turn and look at the mess. The sink lay sideways, balancing on the silver pipes beneath it.

"Oops." Elise took a second to assess the damage before she wrapped her thighs tightly around me and squeezed her muscles, gliding her body up and down on my cock.

"Fuck." I didn't have time to consider the situation before Elise had me coming inside of her. I stumbled, my back meeting the wall as my cock pulsed. Elise held on to me tightly, breathing heavy against my neck. She licked my neck, causing me to shudder again against her. She laughed, happy to have that control over my body.

I lifted her higher to remove my shaft from her warmth before I set her feet back on the floor. Then she scurried away to her pants—shy Elise was back as her wolf was now satiated. I caught my pants when she threw them at me, pulling them on, carefully arranging my cock gingerly in my pants. It was still hard, ready for more.

Elise grabbed a few paper towels from the dispenser and bent down to wet them in the sink that was now precariously held to the wall by the water pipes. The faucet still worked— we hadn't completely broken it. She washed herself up before she pulled on her pants, rolling the waistband multiple times. Watching her clean up made me realize I hadn't done the same, realize that I didn't want to. I liked to keep the smell of her on my skin. I could bathe in the scent of her arousal.

Her hand dipped into her pocket, pulling out the statue she had found among the ash, then she let it drop back in. I grabbed that hand and opened the door, leading her to the bar. Bill met my eyes with some curiosity, and I wondered if he'd heard the sink falling in the bathroom. Nonetheless, we were his alpha couple, so he just poured two shots of whiskey into plastic shot glasses and pushed them toward us.

"The drink I promised," I said as I handed Elise her shot. I threw back the shot, enjoying the burn of the whiskey against my throat. She cringed, not enjoying the burn as much as I did. I nodded to Bill as I took Elise's hand again and pulled her toward the front door.

"Shouldn't we tell him about the sink?" Elise urgently whispered to me as she glanced behind us at Bill.

"Let me worry about it," I said.

Gavrill was there when we exited the bar. The black SUV sat parked but still running right outside the door. I opened the door to the car, letting Elise climb into the back seat. I slammed the door shut before walking to the passenger window. It slid down slowly, revealing Gavrill in the driver's seat.

"Give me your wallet," I said, holding out my hand.

My beta didn't hesitate before digging the brown leather bundle out of his back pocket. "Do I want to know?" he asked.

"Maybe Elise can fill you in," I answered, grabbing the wallet. I knew she wouldn't tell him anything, but I enjoyed knowing she was squirming in the back seat at my suggestion. I turned around and walked back into No Bars.

"What the hell?" Bill's voice carried from the bathroom up to the bar. I pulled out a few hundred-dollar bills from Gavrill's wallet, set the stack of cash on the counter, then walked back out.

12

ELISE

A wolf. I'd been a wolf.

Running had always been a hobby of mine. The way it created endorphins, a runner's high, had always made me feel good. That high was nothing in comparison to running as a wolf—having four legs, the way the cushions of my paw pads had molded around the uneven forest floor. I was faster and all my senses more acute. The urge to run again was strong. My wolf leaped around in the front of my mind ready to be back in the woods.

I lay on my bed—well, Everett's bed, which I also slept in. With him. But not now. He was off doing alpha things, leaving me alone. At least until my mark started to hurt from his absence again. It'd been like this for the last two days—Everett finding me as soon as my mark started pinching, taking the time to soothe and stroke the mating bond between us before he'd disappear again to do his alpha things.

The short times apart gave me the time I needed to process what had happened—my new reality. I held my hand up above my body, examining my short fingernails and smooth skin.

Claws and fur came out of there? I wouldn't have believed it a month ago—heck, a week ago.

Not only was I a Lycan, but I now had new enemies. Witches. Robinson was not a good person, but were all witches like that? Everett seemed to think so. He hadn't seemed happy to see a witch—another threat to his pack. I wasn't happy either. Witches were a threat that would take more of his time away from me.

Now the cabin was gone and along with it my academic goals. My material things being burned up didn't bother me as much as losing the place I'd come to love, even during my short time there. The cabin had been my sanctuary, my home base for the research I'd done. I'd had friends there and a place that was mine. All that had burned to the ground. The summer I'd been expecting was nothing like I'd imagined. I'd submitted no research, and the letter Robinson had given me solidified my failed standing with Northwind University. I was done there, and I knew enough about these research programs to know that he'd likely blacklisted me with any other nearby schools with similar programs. The rot hadn't made it to the lab. No one outside these woods knew what was happening in them, and no one at the university would believe me if I told them Robinson had sabotaged me.

Still, I shouldn't complain. I'd been lucky—at least I'd made it out of there with my life. I hoped Leo's body had made it back to his family like Everett had promised. Leo and his family deserved the closure.

Sometimes closure was all you could hope for.

I let the events of the past few weeks sweep over me. Everett now had Wilder on the loose and Robinson and the witches back from wherever they'd been hiding, on top of the rot that was still ravaging the forest around us. We'd wanted to solve this problem together, but lately it felt like there wasn't much of anything we knew how to do in synch. Other than sex. And that wasn't much of a foundation for a lasting relationship. A true partnership.

The wood planks on the ceiling above the bed joined together in a tongue-and-grove pattern, reminding me of the way plant-bridge grafting worked—creating a connection between two different pieces of wood. Everett and I were two different pieces of wood, forced and tied together, expected to grow into one another becoming a singular piece. All the pieces were there—Everett and I fit together perfectly; I just wasn't sure we'd be able to grow together, to become one. There was so much stacked against us. It felt so easy to fall into step with Everett. To be his luna, to join his pack. But there was something holding me back from being all in. There were still secrets he was hiding from me.

My teeth slammed together, and I inhaled sharply, my head pounding from the pain in my neck. I relaxed my jaw bringing my fingers to my mark, wincing at the touch. It was slowly healing but still tender.

The pounding happened again—this time not inside my head.

"Elise? Are you there?" Kleio's voice drifted under the door.

"Yeah," I said, the doorknob turning immediately after the word left my lips. Kleio flew into the room, a whirlwind of strawberry blonde hair and glitter—actual glitter that rained from her clothing.

"I'm so excited!" She flung herself onto the bed next to me, bouncing the mattress. The movement made the comforter brush against my mark. It burned, so unlike the warm caress from Everett's tongue. "The Deca Party is going to be amazing. Mostly because I have an unlimited budget. Nothing is off limits—wait, that's not true. Everett said I couldn't hire bubble performers." I turned my head and looked at Kleio's flushed cheeks. *Bubble performers?* She glanced over at me. "Okay, okay. I know what you're thinking. But they blow these bubbles and dance with them!"

My neck pinched again, this time harder. I winced, squeezing my eyes shut. How long had it been since I'd seen Everett?

Kleio stopped talking and propped herself up on her elbows, looking over at me. "It's your mark, isn't it? It's been too long." She stood up, pulling me to my feet.

I gasped for breath, taking the short time I knew I had to breathe between the pangs of pain that would soon rack my body.

"Let's go find Everett," she said.

I had little choice but to follow Kleio as she pulled me out of the bedroom and down the hallway toward the large staircase. The next wave of pain hit me as I stepped down the first stair. I groaned, bending my body in half, my hand holding my neck. The waves of pain reminded me of the video our health teacher made us watch in high school of a woman giving birth. One minute she'd be fine, and the next she was hunched over, her body tense with pain, unable to talk or move.

The pain in my neck receded enough to continue down the stairs. I hoped Kleio knew where Everett was. I didn't want the pain to get as bad as it had been earlier.

Kleio led me through twisting hallways lined with identical doors. Good thing I hadn't gone exploring on my own. I would've been so lost. Thankfully we didn't see anyone in the hallways. I could only imagine what stories they would concoct in their mind seeing me in a state like this. *Not only is she a flasher but also can't walk more than a couple feet before falling to the ground in pain.*

I fell to my knees as the next wave of pain hit me. My hand

fell out of Kleio's grasp as I curled myself into a ball to ride it out. I breathed through my nose, trying to find a sense of calm in all the agony. Out of the corner of my eye, I saw her long legs crouched down next to me, and I felt a hand rubbing up and down my spine as my body came back to homeostasis. I lifted my head up toward the footsteps I heard approaching us.

"Elise! What are you doing on the floor?" I blinked my eyes several times, trying to see who was clearly in front of me, not believing my eyesight. "Let's get you up." Stunned, I stood up with the help of my mother. "I've been so worried about you!" She pulled me in for a tight hug. My arms hung limp at my sides, my mouth open in shock.

"She's been well taken care of." Everett's smooth voice floated to my ears from behind my mother. He made his way to my side, wrapping his own arm around my waist when my mother released me. My body involuntarily melted into his side. It was like I was a magnet and he was the North Pole. The burning feeling in my neck subsided. I could breathe freely.

"You're so lucky that such an attractive man came to rescue you from the cabin," Mom said. She reached over and rubbed Everett's arm like she knew him. "The university called last night and let us know the cabin had burned down—but they wouldn't give us more information than that. Something about emergency contact paperwork you never signed..."

She waved her hand in front of her as if she was shooing away a fly, a smile back on her face. "I hadn't heard from you, so I borrowed the neighbor's car and headed straight to the cabin."

"You didn't." I grimaced.

"I most certainly did. But then I had to use the bathroom. You know how important it is to stay hydrated." She patted Everett's arm again between breaths. He kept me tucked tightly to his side, a small smile on his lips. "So, I stopped at a little bar nearby to use their bathroom, and these tall, gorgeous men approached me. I was so flattered that they were talking to me. Your mom's still got it." She winked at me, combing her hand through her hair.

"Mom..." I interrupted her. This was getting to be embarrassing.

"And we got to talking about the cabin, and they told me you were here! It's so unlike you, Elise, to have made so many new friends. You've really grown up in the last month."

"Mom!" I snapped at her. My face was warm. "Why are you here?"

"To check on you! I left your father with the neighbor for the day. I had to see if my baby was okay!"

"As a good mother should," Everett said. My mom beamed at him, a huge smile plastered on her face. *Suck-up.*

"You didn't tell me you had a boyfriend, Elise. And such a handsome one." She took a couple of steps and wound her arm around Everett's free one, placing him between both of us. "He met me at the gate and opened my car door for me. Such a gentleman too."

I shot Everett a look. He was really working to get on her good side. Lucky for him, it wasn't hard to do.

"*Sweetie,*" I said, forcing the smile on my face, "why didn't you tell me sooner that my mom was here? You could've *messaged* me."

He smiled right back and said, "I tried, but your phone must've been on silent." That surprised me. He'd actually tried to mind-link me? I must not have noticed. There was still so much to learn about this Lycan business.

My mom carried on. "He was telling me about how you're staying with him to finish up your summer research. That's so kind of him, especially because of the situation with the fire." That was his explanation of why I was here? She seemed to have bought it. "And a job? The man offered you a job? You really hit a home run with this one."

My eyes shot toward Everett. There had been no mention of a job from his lips. He looked at me with a smirk on his mouth and gave me a shrug of his shoulders.

"You both remind me of Elise's father and me when we'd first met. We couldn't keep our hands off each other either."

I groaned, closing my eyes. She needed to stop talking.

"She's hard to keep my hands off of," Everett said, kissing the top of my head.

I watched my mom melt at the sight. We started walking down the hallway from back where I'd come from, Everett sandwiched between mother and daughter.

"Oh yeah," my mother chirped, as if she suddenly remembered something she'd forgotten, "and lots of sex. That's the indicator of a long-lasting relationship."

Behind us, Kleio spit, trying to contain her laughter. I'd forgotten she was still with us.

"If that's the case, then Elise and I'll last for an eternity." Everett grinned at me. I tried to pull away from him, but he held me tightly, leaving no room to wiggle free.

My mother patted his chest in approval, or just to cop a feel—I wouldn't put it past her. It was so inappropriate that my mother was discussing my sex life with the guy I was currently having sex with. What I wouldn't give to have a prude mother in this situation.

"Is Dad okay?" I changed the subject.

"Yes, he's fine. I told him I'd be back later tonight unless you needed me here." She looked at me expectedly, willing the words *Please stay with me* from my lips.

"You're welcome to stay as long as you want," Everett said. I looked to see if the tip of his nose was turning brown.

"I'm fine here, Mom. I promise. I'm sure Dad needs you."

There was no way she could stay here. I had to convince her everything was okay here. I put a smile on my face. It felt unnatural, but she didn't seem to notice.

"Absence always makes the heart grow fonder," she mused. Funny she was telling me this when I physically could not separate from Everett.

"But really, you should go home." I paused, stopping our threesome.

"Elise, don't be rude. I just traveled for hours to find out if my daughter had burned up with the cabin." She stared at me, giving me those disappointed-parent eyes.

"Stay for dinner. Then you can get back to your husband." Everett interrupted the standoff between me and my mother. Ever the referee.

"It's so kind of you to offer. I'd love to stay for dinner," Mom said. She scowled at me before making doe eyes up at Everett.

We walked to the dining room, full of pack members eating. They sat along long tables and round ones, everyone busy with their dinner. The scrape of silverware against ceramic plates and the low murmurs of conversations filled the air. Kleio had slinked off before we got into the dining room, and I wished she would have taken me with her.

Three large chandeliers hung from the high ceiling, lighting the room. Large windows looked out over the surrounding forest full of green trees and undergrowth. The arena I could see from my room stood directly in front of the windows. Prime viewing for those who were eating. A set of double doors served as an exit from the dining room and onto the gravel around the arena. I could imagine the shifters coming in through the doors after training to eat.

Everett walked over to a small table with two chairs. He pulled out one chair for my mother, and I could almost hear the words of approval bouncing around in her head. Still hanging on to me, Everett pulled out the other chair at the table and sat down before he pulled me into his lap. He ran his hands up and down my arms, taking a minute to nuzzle my neck. I couldn't complain about his warm skin against mine. It felt good. Although I almost complained about sitting on his lap in front of my mother. She'd never seen me so physical with a man before. I couldn't help but wonder what she was thinking. She'd just met Everett, and here he was touching her daughter right in front of her.

"Just like Roger and me," I heard her mumble under her breath as she unfolded her napkin and laid it on her lap. The awkward feeling was apparently only my problem. She and Everett seemed completely fine with what was happening.

Kleio emerged from the kitchen carrying two plates of food in her hands and one plate balancing on her forearm. She set the dishes full of grilled chicken, mashed potatoes, and some purple carrots in front of us.

"Enjoy!" Kleio said, winking at me.

"Do you live here too?" my mother asked her. "There are so many people in this house!"

"I have a big family," Everett said before Kleio could say anything. "I like to keep them all close."

My mother nodded her head humming approvingly as she stuck a piece of chicken with her fork. Kleio bounced away, leaving me to fend for myself.

Everett took my knife and fork from me and began cutting my chicken into pieces. He stabbed a cube of chicken with the fork and brought it to my mouth, feeding me.

I pushed it away. "I can feed myself, thanks."

"You need protein," Everett said, holding the fork back to my lips.

"Yeah, I've got it." I tried to take the fork from his hands.

"Oh, just let him feed you, Elise. It's so cute," Mom said, looking at me expectedly. Everett squeezed the inside of my thigh, and my mouth opened involuntarily, letting out a small gasp. Chicken was shoved into my mouth, and the fork pulled away. I snapped my jaw closed, chewing the chicken, glowering at my mom and Everett. My mom smiled at me.

I couldn't pretend I didn't like it. It tasted too good. I grabbed the extra fork on the table and stabbed a piece of chicken myself and brought it up to my mouth. I needed food. Sometimes I didn't know how hungry I was until I started eating. I finished my chicken and peppered my mashed potatoes and carrots before finishing them as well, while my mom asked Everett questions about the house and his job.

Filling my mouth with forkful after forkful of food, I barely paid attention to the conversation. I also didn't want to say the wrong thing. Everett seemed to have a whole narrative to placate my mom. I didn't know how much of it was true. A job? Finishing my research here? I'd already been expelled. I could tell she accepted his answers. She nodded and smiled encouragingly.

The chandeliers above us glowed brighter as it got darker outside.

Mom wiped her mouth with her napkin and set it down in front of her. "That was wonderful. I feel so good about this," she said, motioning to Everett and me. "I'm so glad you found such an attentive, attractive, and affluent man." Mom was really getting creative thinking of every *A* adjective to describe him. "I give this an A-plus." She beamed, proud of herself. I rolled my eyes.

"Let us walk you out to your car." Everett stood up, letting me slide off his lap. I was only free for a second before he once again seat-belted me to his side with his arm. At least she was going to leave. I wasn't sure how much more pretending I had in me.

Everett offered his elbow to my mom, which she eagerly looped her arm through, and he led us back through the maze of hallways and doors before we came to a larger set of double doors. He opened it up and guided us down the stone stairs to the circular brick driveway with a fountain in the center. Next to the fountain, a black Range Rover sat parked. Mom fumbled through her purse for her keys, which lit up the lights of the car when she unlocked it.

"That's a really nice car," I said. A step up from the family Subaru.

"The neighbor let me borrow it. The ride's very bumpy." She looked at the car with disdain. I didn't want to point out that it was probably her driving and not the car that caused the bouncing.

Mom took a moment to pull me aside. Everett hesitantly let go of me, waiting with his arms crossed, watching us.

"I'm so glad you're okay, Elise. Now that you have a cute boyfriend, don't be even more aloof than you already are. We miss you." She pulled me in for a hug. I wrapped my arms around her, hugging her back. It was nice that she came to check on me. Sometimes I felt like an afterthought between my father and her art.

"I miss you too, Mom. Take care of Dad," I said into her hair. She climbed into the car, and Everett grabbed me, pulling my body close to his.

Mom rolled down the window as she started the car. "Come and visit soon! You too, Everett. Roger will want to meet you!" she said. "Oh, I forgot. Don't worry about the cat either. Bessie's just fine!"

Yeah, I'd been worried about the family cat.

Everett and I stood there wrapped up in each other, waving to my mom as she drove away. We looked like the picture of a happy couple.

13

DAFNI, AGE TWELVE

She arrived as she always did, loudly and without warning. A car door slammed before the screen door flew open. I froze where I was standing next to the bubbling cauldron. The brew was purple and liquid again. Grandmother had ordered me to make it myself after I'd frozen her last batch. The wooden stirring stick I held tightly pushed tiny splinters into my hand, my knuckles white.

There was nowhere to hide. Our cottage had little furniture. Besides the lamp there was a table, two chairs, and a mound of blankets my grandmother and I shared at night. We had a small bathroom off the main living area with running water—cold, never hot, and a toilet that my grandmother said was always "running" although it stayed in one place.

"You've grown," my mother said as she stood in the doorway looking at me. Her hair was the same fiery red as mine and our face shapes were alike, but that was where our similarities ended. Mother resembled a villain from one of my stories. Where my skin was smooth, hers was bumpy and covered in a mixture of pink and brown warts. My nose was straight, although covered in freckles, whereas hers was crooked and hooked at the tip.

"Of course she's grown. You haven't seen her in three years," Grandmother said, leaning against her broom.

Mother spit on the freshly swept floor. Her green poison burning a hole in the floorboard. "Who's running the Coven while you play nursemaid in the cottage?" She didn't wait for an answer. "Do you think what I do isn't important? Isn't necessary for the survival of our kind? We have the Lifestone now. Our kind has never been so fortunate."

I turned back to the cauldron, watching the purple bubbles pop on the surface. Mother was always angry, picking fights with Grandmother. I tried to stay out of it. The last time she visited, when I'd been nine years old, they'd gotten into a fight and she'd destroyed most of the furniture in the cottage. She'd never replaced it. Hence why we had so little. I'd cried, Mother had called me weak, and Grandmother had promised not to lose her temper with my mother again. Years later, I hoped Grandmother remembered her promise.

"Of course, daughter. You never let me forget," Grandmother said.

Mother scoffed at her, looking at me. I stirred the cauldron unnecessarily. My underarms were wet with perspiration.

"Show me what I've missed," Mother ordered.

Grandmother walked over to the cauldron quickly, pulling at the stick in my hand. I held on tight, looking into my grandmother's eyes, sending her a silent plea. With a sharp tug, she took the stick from my hand and took over stirring, her eyes glancing from me to my mother, directing me to go to her. I inhaled sharply as I turned my body toward my mother, my eyes on my feet.

"Has your magic manifested yet, daughter?" I kept my eyes

on my feet, willing my body to stop trembling. "Have you inherited some of my magic?"

Pointing her index and middle finger at a chair tucked under the table, she flicked her wrist, moving the chair with her magic, positioning it in front of her. She placed a hand on the backrest and motioned me to come forward to sit. I walked over to the chair, turning, sitting in the seat with my back to her.

"Can you move things with your magic?" she asked.

I shook my head.

"Hmmm...you're going to make this a guessing game, are you?" She walked along the side of the chair, her finger tapping on her chin. "Can you grow things as I can?"

With another flick of her wrist, her fingers pointed at Grandmother. Quickly, her bottom grew out and upward, making her back arch and her weight shift to her toes. Her eyes widened as she tipped closer to the bubbling caldron. Like me, she kept her mouth closed so as not to encourage her daughter. Mother laughed, flicking her wrist again, and Grandmother shrunk back to her normal size.

"Dafni's taken a liking to killing frogs. She has a collection of them in the icebox." Grandmother thought she was helping. She didn't know they had died by my magic accidentally before I'd learned to control it.

"How'd you do that, daughter? With magic? With force? Either would be acceptable. I'd welcome any sign that you're a witch." Mother acted unreasonably excited. "Do you enjoy it, watching their lives end?" This was the most questions I ever remembered her asking of me. I kept my lips shut. "Fine, I won't ask about the magic you clearly haven't received yet."

She looked at my grandmother. "Was I this moody as a child?" Grandmother grunted, keeping the stick stirring. "You must have at least transformed by now. How old are you now, ten?"

"Twelve," I said.

"Twelve? What was I, six, when I first transformed?"

Grandmother nodded and kept stirring. "Dafni has yet to transform."

"What are you doing out here? She's...twelve?" Mother asked. "For twelve years you've raised her, and she has learned nothing! I gave her to you to train, to raise me an heir. That's the least you could do for me. I'm busy saving our kind while you're here playing house and coddling my child."

Mother grabbed me by my ponytail and pulled me up out of the chair. I struggled to keep up with her fast footsteps as she pulled me out of the cottage. I tripped down the porch steps and landed on the ground on my knees behind her. She let go of my hair and looked down at me with disgust. The screen door slammed. My grandmother stood, watching from the porch.

"If you haven't transformed by now, you will today," she said.

I didn't have time to say anything before she pointed her fingers and flicked her wrist at me. I watched the ground become farther and farther away from me as I floated in the air, dropping onto the wood shingles of the cottage roof.

"Jump." Mother looked up at me from the ground and said, "If you transform before you hit the ground, you won't get hurt." Our cottage wasn't large, only one story tall, but I was small. It seemed like I was up in the clouds, the ground miles away.

Grandmother joined Mother in front of the cottage. She looked up at me with sadness in her eyes. "Daughter, please, she isn't ready,"

"Whose fault is that?" Mother looked up at me. "Jump." I sat down carefully, hoping my wobbly knees wouldn't give out on me. She took in my seated position. "You're supposed to be my heir! Look at you. Worthless." Mother shook her head and walked back toward the cottage. "Leave her up there."

Grandmother followed her, back into the cottage. I stared at the car she'd arrived in. Puffs of smoke exited the pipes in the back. I strained my eyes, trying to peer through the windows that were just as black as the paint on the doors. The car seemed magical, the way the wheels turned without an effort. I've always wanted to ride in one, just to see if it was like flying. Grandmother would never allow it.

"Give me whatever you have made of that anti-nausea potion. It's the only thing that is helping those impregnated."

That was my mother. The cottage had thin walls and a thin roof. From where I perched, I could hear every word clearly, my grandmother rustling through her trunk of potions.

The clinking of glass muffled Grandmother's response. My mother's voice came through clearly. "Because you're the only one skilled enough to make it correctly." The rustling stopped. She must have found what she'd been looking for.

"Can you help in the garden?" Grandmother asked. They were moving close to the door. "The vegetables aren't coming in as quickly as they should."

Mother laughed, her cackles traveling through the roof to my ears. "Not this time. Maybe if she starves, she'll be hungry enough to please me next time I visit."

The screen door slammed, and my mother walked down the porch steps toward the black car. Mother got into the back, shrieking directions at the driver before closing the door behind her. The wheels immediately began to turn, taking Mother back into the woods, away from the cottage.

"Dafni? Are you still up there?"

The screen door slammed again. Another few seconds

revealed my grandmother standing below me, looking up, her hand above her eyes blocking the sun. Of course I was still up here. How would I have gotten down?

With two fingers and a flick of her wrist, Grandmother sent a stream of air toward me that blew my hair behind my shoulders. It was warm and familiar. I stood up on the roof, my arms stretched out on either side for balance. My feet shuffled toward the edge of the roof, and I extended one foot over the side, testing. Grandmother's wind met my foot, supporting the arch and heel. I brought my other foot over the edge, finding the same support. Slowly, Grandmother's wind lowered me to the ground.

When my feet met the dirt, she let out a gust of her own air from her lungs. "I'm getting too old for that."

The anger from my mother's visit overrode my manners, and I didn't thank her for the help. "You shouldn't have told her about the frogs." I stood on the ground with my feet in a solid stance, my arms crossed over my chest.

"You haven't been killing them lately, have you?" No, not on accident anymore. I shook my head. "Then I'm sorry. I thought it might appease her, keep her from tormenting you too much during this visit."

"Why didn't you tell her about my water or air magic?" I asked. That would have appeased her greatly.

"You don't need to be privy to her type of life just yet," she said. "The life your mother leads...isn't for every witch." There was little I knew of the life my mother led outside her random visits to the cottage. "Selfishly, I don't want you to leave me just yet." A rare smile graced her lips. Grandmother was hard on me, made me practice my magic to the point of frustration, but she cared for me. That was more than I could say of my mother.

"We'll keep working on your magic," Grandmother said.

"For now, come inside by the cauldron. I'll tell you one of your favorite tales while I stir."

I followed her inside, ready to escape into whatever story she would weave.

14

____

EVERETT

"It stinks down here," Kleio complained, pinching her nose shut.

"Decaying flesh never smells good," Gavrill said, leading the way through the damp hallways underneath the pack house.

It did stink. I'd much rather be upstairs, in bed next to Elise. That was where I'd tried to be as much as possible after the visit from her mother. I hadn't meant to go so long without contact yesterday—it had hollowed my stomach to see her on the floor in pain.

But alpha duties called.

Groans and screams vibrated the dirt walls, causing pebbles and dust to tumble off them and onto the ground near our feet. The hallways were narrow, with just enough space for one body to walk through at a time. I spent as little time down here as I could. It was always humid and dirty, probably because we were underground. No natural light reached this far beneath the earth.

Beneath the pack house was a maze of hallways and cells. The cells were almost always empty, sometimes holding a shifter for the night that had too much to drink or a pack member that had trouble accepting authority. It was a place mostly used to scare shifters straight. It had gotten a lot more use lately.

The biggest chamber, what we called the Vault, currently held the rogues my father had collected and used for hunting during the Deca Games. As soon as he'd died, we'd made sure they were all gathered so they wouldn't wander off attacking humans. They'd been sitting in there, continuing to rot for the last week. We didn't know what to do with them. It had become a point of contention between us.

We found our way around based on memory and the flashlight Gavrill held in front of him. I left this part of the pack house to Kostas. He never told me, but I assumed he liked it based on how much time he spent down here. There was a dark side to Kostas that he didn't let many people see. He was my strategist and enforcer for a reason. "Calculating" was what his last target had called him.

"He's just through here." Gavrill stopped before a metal door, resting his hand on the handle. "He's been working on him for a while. It's not going to be pretty." Gavrill directed this toward Kleio, probably the most sensitive of us.

"I can handle it," she said.

Gavrill slowly opened the door, lifting the flashlight into the space to illuminate the room. The room was one of the larger chambers. Not the Vault, but one that Kostas liked to use to extract information from those unwilling to divulge. The room was bare, the walls the same packed dirt as the hallway. In the center of the room was a single wooden chair. Stained with blood and other fluids, it had held its fair share of bodies.

A lantern set off to the side cast an eerie glow. It was just enough light for Kostas to see but not enough light for his victim to anticipate his moves. A rope held the rogue in the chair. It was bound around his abdomen, weaving through the spindles of the backrest, keeping him in place. Kostas had gotten him to shift back into his human form—no easy feat. He must've been transformed into a rogue not long ago.

The man slumped over in the chair, his head hanging limply from his neck. His hair, soaked with blood and sweat, dripped onto the ground collecting in puddles in the dirt. Kleio stuck by the door while Gavrill and I walked toward the chair, staring at the sorry state of the man before us. Kostas walked out of the shadows to meet us. His hands were brown from a mix of blood and dirt. The clothes he was wearing were soaked with sweat from exerting himself in this humid environment.

"Here are my friends I was telling you about." Kostas kicked one leg of the chair the rogue was sitting on.

The rogue groaned from the movement and pulled himself up slowly into a seated position with his back against the backrest of the chair. His head still hung limply from his neck, his eyes closed.

"I need you to tell them what you told me." Kostas kicked the chair again.

The rogue's eyelids opened, but his head still dangled, his chin on his chest. Still, he didn't talk.

"They can come back later," Kostas said, "if you need me to give you some more motivation..."

"Fine! I'll talk. He"—the rogue gestured to Kostas— "promised he wouldn't hurt my sister, Molly, if I talked. She's in there with the rest of them."

The rogue directed that at me. I nodded at him, agreeing with his request. I wasn't sure what I was going to do with the rogues yet. It was easy to make empty promises to a rogue who was practically empty themselves. That Kostas had found a rogue in the group of them who could still make coherent sentences was impressive. He probably wouldn't be able to connect his thoughts for long.

"He took us from our pack last year," the rogue said. "I saw them rounding up the younger females, tying them up and forcing them into trucks late at night when everyone was sleeping. Our alpha tried to fight them off, but it wasn't any use. There were too many of them." He took in a couple deep breaths. "I snuck into the truck that my sister was in. The knots they'd tied were too tight for me to loosen."

He closed his eyes, remembering. "I kept quiet as they drove for a couple hours. I was ready to fight when they opened the door. His pack members overwhelmed me and tied me up too. They brought us over to a giant tree and lined us up. Those that couldn't stand up went to the front of the line and were thrown at the foot of the True Alpha."

I knew he was speaking of my father, the *former* True Alpha. The rogues didn't know that he'd died.

"He took turns with each of us, slicing our throats with his knife and letting our blood drain into the ground. He threw the empty bodies in a pile for his pack doctor to sew up."

I inched closer to him, looking closely at his neck. A raised red scar from crudely sewn stitches sat on his skin.

"They threw the bodies into a truck," he continued. "They stacked us, one on top of each other. Some of us were still conscious and others weren't. They brought us to his dungeon and threw us all together in a large cell. They left us to die. Some of us did. Others of us died in different ways, lost ourselves. I tried to help my sister, but she slowly vanished. Turned rogue, like the rest of us."

"Seems like the former True Alpha has been feeding the

forest to stop the rot for a long time," Gavrill, who'd been listening intently, said. I appreciated him not referring to the True Alpha as my father.

"Indeed. This makes things a lot more complicated," I said, standing up and looking at my inner circle. Knowing that the rogues were innocent in their creation, it would become much harder to dispose of them. But it didn't make them any less dangerous. They were hardly Lycans anymore. I refused to follow in my father's footsteps, draining wolves to feed the forest. There had to be another way to keep the rot from spreading. Even without the stone. "Throw him back in." I waved my hand at the rogue, dismissing him. "Wait! You can't! You can't throw me in like this." He motioned to his body in human form. "They'll eat me alive!"

I paused, glancing up and down his human form. He was right—the rogues in the Vault would tear him apart limb for limb if we put him back there in his human form.

"Put him in one of the empty cells," I ordered Kostas. He nodded his head, crouching behind the rogue and untying his hands.

"Thank you—thank you," the rogue chanted. I grunted, turning around to leave the room. "You could stand to be a little nicer, Everett," Kleio scolded. "He gave you the information you wanted."

Kostas dragged the rogue from the room and down the hall to one of the empty cells. I heard the metal door latch shut as Kostas closed him in. It wasn't the most comfortable of accommodations, but it was better than releasing him back into the Vault.

"He's still a rogue, Kleio. We don't know what they're capable of," I said.

Kostas came stalking back down the hallway. I turned to

climb the stairs back up into the pack house. Elise would need me soon.

But first, I looked back at my inner circle. "No one tells Elise what's going on down here. She doesn't need more to worry about."

They all nodded. I looked straight at Kleio, giving her a pointed look. She was the closest to Elise. She'd better not tell.

15

———

ELISE

ONCE AGAIN, I AWOKE TO EVERETT'S SIDE OF THE BED empty. The sheets were still warm when I reached over to touch him, only for my hand to flop onto the mattress. I wondered how long he'd been gone. How much time did I have before my neck would start hurting? I pushed aside those thoughts and swung out of bed, placing my feet against the stone floor.

I got dressed before making my way over to the window overlooking the arena. It felt good to be back in my self-imposed uniform—leggings and a T-shirt. The sun was shining brightly today, and the rays felt good on my skin. I needed to get out of this room today and into the fresh air.

There were no shifters outside with shovels today. The arena was empty, all the equipment put away neatly. I looked to where they'd stood the other day, just beyond the short walls of the arena. A rectangle of freshly upturned black dirt surrounded by a white-picket fence that hadn't been there previously caught my interest. It couldn't be.

The door to the hallway opened easily, although creaking

hinges gave me pause. A brown-haired woman poked her head out of a nearby room.

"Luna!" Her smile was warm and wide. I tried to mirror her ease with my own smile as I stood in the hall. "Do you need help finding your way?"

"No, thanks. I think I know where I'm going," I said. I was still getting used to being called *Luna*.

"If you get lost, don't be afraid to ask any one for help. It's a big pack house."

"I will. Thank you."

The woman smiled again before turning back to her room.

I scurried down the hall and down the enormous staircase, trying to remember how to get to the dining room we'd been in yesterday. There was a door in there that would lead me outside. I probably should've asked for directions from the brown-haired woman. I had forgotten to ask her name—so rude of me. I needed to remember to be more friendly, especially if I was to be their luna.

Still, I didn't want to ask for directions. That would make it apparent that I didn't know what I was doing, that I was winging it. So, I nodded my head in hello to everyone I passed in the hallways, refusing to ask for directions, following the scent of bacon toward the dining room.

Turning a corner, I saw the wide double doors that opened into the dining room just down the hall. I walked quickly toward the room, peeking my head through the crack of the doors before I opened them further. There were pack members milling about talking as they wiped down the tables from breakfast. Everyone paused as I walked into the room, their heads tilting to the side, showing me their necks.

They're submitting to me, I realized.

"You all don't need to...do that," I said quietly. Their

submissions made me slightly uncomfortable. I was new to them; I'd done nothing to earn their respect.

"We'll gladly submit to our luna," an older man said holding a wet rag. The others around him nodded in agreement.

"Well...thank you?" I didn't know how to respond. Luckily, everyone went back to their work or conversations leaving me to navigate the dining room.

Weaving through the tables, I kept my eye on the large windows, trying to peer over the walls of the arena to the picket fence beyond.

The doors to the outside were unlocked, and I pushed them open, closing my eyes to appreciate the sun on my skin and the fresh air in my lungs. I bypassed the arena and walked over to the white-picket fence I'd seen from my room. A tall, white wooden arch framed a gate with a hook-and-eye latch. I flipped the latch and swung the gate open. My feet were bare, but I didn't care. I let the dirt squish between my toes.

It was a garden. A large one with high-quality black dirt that plants would thrive in. Several raised garden beds sat in the dirt. They even had hinged hoop houses to cover the beds to keep the seedlings warm. It was empty, a blank canvas for me to plant. I knew in my gut that this was for me. A garden was something I'd mentioned to Everett in the cabin weeks before.

He'd remembered.

In the corner of the garden there was a crate. I walked over, letting my feet sink into the dirt with every step. I crouched down next to the crate, examining the contents: packets of seeds, a trowel, a pair of snips, and a watering can.

Along the fence next to the crate, there were several potted medicinal plants, already sturdy and thriving. I touched the spiky stalk of aloe and my favorite yarrow. There were even some plants that I hadn't had before in my personal collection.

The oval leaves of a selfheal plant caught my eye. I stroked the leaves. Many believed this was a weed. Little did they know it actually had healing properties. Leaning against the fence was a hoe and rake, brand new.

I squealed, then looked around to make sure no one had heard my outburst. Everything was here, just for me.

It was second nature for me to be in the garden. It'd been a while since I'd worked in one. We'd had one at my parents' old house, but I'd lost access to that when the bank had commandeered the house. My heart sank as I thought about the plants I'd saved and transported from that garden to the cabin. They were crisps now, burned up in the fire.

I'd have to start from scratch. The packets of seeds were mostly heirloom seeds. I thumbed through the packets, looking and deciding what I would plant first...tomatoes, cucumber, squash, and peppers. There was a large selection of medicinal seeds that I immediately recognized: elderberry, witch hazel, chamomile, and garlic. These would do nicely for my initial planting. I smiled, knowing I was already planning to plant more.

The trowel felt good in my hands as I dragged it inside one of the raised beds, making a contour in the dirt to plant my first seeds. It was busy work that kept my mind occupied. Remembering the aloe plant along the fence, I snapped off a stalk. Using the sharp edges of my trowel, I sliced open the aloe stalk lengthwise and peeled the two halves apart. I took some of the delicate jelly inside the aloe and placed it where I wanted the tomato plant to sprout. The packet of tomato seeds easily ripped open, and I carefully placed a seed into the aloe jelly before covering it up.

It became a rhythm, spacing them correctly and covering them up. Patting the dirt on top of them, tucking them into germinate. It was beautiful, creating a new living thing. Despite the loss of the plants that I had nurtured at the cabin, I was creating new life here to restore the balance. I smiled, thinking of the metaphor I just created for my life.

In the second raised bed, I ditched the aloe and made tiny rows for the selfheal to grow. Having fresh selfheal at my disposal would be helpful for healing—if I needed it.

"Lyka, somehow I knew I'd find you here." His voice met my ears. The same one that whispered *mate* into my ear while he thrust into me, making me feel desired. Also the same voice that he *didn't* use—keeping quiet to keep things hidden from me.

"You did this, didn't you?" I asked.

"Well, it was my idea, but some of the younger pack members dug the garden and put up the fence. Bunny found all the supplies and shopped for the seeds."

"Thank you. This is amazing." I said, biting my lower lip.

My eyes bounced around the garden and the surrounding tall trees just beyond the stone fence surrounding the property. Ever since I'd come to the pack house, our interactions had been in the bedroom or included other people—the time together in the woods seemed like forever ago now, almost like a dream. I didn't know how to just *be* with him anymore.

"It's the least I could do." Everett tucked a piece of hair behind my ear that'd fallen out of the bun on the top of my head. My eyes returned to his face. "I know it hasn't been easy for you—transitioning, moving here."

I squeezed my toes in the dirt. It hadn't been easy. Not one bit of it. But here, with my toes in the dirt and earth pressed under my fingernails I felt like myself again.

"You planted all of this today?" Everett looked down at the raised planter beds where I'd spent the day digging and planting.

I brushed a drip of sweat that fell from my hairline, down

my forehead, my fingers smearing dirt across my skin. Everett took a step closer, reaching out with both hands. One palmed the back of my skull, tilting my face toward his. The other slowly rubbed the smear of dirt from my skin, his thumb moving in tight circles against my forehead. My eyelids flickered at the sensation. His physical presence had a hold on my body; it always reacted for him.

"I'm impressed," he said, still holding the back of my head in the palm of his hand. This time, the sound of his voice broke me out of the trance he'd put me in with his touch. I took a step to the side, breaking our contact.

"I got excited when I saw everything," I gestured to the garden space. "It's probably too much."

"I'd argue it's not enough," Everett said. "You don't yet realize what you bring to the pack. The way you can work with the dirt, make things grow...it's not something that comes easily to us."

There it was again—him referring to the pack as "us" and me as something separate. I was different, yes, but that didn't mean he could keep things from me. I'd been completely blindsided when he'd mentioned a job in front of my mother the other day. You'd think he'd discuss that with me before getting her hopes up.

"We need you—I need you here. I can get you more planting supplies, seeds? I can get you seeds. Do you need anything else?"

I looked down at the neatly planted rows of seeds and the tools that'd become muddy from use. Whoever had organized the garden had done a good job. "No, I have everything I need."

"How about outside of gardening?" he said. "Do you need anything here at the pack house?"

Everett stepped closer to me, wrapping his long arms around my back, pulling our chests together. I held in a moan at the contact between us. "I know I've been busy, sometimes absent, but just tell me—tell anyone if you desire something, and we will get it for you."

I took a step back, still wrapped in his arms. I stared at his yellow eyes, watching the way they swirled as they looked at me. This was the Everett I'd known back at the cabin, before we'd come to the pack house. That Everett had been vulnerable. He'd let me in. Everything had sped up since that day in the woods—the one where he had completely changed my life. The Everett I'd known since then was different. Colder, closed off, and hiding things from me.

"I'm good. I have what I need," I whispered.

Right now, in his arms, that was true. Everett slid his hands up the sides of my body and up my neck, capturing my face between his palms. He pulled me closer, his lips pressed against my forehead. My body buzzed from the kiss, my arms wrapping around his torso. I needed to be closer.

"Yoo-hoo! Madame Gardener! It's time for a break!"

I brushed some hair out of my face, smearing more dirt across my forehead. Looking up, I saw Kleio in the window of what must have been our room. She'd opened the top part of the window, half of her body hanging out. Everett kept me close, his chest vibrating as he growled at the interruption.

"You've been out here all afternoon," she said. "We have the party, remember?"

Kleio looked down at me, my eyes following hers. The white T-shirt had been a bad idea. Smears of black dirt covered it. My leggings didn't fare any better. The rich black dirt clung to my feet and hands, making it impossible to stay clean.

"We have a lot of work to do," Kleio sang, all cheerful, from the window. I supposed we did. I couldn't get introduced to the pack like this. "Get up here!" She pulled herself back into the room and closed the window.

I let go of Everett's waist, cold air filling in where our bodies had made it so warm pressed together. I reached down for the rake and hoe I'd left on the ground, my hands coming up empty as he grabbed both before I could.

Time had gone by quickly. The sun was on the other side of the pack house, shade creeping over the garden. I'd used my time efficiently.

I looked over my work. Neat rows of seeds planted, tucked in tight to germinate. In several days, little green sprouts would pop up in the black dirt. I brushed my hands off the best I could before I closed the hoop houses. It felt like putting them to bed.

Everett placed his palm on the small of my back, guiding me back toward the pack house. There was a party to prepare for.

"Oh, gosh." Kleio looked at me up and down when we made it into our room. Bunny was behind her, fussing with the shower in the bathroom. "We need to find you some rubber boots."

Everett choked down a laugh from where he stood at the side of the room. I looked down at my feet. I'd done the best I could to brush away the mess as I'd walked, but my feet were black with the fine particles of dirt from the garden. The dirt had even pushed underneath my toenails. Boots might be a good idea.

"You should start with a shower." Kleio pulled me into the bathroom. The air was already steamy from the hot water Bunny had started. She tsked at me as she walked past, like a disheartened grandmother. I was a bit of a mess.

Kleio and Bunny left me to undress, and I put my dirty clothes into the hamper next to the shower. They might just have to be thrown away.

The bottom of the shower turned black when I stepped into the stream. The dirt mixed with the water, formed a muddy substance that ran down the floor drain. It took a couple of minutes for the shower water to run clear.

The door of the bathroom creaked open. I peeked my head out of the glass door, looking beyond the foggy glass to see who had intruded. I wouldn't put it past Kleio to think I needed help bathing.

Everett stood in front of the door, looking as broody as ever. "You missed a spot." He pointed to his forehead. I lifted my hand to my forehead, pulling it away to look at my palm. There was still dirt there.

The steam in the room picked up Everett's scent and brought it over to my nose. His fresh scent in my nose prompted the mark on my neck to pulse. I grimaced at the feeling.

"Lyka," Everett whispered. He pulled down his pants and peeled the shirt from his back. In two steps, he was next to the glass of the shower. I opened it wider to accommodate his large size. The minute his body touched mine under the water, I relaxed, the mark on my neck calming.

Everett pulled me close to him, our skin pressed so tightly against one another that the water from the shower ran around us instead of between us.

"Our bond is strong. It's always hungry." He lifted my chin with his finger, so our eyes met. The golden swirls pulled me in. "I'm not complaining."

He held on to my chin and twisted my head to the side to give him access to my mark. I felt it ache under his gaze. He moaned as he brought his head close to my skin and began licking the mark, cleaning it as if the shower wasn't sufficient. His tongue against my sensitive skin sent shivers down my body, making my pelvis twitch suggestively toward his. I pulled my neck away from his mouth, the sensation becoming too much.

Everett pulled me back forcefully. "Let me take care of you," he growled against my neck. Sharp fangs grazed my skin between laps of his tongue over the mark on my skin. My breathing quickened, the feeling of the warm shower water and Everett's tongue making me throb between my legs. He was sweet, taking care of me. My discovery today showed that he had been listening and thinking of me.

"Thank you again for my garden," I whispered.

"I hope it will continue to be to your liking." Everett said. I nodded my head. It was more than enough. "I want you to be happy here." His heavy breathing met the pace of my own.

Loud pounding on the door followed by Kleio's voice broke the spell we both were under. "Finish up! Don't make me come in there!"

I could feel Everett's chuckle against my neck. "We'll have to come back to this later. It's time to get ready."

Get ready? Oh, right. I rubbed my forehead against his chest to clear my mind. It took a large amount of willpower to separate my body from his. The bond between us was so strong. He was right—it was always hungry, starving, wanting to be fed.

Everett turned off the water and grabbed two rolled towels from the basket next to the shower. He wrapped one around my shoulders before securing the second one around his waist. His lips brushed my cheek before he opened the door, letting out a cloud of steam.

I pulled the towel around me further, watching the trails of water that still dripped down the panes of his muscled back. We would definitely come back to this later. I sighed.

First, I had a party to attend.

16

ELISE

THE DOOR LATCHED AS EVERETT LEFT OUR BEDROOM. I emerged from the bathroom with my towel wrapped around my chest, held up by the squeeze of my armpits. Three dresses had been laid out on the bed: one gold, one red, and one green. There was a vanity that hadn't been there earlier, with a variety of hair torture instruments sitting on top of it with long cords plugged into the wall. A plush stool tucked underneath the vanity, and a mirror was perched above it. Powders and liquids in all different colors sat next to the hair torture instruments along with brushes of varying puff sizes. Apparently I'd be getting ready for this big fancy party by myself.

Joke was on them, because I had no idea how to do my own hair and makeup let alone pick out a dress.

I picked up one of the poofy brushes, brushing it up and down the top of my nose. How was I supposed to use this? Which powder did the brush belong to? I picked up a circular container filled with light pink powder and held it up in front of my face, looking in the mirror to compare it to my skin. Close enough. I popped open the top of the container and swirled the brush through the powder several times.

Leaning over the vanity, close to the mirror, I dragged the brush down the top of my nose again, a dark pink trail of powder following the brush. I gasped. It looked like I'd been sunburned. I brought my white towel up to my nose to rub it off, but the powder mixed with the moisture from the towel made a pink paste that smeared all over the white terrycloth.

Dang it.

Forget the face powder. I'd watched Jenny painstakingly coat her eyelashes with mascara. How badly could I mess that up?

The tiny brush squished out from the tube coated in black goop. Was this right? I held the brush up to my eyelashes, begging my hand to stay steady.

It didn't listen. My hand shook as I brushed my eyelashes with the mascara, clump after clump falling off my lashes and onto the skin below my eyes. Every swipe of my fingers brushing it away smeared it further, black streaks forming underneath my eyes. How did people do this every day with such precision? Taking samples from a red mulberry tree was easier than this.

Okay, makeup was a bust. Hair. My hair was still wet—curling it wasn't an option. I spied a hair dryer on the vanity, its cord coiled on the floor underneath the outlet. Perfect. I could do this. The hair dryer was loud, blowing my hair in every direction. It was also hot. Sweat formed at my hairline both on my forehead and the back of my neck.

I flipped the hair dryer off when I'd had enough, taking time to run my fingers through my dried strands. I don't know what it was about the hair dryer, but it made my hair so much fuller and frizzy. A bead of sweat traveled down the back of my neck and between my shoulder blades. Just what the pack wanted to see—a sweaty luna who looked like she'd just been electrocuted. I dragged my hands down my hair from the part to the ends, trying to smooth it down. What was I supposed to do?

Dresses.

I turned to the three beautiful dresses laid out on the bed for me. They all looked to be my size. I picked up the red one. Red meant power, right? That was what I needed to channel tonight.

I let the stained towel fall to the floor as I picked up the silky fabric, admiring the thin straps and ruffles that traveled from the bottom of the dress, up the leg slit on the side. Finding the top of the dress, I stepped in, wiggling the fabric over my rear and up my stomach. I looked down to where the shoulder straps should be. My right one was there, but the left one had disappeared. I pulled the right one up my arm and tugged it over my shoulder, a tugging feeling suddenly developing between my legs.

The left strap. It was between my legs, snuggly tucked between where I'd forgotten to wear underwear—it was up there, tight. The strap on my right shoulder felt like it'd gotten tighter since I'd pulled it up, unwilling to budge from where it cut into the notch in my shoulder blade. I tucked my fingers beneath the strap, trying to make room for it to move, but it only made the strap between my legs pull up even more, almost cutting into the sensitive skin down there.

I let out a breath, my shoulders slumping, my head hanging low. I wasn't good at this. If this was what it took to be luna, then I'd already failed.

I caught some of my movement in the mirror, bringing my attention to my haggard appearance. The dress covered my breasts, but it was apparent that it didn't fit correctly. I was alone in this big room, stuck in a dress. I couldn't do this myself.

The laugh of someone in the pack house filtered through the door and into the silent room. The pack house. Kleio had said at one point that they were just one big family. All my life I'd been waiting to find a close group of friends—friends I could trust and rely on, and here I'd been wallowing when there was a whole house of shifters who could help me. Namely the shifter who had boasted about the benefits of being part of a pack.

"*Kleio,*" I said through mind-link.

"*Elise?*" she responded.

"*So...maybe we could get ready together?*" Looking in the mirror at the way my hair looked and how my dress currently hung from my body...I needed her.

"*Fun! Why didn't I think of that?*" she squealed in my mind. "*I just finished my makeup. I'll grab my stuff and be over in a minute.*"

I tried to sit on the bed, but the strap between my legs rode up even further when I bent over.

Kleio burst into the room, arms full of hairbrushes and makeup and a long dress hanging from her shoulders. She stopped abruptly when she saw me, a comb falling from her hands and onto the floor. "What did you do?"

I pulled my shoulders up to my ears, my teeth pressing together, my eyebrows raising up. I wasn't sure what I'd done—but it wasn't good.

"I'm calling Bunny in for reinforcement."

They scrubbed, brushed, and plucked me within an inch of my life. I didn't have time to say anything between all the complaining about my hair that Bunny did and Kleio's pointed sighs as she polished my fingernails and applied makeup to my face. It felt like an eternity sitting there, getting prodded and groomed. For some, I was sure it would have been a luxurious experience. It was akin to torture for me.

After using small scissors to cut the strap of the dress currently tangled around me—she'd insisted that Everett could afford to waste a dress—Kleio helped me slip into the green floor-length dress after picking out some lacy undergarments she insisted I wore. Behind me, she zipped up the dress that fit perfectly. It was a knit dress that looked like tiny elves had made it with the tiniest of knitting needles and yarn. You had to be close to the dress to even see the small stitching that knitted it together. It stretched against my body, hugging every curve.

She pulled the straps off my shoulders, letting them hang along my triceps. The sweetheart neckline made the dress look feminine. The corset beneath it pushed my breasts into a perky position.

Bunny pulled up a stool and climbed on top of it, getting to work pulling the hair in front of my face back and securing it with a clip. She ran her fingers through my brushed hair, busy separating imaginary tangles.

"There. Now she looks like a luna," Bunny said, satisfied. She came around in front of me and stood next to Kleio. They both looked pleased with their effort. Kleio pulled me in front of the standing mirror that leaned against the wall next to the armoire.

I looked at the girl in the mirror and didn't recognize myself staring back. I looked regal in the dress. The hunter-green color highlighted my eyes and made my brown hair look extra shiny. Or maybe that was Bunny's doing. The hair clip she chose had small diamonds that sparkled in the light.

I walked closer to the mirror to look at my face. Kleio had done a good job on my makeup. The dark brown eyeliner matched the color of my hair, and the light pink blush made me look vibrant. I was glad she hadn't painted me into someone I wasn't.

"One more thing," Kleio said, pulling open the bottom

drawer of the armoire. The drawer was so low it almost scraped against the ground when it opened. She pulled out a pair of nude-colored heels with a pointed toe. I groaned when I saw them. Tennis shoes were more my style. "They aren't that high. You can suck it up for a night."

I looked at the heel. Kleio was right; they weren't that high. She placed them in front of me, and I stepped into them, instantly gaining three inches in height. They had hemmed the dress especially for the shoes, and the bottom of the fabric brushed against the floor, hiding my feet.

"I'll let Everett know you're ready," Kleio said.

I grabbed her hand before she could turn away, then I looked behind me at Bunny and grabbed her hand as well. Gratitude overwhelmed me. They didn't need to spend all this extra time helping me to look presentable. I felt thankful that I looked put together enough to be introduced to the pack. It made me feel a lot more confident. I could be their luna for the night.

"Thank you both. It means a lot that you spent so much time with me," I said, looking them both in the eye. I was of few words. The ones I spoke aloud I always tried to make count.

Bunny shushed me, batting my hand away as she cleaned up the mess they had made creating my look.

Kleio kept my hand in hers. "It's our honor to help you on such an important night."

A knock interrupted our moment, and the door opened to reveal Everett standing in the frame wearing an all-black suit with a matching dress shirt underneath. He didn't wear a tie, instead leaving the top two buttons of the shirt undone.

"Damn."

Kleio stole the words from my mouth. Everett looked good. The suit exuded power, and he looked every bit an alpha in it.

His eyes locked onto mine before they trailed down my body and then back up.

"I've never seen you look like...that," I said, walking forward carefully on my heels. I was used to Everett in a T-shirt and pants...or nude. The suit might've been doing more for me than his naked body ever did. My heart skipped a couple of beats as I traced the folds of his suit with my finger. His tattoos stuck out from the collar of his shirt, encouraging me to follow them to what was underneath.

Everett grabbed my hand off his chest and twirled me around, making the skirt of my dress flow out into a ring around me. "You look very much like a luna—a powerful one. A luna that I'm proud to have by my side," he said, pulling me close to him.

The bond hummed between us. This luna business was all new to me. I hadn't met many members of his pack before today, and I felt nervous. He could sense my apprehension.

"I've kept everyone away while you've settled in, but it's time that everyone meets you. Everyone will love you."

"How many is everyone?" I asked. A ballpark number of people would be nice.

"Only three hundred or so."

"Three hundred?" That was way more than I'd assumed would be there. My head already ached at the onslaught of voices soon to enter my brain.

"It's the first time you'll be formally introduced to every-one. Their thoughts might be a little...intrusive. Have you been using your mind-link?" Everett asked.

I nodded to my friend. "I called Kleio earlier."

"Good." Everett called her over. "Try to mind-link her," he commanded.

It only took a second for Kleio's voice to enter my head.

"You gonna hit that tonight?" I rolled my eyes as she smiled at me.

"Next time she mind-links you, I want you to pretend a brick wall is between you and her voice, blocking it out."

Sure, not a problem, I thought. *Blocking out Kleio's suggestive comments should be easy.* Everett gestured for her to try again.

"He's..."

I closed my eyes, imagining red bricks being placed on top of each other, the wall getting taller and taller. Kleio's voice grew more and more quiet as I built the wall between us.

"She did it. I'm closed off," Kleio announced.

I opened my eyes to find her smiling at me proudly.

"Good. Do that when the voices become too much. Some of the pack members aren't as courteous as others," Everett said.

"And some will test you, see if they can overwhelm you," Kleio added.

I nodded my head once. I could handle that.

"Everyone is excited to meet the new luna. I have to say that I'm excited about introducing her." Everett offered me his arm, which I accepted, weaving my hand through it, resting my fingers on the crook of his elbow.

"We haven't talked about what a luna is, what I'm expected to do," I said. "I don't even know how long I'll be staying here..."

He put his index finger on my lips, quieting me. "Let's focus on tonight," he said. "Everything you do will be perfect. You can't do anything wrong."

"What if I fall on my face or what if I throw up on the floor?" Every worst-case scenario ran through my head as he led me to the door.

"You won't fall because I'll keep you here." Everett patted my hand in the crook of his elbow. "And you won't throw up because I know you haven't eaten anything today." He tsked me, reminding me of Bunny.

My stomach growled in reply.

17

ELISE

Everyone stopped talking when Everett and I got to the top of the grand staircase. I could feel hundreds of eyes on me as everyone took in their new luna. I sent a mind-link of thanks to Kleio for finding me this dress. It made me feel confident—or as confident as I could be in the spotlight. Everyone below us wore long dresses and tailored suits.

"Is that the new luna?"

"Where did she find that dress?"

"The True Alpha looks so happy."

"When's dinner?"

I closed my eyes and built my brick wall, as Everett had taught me. The voices faded, and I opened my eyes to take everything in.

Evergreen boughs with white and red berries sprinkled between the branches adorned the banister of the stairs. It almost looked like Christmas, though it was only the middle of summer.

Everett kept to his promise as we descended the stairs, keeping my hand nestled in his elbow. We went slowly down the stairs so I wouldn't trip in the small heels I was wearing. He paused in the middle of the staircase and looked at me before he spoke.

"I've been an alpha for many years," he said, his voice carrying throughout the open area surrounding the stairs. "Some have been good, and some have been bad. None of those years compare to the year I'm currently having."

The crowd laughed. I looked at Everett as his eyes caught mine. He smiled before he looked back at his pack.

"We have much to celebrate this year. The Deca Tournament is over, and there are many changes within our pack. Not only do I have the honor of being named True Alpha, but I've also found my mate, all within the last month." The crowd exchanged whispers with each other. "I want to introduce you to my mate, your luna—Elise Wilson Silas."

Everett looked at me with pride in his stare. The heat of everyone looking at me set my cheeks aflame. So, he assumed I was taking his last name... "I know you're all eager to get to know her, but let's not overwhelm her. I want her to stick around."

He wrapped his arm around my waist and pulled me in to kiss my cheek. The crowd clapped, and Everett guided me down the stairs. I exhaled as my feet met the stone floor at the bottom of the staircase. I hadn't tumbled down the stairs.

First mission accomplished.

The crowd parted, letting us pass. They left just enough room for both of us to fit through. I could feel the heat of their bodies radiate onto my own. There was little consideration for personal space.

We walked, leading the pack to the dining room. They'd arranged it for tonight's festivities. Tall cocktail tables scattered around the room, each covered with a black tablecloth. The evergreen theme continued, with large pots filled with boughs and branches and red-and-white berries. A wooden dance floor was in the corner of the room, complete with lights and a DJ booth. Twinkle lights hung from the wooden beams on the ceiling, creating a magical glow in the room. Servers dressed in white dress shirts and black bow ties carried trays of steaming food to long tables lined up against the windows. My stomach growled.

Kleio popped up next to me, grabbing my free arm. "Isn't it just wonderful?" she asked, as if I'd already commented on the state of things, but honestly, I was still taking it all in.

"I barely recognize the place," I said. This hardly looked like the dining room I'd walked through earlier. The shifters in the room looked different too—everyone was dressed up and groomed to perfection.

"You did a great job, Kleio," Everett said.

"See what happens when you give me an unlimited budget?" she asked. "I even hired catering staff for the event. Everyone has to be on their best behavior!" She pointed to her fangs. "They're human."

She giggled before trotting off, stopping to talk to this person and that person. The woman was in her element.

It wasn't long before Everett and I got bombarded with pack members wishing us well and wanting his ear. I stood there next to him, half listening and nodding, accepting everyone's words of welcome. It was completely overwhelming. There was no way I could memorize everyone's names.

Everett seemed to have no problem remembering everyone he talked to. He greeted them by name and often inquired about their families or hobbies. It was impressive. I recognized a few faces from around the pack house and the guards that I'd snuck by the other day, but there were so many shifters—many of whom I'd never seen before.

"Is everyone here a part of your pack?" I asked after Everett finished speaking to a sweet couple who'd just welcomed me wholeheartedly to the pack.

"*Our* pack," he corrected.

I looked down at my toes hidden beneath my dress. I kept forgetting that.

"Some of the pack lives here in the pack house, but most live in their own homes on pack lands. They come to the pack house for events like this or for pack meetings."

I nodded, smiling at the next pack member approaching us. Everett kept my hand tucked in the crook of his elbow, often checking on me with his eyes. As long as he steered the conversation, I was happy to stand there quietly observing.

My attention piqued when a girl with long platinum-blonde hair that reached to her butt weaseled her way to the front of the receiving line. She was wearing a tight blue mini dress and sky-high stilettos. The girl cozied up to the free side of Everett's body, making sure her own body was flush against his. Her arm wrapped around his free elbow, attaching herself to him. Looking across Everett's chest at her face, I noted her hand with makeup was far more advanced than mine. Her eyes were lined with black eyeliner, her long fake lashes fluttering as fast as hummingbird wings as she looked up at Everett. I felt a growl vibrate in my chest.

"Bethany," Everett said, stiffly acknowledging the girl plastered to his side.

"I'm so glad you're back. I've missed you." Bethany's hand ran down the lapel of his jacket. Her shiny red fingernails caught the light. I tightened my grip on Everett's elbow. "Thank you for inviting me tonight. I know before you left for the games, we both said things we didn't mean."

She continued talking to Everett, ignoring me completely. I cleared my throat, drawing Everett's attention. He pushed her away gently, unhooking himself from her grip.

"I told you earlier, Bethany. We're over," Everett said, firm with his words.

This was news to me. How much earlier had they talked? A week ago? An hour ago? Was this his ex? When had he cut it off?

I suddenly felt the need for information about this Bethany girl who was encroaching on my territory.

Ugh, now I was sounding like a wolf.

Bethany's eyes met mine, then narrowed as she slowly ran them down and then back up my body, sizing me up. Was this what Everett liked? I was nothing like her. My self-consciousness crept back, and I felt my shoulders slump.

Kleio appeared next to me, grabbing my arm that had made its way across my stomach, trying to hide myself. She had Jack behind her, with a big smile plastered across his face. She took one look at Bethany standing next to Everett and barred her teeth at her, flashing her canines.

Bethany's eyes widened, and she turned around, retreating into the crowd.

"She's such a bitch," Kleio said under her breath. I turned my attention from where Bethany was walking away back to my friend.

"I need to steal Elise for a bit," Kleio said, pulling me away from Everett.

He looked at me, trying to gauge how I felt.

"I need a break," I said. The line in front of us was still long, full of Everett's pack members wanting to speak to him. I also needed to get the details on this Bethany girl. I was sure Kleio would be full of information.

"Only for a little bit," Everett said, speaking to Kleio. He turned back to me, bending down and whispering into my ear, "I need you by my side."

I nodded at him, letting Kleio pull me away.

"Who was that?" I asked, bending in close to keep our conversation private.

"Jack told me that nightmare, Bethany, was sticking her claws where they don't belong. I had to save you."

I looked back at Jack, who trailed behind us.

"You're welcome!" he said, flashing me a smile.

"I don't know what she said, but you probably figured out that she's Everett's ex," Kleio said as we walked around the perimeter of the room. "She moved out of the pack house after Everett ended it—after he saw you at No Bars. I didn't think she'd have the nerve to show up."

I glanced around, spotting Bethany standing with two other girls, all of them staring at me.

"I'm sorry," Kleio said. "I should've told you about her."

I shook my head, accepting the apology. Things between Everett and me had been so intense that the thought of his ex had probably slipped her mind.

"Before Everett met you, she was convinced she'd be named luna. She had Everett wrapped around her finger. It was disgusting." Kleio frowned. "Bethany tried using her influence over him to separate Gavrill, Kostas, and me from Everett, whispering all sorts of untrue things to him to change his opinions of us."

I was surprised Everett would entertain anything Bethany said. He and his inner circle were so close.

"She hasn't taken the news of you entering the pack well. She and her posse have been scheming since you got here. They haven't had access to you until tonight." Kleio nodded her head toward the girls, standing by Bethany, still staring at me. "Watch out for them. Everett broke it off with Bethany that night he saw you at the bar with Wilder," she said, "but I wouldn't put it past her to attempt something to scare you away."

The three girls whispered to each other while continuing to stare at me, obviously talking about me. I shook my head, looking away.

Our walk around the room brought us to the large windows with tables of food served buffet style. Kleio followed me as I filled my plate with food. Steaming vegetables, cuts of tender meat, and bread filled the plate that I realized was much too small. Champagne flutes set in neat rows ended the buffet, and I reached to grab one.

Kleio caught my wrist, balancing her own plate full of food. "That's wolf wine. It's strong, especially if you aren't used to it."

I pulled my hand back, heeding her warning. I grabbed a glass of water instead and followed her over to a high-top table. My empty stomach appreciated the food I filled it with, and I could feel a smile on my lips as I listened to Kleio chat next to me with whoever came to our table. There was a lot of gossip that she both acquired and dished out. I didn't know any of the individuals she was talking about, but it was entertaining none-theless.

I looked around the room, locking eyes with Everett. He was chatting with an elderly man who looked like he enjoyed the sound of his own voice.

Everett eyed the empty plate in front of me. "*Come here, Lyka. I need you.*"

My hand brushed Kleio's shoulder to tell her I was leaving without having to interrupt her conversation. Everett had so much patience, standing there listening to each of his pack members individually. I was sure a lot of the conversations were unnecessary, but Everett looked at every one as if they were just as important as the next one.

I felt eyes on me as I walked across the room, and suddenly I felt exposed walking alone. I'd had Everett or Kleio next to me the entire night. With my shoulders pressed down and back and my eyes up, I scanned the crowd as I walked, making eye contact with the shifters looking my way. Everett had introduced me as luna, and I needed to assume the role.

Flashes of blue and platinum-blonde hair registered in my peripheral vision. Across the room, parallel to me, I saw Bethany making her way to Everett. She was walking fast, her blonde hair flowing behind her body. Was she trying to talk to him again while I wasn't there? My wolf growled, my fists clenching tight.

Bethany noticed me as we both came closer to Everett. The line of pack members waiting to talk to him was still long, wrapping around a portion of the room. He was deep in conversation with a family, their children swinging from his arms and giggling.

I stopped, not wanting to interrupt, despite the situation. My heart warmed at the sight—the way the children squealed as he lifted them up and down with his arms.

"Don't get too comfortable in Everett's bed. I don't want my side to be sagging when I climb back into it."

I turned around, finding Bethany standing directly behind me, her face close enough that the words she'd whispered hadn't been heard by anyone else. I looked up and down her body. What was she talking about? She was the same size as me.

I thought back to Kleio's warning earlier. I couldn't play nice with her. She needed to be dealt with. Bethany didn't seem to accept that Everett was done with her, that I was the luna.

I didn't want to draw attention to myself, but she was targeting me.

I took a step closer to her, surprising myself with my courage. The black smoky cloud overwhelmed my head again, taking over. "I plan to get very comfortable in his bed," I said, "and in his shower, and on his couch…"

A large hand wrapped around my stomach, pulling me back.

"Don't tease me, Elise." Everett spoke loud enough so that Bethany could hear.

Her hands formed into fists, and she sneered at me before walking away to the comfort of her minions.

"You were seriously with her?" I asked Everett, turning to face him.

He ran a hand over his jaw. "She was nothing but a temporary fling who let the power of my position get to her head." Everett cupped his hand to my cheek, rubbing his thumb back and forth over my chin. "None of my other relationships ever went beyond casual. I was always waiting for you."

"Well, she seems to think otherwise." I grabbed Everett's wrist.

"I like when you get riled up and possessive," he said. I scoffed at him, looking away. He took his other arm and pulled me close to him. "I'll show you tonight what real possession is."

His hand left my cheek and gripped hair, forcing my head to the side. He dipped his face down to my mark, and he placed a kiss over the healing skin, sending shivers down my spine.

I opened my eyes, my face looking out into the pack. Many of the pack members had stopped their conversations to stare at us. I blushed, pushing away from Everett. He didn't seem to take notice of the attention and led me over to the DJ booth, holding my hand.

Grabbing a microphone, he tested the volume before speaking to the crowd. Everyone gathered around us, leaving Everett and me little space to move. Gavrill and Kostas appeared at his side, holding ropes that hung from the beams above us. I looked up and saw that they were attached to a pulley system. Kleio came to my side, also holding a rope. She smiled at me, and I relaxed a little.

"Before we start the party"—someone yelled "Whoop!" from the crowd excitedly—"we need to raise the flags. There are three flags that remind us we are one pack, stronger together," Everett said. "These should remind all of us that the actions we take not only affect ourselves, but everyone in the pack as well."

Three young children walked forward, each carrying a bundle of colored fabric. Their smiles were contagious, each looking so proud to be a part of the ceremony. They handed their bundles off to Kostas, Gavrill, and Kleio before returning to the crowd.

"The first is the Cedar Moon Pack flag," Everett continued.

Gavrill clipped the flag to the rope before he used the pulley system to raise the flag to the ceiling. It was the black flag with a cedar tree that I was familiar with from the tournament.

"The second is the Great Northern Pack flag."

Kostas followed Gavrill's motions, clipping the flag to his rope before he pulled it up to the ceiling. The flag was a deep brown with a white circle in the middle representing the moon. A single wolf sat on its haunches in the center of the moon with its snout pointed at the sky in a howl.

"And the third is a new flag, one that I acquired from my late father. It's the True Alpha flag."

Gasps and awe filled the room as Kleio attached the flag to her rope. This was exciting for everyone in the pack. She started pulling the rope swiftly to raise the flag. I looked up, like everyone else, following the flag's path to the ceiling.

Out of the corner of my eye, I saw a flash of blue. I looked down in time to see long red fingernails grasp a piece of green yarn that hung from the bottom of my dress and wrap it around the moving rope. I felt a tug and stood there in shock as I watched my dress unravel around me.

The green string followed the rope up to the ceiling, spinning in circles around my body, slowly making my dress shorter and shorter. Kleio was so focused on raising the flag quickly that she didn't notice the string that shadowed the rope upward.

I held down my skirt as I watched the rows of knit pull apart, hoping it would stop before my lacy underwear began to show. Everyone's eyes were on the flag when it reached the ceiling beam, but mine were on the much shorter hem of my dress. It now ended well above my knees.

I scanned the room quickly, landing on two beady black eyes with fluttering eyelashes a couple of feet away from me. A smirk grew on Bethany's lips as she took in my situation. She *was* a nightmare. We were the only ones not looking at the flag right now.

Time slowed. Parallel to the brown rope, the green string of my dress hung, and I followed it up to the ceiling. Sounds of oohs and aahs from the crowd echoed in my head as they stared at the hunter-green flag that matched my dress. The white teeth and jaws of a wolf's mouth, open and ready to bite, encircled the flag.

I glanced back to Bethany's smug face. It would only be a couple of seconds before everyone looked back down, following the string, and realizing what had happened.

Acting on instinct, I bent over, grabbing the yarn that was still attached to my dress and put it between my teeth, biting down hard on the string and grinding the fibers until I felt it snap apart.

Bethany's eyes went wide as she watched me drop the string and slide my arm into Everett's elbow, clapping with the rest of the crowd. I looked up at Everett and smiled, and he returned it.

Back where Bethany had been standing, I now saw an empty space. I'd won this round.

Kleio caught my eyes as she looked at my dress and the green yarn hanging next to the rope she had just pulled, putting what had happened together. She mouthed *That bitch* at me before looking around for Bethany.

I put my hand on her shoulder and shook my head at her. I didn't want to alert Everett about what had happened. He had enough to deal with without having to worry about me and his ex-girlfriend fighting. Kleio was my friend. She'd help me deal with Bethany.

"I have to say the short dress does amazing things for your legs," Kleio whispered to me. "I bet Bethany is really regretting her idea of vengeance right now."

I smiled to myself, looking down at my legs in the dress. My heels, now visible, made the muscles in my calves pop. I did look good.

The surrounding crowd murmured to each other. A few people pointed to me, confused.

"Fancy dress there," Everett whispered to me. "Kleio really outdid herself with the outfit change. First time someone has changed dresses during the Deca Party." I felt his gaze linger on my thighs that were now very visible. Clearly he had thought this had been planned and didn't know that I had been targeted by his ex.

I wasn't going to let Bethany make me feel inferior. I smiled, picturing her blood boiling as she looked at us from wherever she was hiding now.

Taking advantage of the attention, I stood on my tiptoes to kiss Everett on the lips, and he leaned down to meet me in a deep kiss. I made sure Bethany saw that he was all mine. This new possessive attitude of mine suited me. I felt good. It was like there was a new, more confident Elise that had taken over.

After, I grabbed Kleio's elbow and left Everett standing at another receiving line as he shook hands and greeted pack members he still hadn't talked with. I felt his eyes follow me over to the table that had champagne glasses lined up in neat rows.

As soon as someone took a glass, it was immediately replaced, keeping the lines neat. I grabbed two glasses by the stems and handed one to Kleio. I needed some liquid courage to deal with Bethany.

"Are you sure?" Kleio asked me, worried. "This stuff can really do a number on you."

"Bethany doesn't get to win. I refuse to let her ruin the night." I took a sip of the wolf wine. It was light pink and bubbly. Tiny bubbles danced along my throat. Delicious. I dumped the rest of the glass into my mouth before grabbing another one off the table.

Kleio watched me, astonished. "Okay, okay, you made your point. Slow down." She walked me away from the drink table and brought me to one of the tall cocktail tables in the room.

It took only a minute for the bubbles to hit my bloodstream. It was weird. I could feel the bubbles dance along my veins. They traveled from my chest to my fingertips, making my hand feel fizzy. I held my hand in front of my face, turning it over, expecting to see the bubbles underneath my skin.

Kleio looked at me, her drink still full. "Oh boy, here we go."

18

DAFNI, AGE EIGHTEEN

Eighteen years of living in the same cottage. Wandering the same grasses, completing the same chores. Every day the same—except for the days Mother came to visit. Those days were always different.

My fingers wound the long grasses effortlessly into a braid. I didn't even need to look at my hands anymore. I had done it so many times. Tiny purple flowers grew on a vine up the trunk of a nearby tree. Its green vine had grown tiny green claws that dug into the tree bark, attaching itself to the tree.

I plucked eighteen purple flowers off the vine. One for each year on this earth. Each uneventful year.

Grandmother said I would look back on these years with fondness, a simple time. But at this moment, I couldn't see things the way she could. An old woman who had lived her life before settling down to care for her granddaughter. I was young, able, and deprived of adventure.

We were always waiting. Waiting for my magic to appear. Waiting for my first transformation. Waiting for my poison to come in.

The wait was over for the first two. My magic had manifested early and powerfully. Under Grandmother's tutelage, I'd become a stronger air wielder than she was. She often looked to me to brush the leaves off the porch with my magic instead of the broom she now had trouble maneuvering.

My transformation powers had come later than most, but they had come nevertheless. Now we were waiting again, this time for my poison to come in.

Grandmother had worried when I'd had my seventeenth birthday and there'd been no green poison dripping from my gums. As the days and months had gone on during my seventeenth year, she'd become increasingly anxious, waking me each morning by lifting my lips to examine my gums. Gums that still didn't have poison.

I tucked the stems of the purple flowers between the weaves of my grass braid before tying the ends together in a knot. I placed it on top of my head as I had done every birthday before, built my own crown. It was in the quiet moments like these that I could breathe. Frogs croaked around me, having repopulated themselves from the killing spree I'd gone on when I'd been younger. Grandmother still had my stash in the icebox. They were probably white with frost by now.

Every rustle of leaves or acorn falling from a tree startled me. It'd been six years since my mother had last been here. Memories of her visit had faded, but the winter we'd suffered through after she'd left hadn't. Her refusal to use her magic to grow the plants in our dilapidated garden that year had been devastating to our winter stores. We did the best we could to survive with what small amount of food our garden produced and by beheading too many of our hens. Luckily our garden had grown hardier in the years that had followed, helped by the growth of my powers. I could blow in the occasional rain cloud when our garden was dry and blow the stray cloud away that covered the light when our garden needed sun.

"Dafni!" Grandmother's voice echoed through the meadow to where I sat. Quiet time was over.

I used my air magic to bow the long grasses, clearing a path that wouldn't leave dried grass stuck to my green dress. Grandmother was waiting on the porch, her dress robin's egg blue today, broom in her hand. Recently she used it more as a cane than as a sweeping device.

"Your mother will be here soon to collect you." Her voice wobbled a bit. She had raised me for eighteen years, until I'd become mature enough to join my mother's Coven. Grandmother never said the words, but I knew she was dreading today.

It was a bittersweet day for me, one I'd always known would come. The day when I left everything I'd known, the only place I'd known, to join my mother. I'd never let my grandmother know that I was also eager to see life outside of the cottage.

"She isn't going to be happy," I said.

"We don't know how she'll react," Grandmother said.

"Yes, we do. I have yet to get my poison. She'll be disappointed."

Grandmother turned and made her way into the cottage, using the broom for support. I knew she expected me to follow. "Whatever happens today, we'll accept and move forward. You're the most powerful air wielder I've encountered. You also have water magic. She won't be disappointed in that."

"You know she's unpredictable."

"Don't insult me, Dafni. I know my daughter. I know you. You're powerful and worthy of her respect." Grandmother wobbled over to the cauldron that always hung above the fire and stirred it. "I just hope she sees it."

The screen door flew open, hitting the wall inside the cabin.

"Happy birthday, dear daughter." My mother's voice always sent chills down my spine.

"Mother," I said. I wasn't as afraid of her as I had been when I'd been younger. She wasn't as tall as I'd remembered. Or maybe I had grown to her height. Looking at her was like looking in a mirror. We had the same hair and face shape.

"Tell me you've transformed?"

There were never any niceties with my mother. That I had received a "Happy birthday" earlier was surprising.

"Yes," I answered.

"And your poison?"

I was silent. So was Grandmother. *Frogfeet.*

The silence lasted too long. "Tell me you got your poison," Mother said, this time with more venom laced in her voice.

"It has yet to come in," Grandmother said.

"Eighteen and no poison?" I watched as Mother's jaw dropped. "This is unheard of! My own daughter with no poison at eighteen?"

Her face grew red, her fists clenched at her sides. The ground crackled underneath the cottage. Would vines shoot up from the floorboards? Would furniture fly? "Why? Why have you not gotten your poison?"

Mother stomped over to me, unclenching her fist to lift my upper lip. Her fingers tasted of fish. Seeing no poison dripping from my gums, she let my lip fall back to cover my teeth. I stuck my tongue out to lick them, only to be surprised by the hand that slapped my cheek.

"You..." She turned away from me and stalked toward Grandmother. "Eighteen years I left her here with you. What did you do?"

Grandmother stood strong by the cauldron, still stirring, "I raised your daughter as my own for eighteen years. Is that not enough for you, Matilda?"

"You did something, something that's kept her poison away. Probably fed her one of your special brews." Mother spat poison on the floor as she spoke. Small tendrils of smoke rose from the wooden floorboards.

"I did no such thing. I raised her to be a strong witch. Just because she doesn't have poison—"

"No daughter of mine will be without poison," Mother interrupted, looking back at me, my hand on the cheek she had slapped, which still stung. "You...you will never be a part of my Coven. Never be my heir. All this waiting, eighteen years! For nothing. The Lifestone could've been yours."

Mother stomped over to Grandmother and grabbed her arm that stirred the cauldron. She pulled, the stirring stick flicking out a blue potion as it exited the cauldron. "You disappoint me, Mother."

Grandmother's eyes were wide, her body too weak to fight back as Mother leaned over Grandmother's arm and grabbed her hand. The popping sound of her teeth piercing Grandmother's skin reverberated in my ears. Grandmother's skin was thin. Mother knew what she was doing when she broke the skin. Green poison dripped from the bite mark on her arm after Mother let it go.

Grandmother stumbled back, her shoulders hitting the hearth. She looked down at her arm, at where her daughter had bitten her, before she looked back up at me. We both stared at each other for a moment, slack jawed.

Time seemed to have frozen for a moment.

She'd just poisoned Grandmother. A witch's bite was deadly—the poison, a toxin that went straight to the heart.

This couldn't be happening.

My grandmother's words echoed in my head. *You're powerful and worthy of her respect.*

I was powerful. Even without my poison, I was powerful.

Time reeled quickly back to the present.

I darted over to mother, my eyes unblinking, arms outstretched to grab hold of her hair. My fingers tangled around the red strands as I curled them into my palm. I yanked back with both hands mother's head coming with the hair. I felt the popping of her hair follicles as I pulled.

"You little harpy!" Mother screamed as she stumbled away from my grandmother, her hands now locked around my wrists. She pushed her pointed nails into the soft skin on the underside of my wrists, the pain causing me to release the hair between my fingers. Mother turned, flipping the hair I'd pulled back over the top of her head revealing her eyes and her mouth, her lips pulled back, teeth still dripping with poison.

"Now you've really done it. How dare you put your hands on me." Mother took a moment to brush the dripping poison from her chin. The sound of poison sizzling as it hit the hardwood floors filled the cottage.

I scampered over the small smoking holes in the floor toward the fireplace—toward Grandmother. She stood with her back against the brick of the hearth, her hand over her heart and her eyes closed.

"Grandmother?" I touched her cheek. It felt cool even as she stood by the warm fire.

Her eyes peeled open slowly, stopping halfway. "Dafni..." Her lips opened, my name slipping from them.

Tears fell down my face. I grabbed her hand, holding it between both of mine. Just like her cheek, her hand was cold.

"You're the chosen one," Grandmother whispered. Her thumb moved back and forth on the top of my hand. She shouldn't be comforting me; I should be comforting her. I squeezed her hand tightly between my own. "Your mother knows this—don't let her make you believe otherwise."

I looked over my shoulder, where Mother was smoothing the hair I'd pulled out of place.

Grandmother coughed, black goo oozed from between her lips—her blood mixed with my mother's poison.

She's almost gone, I realized.

"I spent the last years of my life...my best years...here with you. You've become not only a powerful witch, but a fair one. That's what I'm most proud of." Grandmother's eyes fluttered, almost closing.

"Don't leave me. You can't leave me with her," I begged.

"Continue to make me proud," she whispered, her eyes opening once more as she spoke. They slid closed slowly, as if she was fighting to capture every detail before they closed forever.

I couldn't speak. My voice didn't work. So, I nodded. I squeezed her hand tightly so she knew—knew that I heard her, that I'd make her proud.

My head flew back, my spine popping and my scalp burning. I tried to reach out to Grandmother as I was pulled away, to hold on to her, but my fingers only met air.

My body hit the floor, my mother releasing the hair on my head she'd pulled me back with. I pushed myself up onto my elbows, wincing at how my neck twinged as I moved. Mother's back was to me. She was whispering something into Grandmother's ear. Grandmother's eyes were still closed, but I believed she could still hear.

A simple push sent Grandmother into the hearth, knocking over the cauldron, spilling the potion down Grandmother's front. The flames licked the potion. Propelled by its properties, the flames grew higher, engulfing Grandmother, turning the blue dress she wore brown and then black.

My throat burned as I screamed, scrambling trying to stand. The pain in my neck made it difficult to move my body. Grandmother didn't scream as the flames consumed her. She didn't fight. Her eyes, once again open watching me, closed slowly, flickering once or twice like the fire that surrounded her. My stomach felt sick. I gagged, heaving over the wooden floor.

I didn't hear the clicking of mother's heels before her fingers gathered the collar of the back of my dress. I scrambled, flailing my body around, gritting my teeth at the pain in my neck.

Mother didn't let me watch any more. She pulled me out of the cottage by my dress, my heels dragging along the ground. I coughed as the collar pushed against my windpipe. I spit the sour bile that'd come up from my stomach out of my mouth, and it ran down my chin as I couldn't get enough air to propel it away from me.

"I should've left you at the Academy the minute you left my womb," Mother muttered to herself as she pulled me away from the cottage. She stopped for a moment, turning to face the cottage.

My legs gave out, and I sat in the dirt on my butt. Orange flames flickered in the window before they climbed out the front door and onto the porch. A minute later they engulfed the structure...and my grandmother.

"See that, Dafni?" Mother said. "It's gone. She's gone. You have nothing left. Nowhere to go." She yanked the collar of my dress again and continued dragging me. I let her pull me along the grasses and roots of the forest floor.

I couldn't stop staring at the cottage. The way the flames licked around the door frame, the way they illuminated the cabin through the windows. My hands felt cold as they dragged along the dirt, my heartbeat thumping in my ears as I watched the cottage slowly become smaller before disappearing altogether.

I couldn't breathe. My fingers dug between my neck and the collar of my dress, forcing space for my windpipe. I coughed, fighting for air as she continued dragging me for what felt like miles.

Suddenly Mother stopped and let go of my dress. I fell onto my back, dragging air into my lungs at a rapid pace.

"I should've left you in the cottage back there to die. But you deserve to suffer like I have all these years waiting for you, waiting for my heir." Mother's face was red, but not from the exertion of dragging me. "All that waiting? What did it get me? A worthless heir—a worthless daughter."

Mother's head blocked out the sun as she leaned over, her face inches away from mine. "Your suffering will end. Maybe in a few days? A week? But mine will continue. I have no heir. I'll have to start again." She stood, towering above me. "Goodbye, daughter."

A slight brush of leaves was my only warning before her foot contacted my head. Sending me into darkness.

19

―――――――

EVERETT

ANOTHER LINE FORMED IN FRONT OF ME OF PACK members waiting for my attention. It was important that I took the time to listen to them, but I just wanted the night to be over with. They each wanted face time with me, either to congratulate me, ask for something, or maneuver themselves within the pack hierarchy. I was the True Alpha now, and everyone looked to me for leadership. There were rogues in the Vault beneath the dining room needing to be dealt with and new wolves, leaving from my father's pack, joining mine every day. It was a lot to deal with.

Bethany wasn't helping either. I regretted ever having laid a hand on her body. I hadn't lied when I'd told Elise that she'd been nothing but a fling. My inner circle had never liked her. I'd never truly cared for her. Most of the time, I'd tuned her voice out when she'd spoken to me. She'd been a warm body during a time I hadn't wanted to get attached to anyone. Maybe that made me an asshole. I hadn't realized how attached she'd become to me. She'd always played it off like the relationship was casual, agreeing to the terms I'd laid out. No promises, no attachments. Obviously she cared a lot more than she'd let me know. Tonight she'd turned Elise into something I barely recognized. A ferocious little thing that had a lot of bite to her bark.

Between speaking to the pack members, I turned to my left, where Gavrill was standing a step behind me. "Keep an eye on her. Let me know if she gets out of hand." I nodded toward Elise. I needed eyes on her while I focused on the line of pack members before me. There was a glass of wolf wine between her fingers, which made me nervous. I hoped Kleio had control over the situation. I shifted my weight between my feet.

"Her wolf's starting to show more and more," Gavrill said as the next pack member reached out to shake my hand. "I heard her speaking to Bethany. She's going to be a feisty one."

I didn't have time to respond before the person before me took my outstretched hand and started giving me compliments. It didn't take a few sentences before their tune changed to asking for a favor. This time it was to move apartments in the pack house. Something bigger and better, I was sure.

I granted their wishes and turned back to Gavrill before the next person walked up to me. "Oh, I know. I met her wolf the other day," I said. It was early for that to happen. She'd just transitioned a few days ago, but Elise was surpassing expectations in every way.

"She turned all territorial around Bethany. I've never seen her act like that before. Her wolf must be strong," Gavrill said.

He had a point. The way she'd spoken to Bethany earlier had been so unlike her, so possessive. I had to actively try not to adjust my pants as I remembered the words that had shocked Bethany.

I glanced back to the table where Kleio and Elise were standing. Half of Elise's second glass was gone. She threw her head back, laughing at something, her long brown hair falling behind her body, brushing her ass that was covered by a too short dress. It was like she was asking for me to flip her over my shoulders and carry her to our bed.

Her hand reached out clumsily across the table to bat at Kleio and knocked her glass over, spilling the rest of her drink. Good. She didn't need any more of the wolf wine. One glass often left me with a buzz. Elise probably felt like she was floating on a cloud one and a half glasses in.

Kleio picked up the glass and looked apologetically at the server who'd come over with a towel. Elise made a show of trying to grab the towel to wipe the wine off the floor, laughing and teasing the poor server, who looked intimidated by the two beautiful women standing before him. Kleio wrapped her arm around her shoulder and steered her away from the mess. Elise walked next to her friend, wobbly in the heels she wore.

I turned my attention back to the next pack member that approached me, hoping that Gavrill was keeping an eye on her.

A loud screech interrupted my conversation, and both my pack member and I stopped talking to turn and investigate the noise. Elise had broken free from Kleio and was darting across the dining room with purpose. She slammed into a petite girl with blonde curly hair, who I recognized now as her friend Jenny, wrapping her arms around her and rocking her side to side in the embrace.

"Oh, shit." Gavrill left his place beside me and stalked over to the two women who were still hugging each other.

I excused myself from my conversation and followed. The receiving line would have to wait.

"What are you doing here?" Elise asked, finally releasing Jenny from her arms.

Gavrill stood behind Jenny, towering over the girls, and I took my place behind Elise, turning to dismiss Kleio with a flick of my wrist. She'd just caught up to Elise. Some chaperone she was.

Kleio put her hands up in defeat, releasing Elise to my care before walking into the crowd, probably in search of Jack.

"Oh, I see." Elise took in Gavrill where he stood behind Jenny. "I guess I'm not the only one who likes a little shifter dick."

I slapped my hand over Elise's mouth before I pulled her back to my chest. She'd definitely had too much wolf wine.

I let my lips touch her ear. "Now, you know as well as I do that my shifter dick is not little." I placed my hand on her stomach, pulling her ass against my pants to prove my point.

Elise pushed my hand away from her face. "Everett fucking Silas! Don't you dare cover your luna's mouth!" She snapped her teeth at my palm drunkenly laughing.

"I heard there was a party," Jenny interjected. She looked back and up at Gavrill, clearly pissed.

"A huge party!" Elise waved her arms in front of her body.

"She's had a lot to drink," I said, smoothing her hair on the back of her head.

"You were supposed to stay in my room," Gavrill said, grabbing the back of Jenny's neck.

"You expect me to stay in your room when there's a party downstairs?" She stepped out of Gavrill's grasp and smoothed the pink dress she was wearing. It didn't cover the bandages on her legs. "I found the dress in your closet," she said. "Hope the girl who owns it sees me in it and gets jealous."

Jenny sauntered away from us, turning her head to see if Gavrill was watching, which he was. Gavrill groaned, rubbing his hand on the back of his neck.

I tucked Elise into my side. She wobbled on her heels, drunk, with a blank look on her face.

"What are you going to do about that?" I asked my friend, motioning my head to the feisty blonde who'd just walked away.

"I don't know, man. She kind of attached herself to me at the bar that night and hasn't let go," Gavrill said.

I smirked at him. He couldn't admit it to himself he liked her. He wouldn't have rescued her from the burning cabin and kept her in his room for days if he didn't, which I knew about thanks to Kleio. She wasn't a good chaperone, but she was an excellent gossip.

"Everett, I don't feel so good." Elise stared up at me with wide eyes and a salivating mouth. Shit. This wasn't good.

"Can you finish up?" I asked Gavrill, motioning to the line of pack member still waiting to talk to me. They'd have to settle for my second tonight.

"That's a lot to ask, man. I've got Jenny on the loose."

That was his own problem.

"Handle it," I commanded. He nodded, turning to the line of people and walking away.

I guided Elise's wobbly legs toward the door of the dining room. Her steps were unsure and slow, and I felt her head slump against my arm.

She was done for. There was no way she was making it up the stairs to our room. I bent down and wrapped my arms around the backs of her thighs, hoisting her up over my shoulder. Her arms and head dangled against my back, and I carried my luna toward the stairs.

"Oh god," Elise said before I felt her stomach clench and warm moisture flooded the back of my suit. "I'm so sorry." She alternated between apologetic crying and retching, covering my suit with her dinner and the sweet scent of wolf wine.

I stood there while she emptied her stomach down my back, rubbing the back of her legs with my thumb. Better she throw up down my back than on herself, and at least we were already out of sight of the rest of the pack.

When she was done, I continued toward the stairs, taking

two steps at a time, and marching to our room with my girl hanging off my shoulder. I mind-linked Kleio, asking her to send someone to wipe the floor, and then mind-linked Bunny to start a bath.

She greeted me at the door of the room and started fussing over Elise as soon as I set her on the couch.

"You let her have wolf wine?" Bunny smacked me on the arm.

"Bethany got to her," I said.

Her eyes closed for a couple of seconds before she opened them, shaking her head. "That girl's always been trouble. I told you to stay away from her. But you always let your little pecker lead the way." She looked at my pants, shaking her head again.

What was with everyone tonight talking about my dick as if it was small?

"I realize that now."

"You need to protect this one." Bunny motioned to Elise's limp body lying on the couch. "Your mother would've liked her."

I tensed at the mention of my mother. I'd never gotten to know her before she'd died. Bunny had been my surrogate mother growing up, taking over raising me, her nephew, after her sister had passed. Her judgments were as good as my mother's would have been. "Let's go check the bath."

Bunny limped toward the bathroom, favoring her right hip. It made me sad to see her get older. She had just as much stamina as she had when I'd been growing up, but small signs of her aging had become apparent.

I picked up Elise in my arms and carried her to the bathroom. She mumbled something into my neck that I couldn't understand. Even with terrible breath, she still smelled good to me.

My cock twitched in my pants at the thought of peeling off her dress and bathing her.

I shut down any thoughts of sex tonight. Nope, tonight Elise needed me to hold her while she slept and came down from the wolf wine high. Watching her breathe and holding her body close to mine would have to be enough for tonight.

20

———

ELISE

Opening and closing my mouth, I tasted my tongue. Gross. A mix of iron and sour wine coated the inside of my mouth. I lifted my head to find Everett sleeping soundly next to me. His hand splayed possessively over the small of my back.

Ouch, my head hurt. I buried my face into my pillow, wishing the snippets of memory from last night would stop appearing in my brain. Wolf wine, knocking over glasses, Bethany, Jenny.

Lifting the sheets, I looked down at my naked body. *When did I undress? Or should I say, when did Everett undress me? I* thought. *Did we...?* I looked over at Everett. *We didn't. He wouldn't have taken advantage of me like that.* My hair fell over my face, and I breathed in the smell of Everett's shampoo. Why had I washed my hair?

It hit me like a ton of bricks. Puke. Upside down, puke everywhere. I groaned, rolling over to my back and staring up at the ceiling. Had anyone seen? I hadn't acted very luna-like. I was disappointed in myself. I should've listened to Kleio about the wine.

Sitting up, I looked at the nightstand for water to rinse the taste from my mouth. A fresh bottle of water sat on a coaster, ready to be drunk. Cracking open the cap, I opened my lips, letting the cool water wash out my mouth. After several long pulls from the bottle, I set the water bottle on top of my leg, waiting to catch my breath.

Swirls of pink floated in the water. I lifted the clear bottle up to eye level to get a closer look. What was that? It looked like blood. I ran my tongue around my mouth, feeling for a cut. An iron flavor filled my mouth as my tongue was pierced by a sharp point in the front of my mouth. My hand slammed over my lips, and I froze. It couldn't be.

I smacked Everett on the back, waking him from his slumber.

"What is it, Lyka?" His sleepy eyes opened fast when he saw me. "What's wrong, Elise?"

"Something's wrong with my mouth," I said from behind my hand. It sounded like I had a lisp. I tensed as my tongue ran over a sharp point again, this time on the other side of my mouth.

Everett grabbed my wrist and pulled my hand away from my mouth, scooting closer to me.

"Open up," he said in his alpha voice.

My lips opened involuntarily. Not fair. Saliva pooled out of my lower lip, and I wiped my chin with my hand. My fingers came back red.

Everett peered into my mouth and smiled.

"What? What is it?" I asked.

"You got your fangs."

I snapped my mouth closed, piercing my tongue again. I cried out in pain.

"You'll have to get used to those," he said.

I scurried out of bed and ran to the bathroom, keeping my

hand over my mouth. I spit the blood out into the sink before I lifted my head to look at myself in the mirror. Streaks of red blood covered my chin.

Slowly, I opened my mouth and pulled back my lips. Two small teeth that hadn't been there last night graced the gums on the roof of my mouth, right next to my incisors. No wonder I was in pain. They had pushed through my gums and weaseled their way between my teeth that had been in the same place all my adult life. Maybe it was good I'd been unconscious last night; I hadn't had to feel it.

I grabbed a toothbrush from the holder and smeared some toothpaste onto the bristles. I scrubbed the entirety of my mouth, washing the blood and stale wine taste down the drain.

I found Everett lying on the bed waiting for me after I'd finished.

"How do they look?" he asked.

"It's weird," I said. "You didn't tell me this would happen."

"I didn't even think to. It's just something all of us shifters go through growing up."

"It would've been nice to know," I said.

Everett motioned me over to the bed, and I climbed in, letting him wrap me up in his arms. The skin-on-skin contact always felt good.

"Having fangs isn't all bad." He dragged his fangs along the skin of my neck. I shivered even with his body heat against me. "There're a lot of fun things they can do." His tongue licked the mark on my neck, and I shook against him. "I think you like my fangs."

"Yes," I murmured.

"I'm going to like your fangs just as much as you like mine."

I snapped up, looking at his face. "Can I...mark you?"

"Now you can. I imagine you'll want to mark your territory after how possessive you were last night."

I thought back to last night. I'd stood up to Bethany. Something inside of me had snapped. She'd made me so mad I'd lost control over my emotions. A different Elise had taken over.

"Sorry about that too," I said. There was a lot to be sorry for this morning.

"I like your wolf. She's endearing."

"My wolf?"

"She came out a little strong last night. We'll have to work on holding her back," Everett said. That would explain the lack of control over my words. "But she takes what she wants. I like that." He traced a line with his fingertips along my collarbone, stopping when he reached my mark.

"I watched you sleep last night and imagined putting one of these"—he brushed his fingers over the mark, eliciting a gasp from my lips—"somewhere else."

"Why would you do that?" I asked.

"To make you feel good." Everett closed his mouth over my mark, teasing it with his tongue. It was like the mark had a direct line to the nerves between my legs, sending currents of pleasure down my body. "Doesn't this feel good?"

"Yes," I whispered. My eyes were closed. I opened my mouth to help with my increased need for oxygen. My fangs hit my bottom lip.

"Imagine me biting you here." Everett brought his fingers to the side of my breast, my nipples instantly pebbling. His head dipped down to lick the soft tissue. I moaned as his tongue wet the skin. "Yes, that would taste good."

He pulled down the blankets that had been covering us, exposing my entire body to the cool air of the bedroom. Kisses from his lips traced the curve of my waist to the bone of my hip.

Everett settled himself between my legs, lifting one leg and bending it at the knee. He let my knee fall to the side, exposing my pink flesh to him. Everett's eyes zeroed in on the glistening skin between my legs. I knew what I looked like, wet from the attention he had been giving me. I could feel liquid seeping from between my folds, readying my body for him. Watching him take it in excited me even more.

A head of brown hair dipped between my legs. I could feel his tongue on my inner thigh that lay open on the bed, right in the sensitive space between my leg and my center. "Or maybe here," he said.

My knee snapped up, closing his head between my legs. I lifted my head to see Everett smiling at me before he tucked his head and dragged his tongue between my folds. I squealed, opening my knees and releasing his head. "Yes," he said. "I think this spot would be best."

I didn't have time to protest. Everett took advantage of my open legs and sunk his fangs into the muscle between my leg and my center. I screamed, both in shock and in pain. My fingers twisted into his scalp, pulling his hair, trying to remove him from my body. He didn't budge.

When Everett had marked my neck, I'd been all but unconscious. I didn't remember it being like this. It felt like I had fallen into a fire. My body was blazing. After a few seconds, the warm heat of his mouth soothed the initial pain. This bite was even closer to my center than the one in my neck. It didn't take long for pleasureful feelings to reach the nub between my legs, making it throb.

"Everett," I moaned, releasing the tension on his scalp.

He pulled his fangs from my skin, then replaced the cool air that slid over the mark with the warm moisture of his tongue. Taking his time, he lapped at the new mark, making sure it wouldn't drip blood. I watched him from my vantage point, looking down at his mouth. His eyes flicked up to meet my gaze. The heat from the bite spread throughout my body, making my muscles tremble with need.

Something in my head flipped like it had yesterday when I'd spoken to Bethany. A dark shadow spread over my thoughts, taking over my brain. Was Everett right? Was it my wolf? It didn't look like a wolf. It looked like a dark cloud, consuming me.

The shadow pushed against my willpower, testing how far it could push. I let it through, and it quickly spread, taking over my emotions and thoughts. My heartrate increased. My self-confidence increased. It was time to take what was mine.

I squinted my eyes at Everett's, letting the new feeling take over. His mouth left my skin, his eyes widening as he watched the sensation consume me.

"There she is," he said.

I sat up and pushed Everett onto his back. He fell easily, waiting for me to make the next move. "Let her take what she needs."

Everett's pupils were large, covering most of his golden iris. They looked animalistic. The tattoos that covered his arms and chest twitched over the tense muscles beneath his skin. He was waiting, preparing himself for what I would do.

I climbed on top of his body, straddling my legs over his stomach, letting my wet center rest against his abdomen. The bond between us hummed with anticipation. Placing my palms against his chest, I slid my core down his abs toward the hard length that lay against his stomach. Reaching between my legs, I picked up his warm shaft and used my thumb to wipe away the bead of liquid that had formed at the tip. Everett sucked air between his teeth, tensing at the feeling of my hand wrapped around him.

"Stop teasing me, Lyka," he hissed, using his pet name for me. I growled at him, showing my teeth. Everett smiled at me knowingly. "My wolf wants me to take what is ours, but I'll hold him back. It's your wolf's first time with us. Let her out, Elise. I want to see what she can do."

The wolf inside my head, which looked more like a shadow, took Everett's invitation greedily. I pushed his tip between my folds and lowered myself down, letting him slide into me, stretching me. I put both of my hands on his pectoral muscles, anchoring myself to him as his tip reached the deepest part of me. My head tilted back, and my eyes squeezed shut as I let my muscles relax around him. His hands gripped my hips, lifting me up before releasing me, letting me impale myself on his shaft.

I looked down at Everett. His lips were parted, eyes still dilated.

"What now?"

His question was encouragement enough for me. I bent over, letting my bare breasts press against his chest. I gripped the fitted sheets above his shoulders, bunching them tightly in my fists. My face tucked in the sweet spot between his neck and shoulder. I took a deep breath through my nose. The smell was intoxicating. Even more than the wolf wine that had rendered me stupid. A mix of the fresh air of outside and a woodsy smell—maybe it was evergreen. I smashed my nose against the skin of his neck, trying to inhale as much of the scent as possible.

I could feel his pulse beating quickly underneath the cords of muscle. My hips moved back and forth, letting him slide in and out of my center but never letting him fully withdraw. The back-and-forth motion had my clit rubbing against the rough expanse of hair above his shaft. The friction of the movement and the smell of his skin had me quickening my pace, chasing my pleasure.

A knot deep in my center tightened, getting close. I breathed heavily against his neck feeling the muscles inside of me tightening around him. His hands found my hips again, his arms taking over the movement as I lost myself to my release. I was tumbling inside my head, my body shaking against his.

Lips parting against his neck, my new fangs pulled against his skin, getting caught on the short stubble of his beard. Everett's breath hitched as he felt the tiny points. Instinctually, I pushed my teeth through his skin. A small popping sound reached my ears as they broke the dermis. Warm liquid filled my mouth, bubbling up from the mark my teeth made. I used my tongue to lap it up, keeping my teeth buried in his flesh.

Everett's body froze for a moment before he roared, thrusting once into me, shooting his release into my body.

"Take it easy." Everett grabbed the back of my neck, holding me in place.

I stiffened, the shadow retreating, letting me comprehend what I had just done—or what my wolf had just done.

Everett closed his fist around my hair, wrapping it around his wrist until he had a tight hold. Slowly, he lifted my head from his neck, pulling my teeth out of his skin. I sat up, straddling him with his softening member still inside of me. My hands flew up to my mouth, covering the blood-soaked fangs inside.

I watched Everett as he brought a hand up to his neck, feeling the two holes I had left in his skin. He pulled his hand away and held it in front of his face, rubbing the fresh blood on them between his fingers.

"Little help?" he asked.

I looked down at the mark on his neck. Blood pooled around the holes, slowly bubbling up from the breaks in his skin. Using the hand that was wrapped tightly around my hair, he guided my head back down to the mark. I stuck out my tongue, licking to catch a drip that had traveled onto his collarbone. I traced the line of blood to the holes and set to work licking the wound.

The effort was instinctive, as it had been for Everett taking care of my mark. He held me there while I cleaned him, using his other hand to rub my back, making small circle motions.

When the mark stopped bleeding, I raised my head to look at his face. "I'm sorry."

"You need to stop apologizing all the time. Following your instincts is nothing to be sorry about." Everett pulled out of me and wrapped his arm around my shoulders, pulling me against his side.

"But I hurt you," I said, looking at the red angry mark on his neck.

"I've told you before—nothing you do in the bedroom can hurt me." His hand reached around and fluttered against the mark on my neck. I held my breath at the feeling of pleasure shooting through the nerves of my body. "It felt good. Just as yours does. It feels even better to know that you've claimed me as your mate."

I supposed that was what I'd done—given him my mark so that everyone knew that he was mine.

"I felt like I wasn't even in control," I said. The shadow that had overtaken my actions and thoughts had been domineering. It'd been like a dark cloud covering the sun, making it dark enough that I couldn't see clearly.

"You are. Your wolf wouldn't do anything you didn't subconsciously want to do," Everett said. "It takes practice to control them, not let them take over so completely."

I sat up next to his body and pulled my knees into my chest. It was a lot to take in. A lot of change happening so quickly, so much of it was out of my control.

Everett kept his arm around my waist. He had been nothing but loving since he'd brought me here, taking care of me when I was sick and building me a garden. He was the anchor that kept me reinforced. Literally—I had to touch him every so often so I didn't fall over in pain. It was getting better; I could go longer and longer without needing his physical contact. But I enjoyed his touch. His warm skin against mine always helped me relax and breathe easier.

I couldn't deny the attraction between us. It was electric. It felt good to have him in my life. I thought back to my conversation with Kleio. I needed to give him more of a chance. More of me. He had my body, but it was my mind that I needed to make more accessible. Stop fighting it. Embrace it. My mother even thought this was a great thing. Not that it counted for much, but it still counted.

"Are we really doing this?" I asked.

Everett looked at me, confused.

"This." I motioned around the room. "This 'shifter' thing, this 'us' thing, this 'luna' thing."

He sat up next to me, leaning against the wooden headboard. "We've been doing 'this' since the day I saw you. There's no escaping 'this.' No running away and hiding. We are linked"—his fingers grazed against my neck—"forever."

He pulled my chin with his hand, so my eyes met his. "You are mine, and I am yours. Nothing can stop 'this,' and nothing will finish it."

I closed my eyes, accepting his words.

"Fine," I said as I handed him my heart.

21

———

EVERETT

KLEIO SCOFFED AT THE SIGHT OF THE BOTTOMS OF MY shoes as she walked into my office, followed by Jack, Gavrill, and Kostas. I ignored her. It was my desk; I could cross my legs on top of it if I wanted to.

"How was the rest of the party?" I asked the group. They pulled out chairs and sat around my desk.

"Jenny made quite the splash," Kostas said, looking to Gavrill for a rebuttal. Kleio giggled into her palm, trying to hide her amusement. "How many girls did she end up slapping? Two? Three?"

"She seems very defensive of you, Gavrill. I don't think any of the girls will talk shit to her face anytime soon," Kleio said. "And in that dress? Macy was pissed. You should've thrown the dress out months ago."

Gavrill ignored their prodding. "Convenient of you to leave. You left me with a line of pack members disappointed that I wasn't the alpha."

"Anything interesting?" I asked.

"Just the nail marks on Gavrill's arms," Kleio said. Jack shook his head, amused.

I glanced down to where Gavrill quickly pulled down the rolled-up sleeves of his plaid buttoned shirt. He covered them up quickly, but not before I saw the red marks Kleio was referring to. I raised an eyebrow his way. Gavrill shook his head, begging me to drop it.

"The party was busy last night," Kostas interjected, ending the standoff. "A lot of new faces. Many of them smell...off."

"There was a weird smell to a few of them," Jack said while rubbing the back of Kleio's neck.

My own neck started to ache—I was missing my mate. What had happened between us this morning wasn't enough. I'd never get enough.

"Probably members of my father's pack." I brushed my fingers over the new mark on my neck. The touch sent shivers down my body.

Part of me wondered if I'd gone too far with Elise. She'd begged me to open up to her, but the only thing I'd regularly opened was her legs. She hadn't complained—but she needed more from me. I'd never been open with someone before, sharing feelings, especially the new ones I felt brewing in my chest. It wasn't just lust. It felt like another four-lettered *L* word that I'd never thought I'd feel. I wasn't sure how to give that side of me to her, especially when it was also new to me.

I brushed off those emotions. There was no space for feelings in this room. "We'll have to stand tough among the new members. They aren't used to order and never learned how to behave within a pack."

Everyone surrounding the table nodded.

"I can't allow them to perceive me as weak. I must be in control." My reason was simple. I was new to the True Alpha position. Any pause or mistake on my part would make me appear weak. "We need to watch out for those Lycans seeking refuge." I motioned toward the closed door. "We don't know what they'll do when given boundaries and pack rules to follow."

"I agree," Kostas said. "We need to keep a close eye on them. We can't trust them yet."

"You're not your father, Everett." Kleio walked over to me and grabbed onto my arm. "He was strong but also cruel. You don't have to be cruel to be strong."

I ran my hand through my hair. I wasn't anything like my father. I'd purposefully left his pack all those years ago to distance myself from him.

"How's it coming with the rogues?" I asked them. "Your week's almost up."

Kleio looked at me, disappointed that I'd changed the subject. "I need more time! Nothing I've tried has helped. Their souls are still there—I just know it."

"You can be hopeful all you want, but I'm sticking to my word. A couple of days and then we dispose of them."

She sat down in her chair opposite my desk. "You shouldn't be keeping all of this,"—she motioned around the room—"from Elise. She'll resent you for it. She's part of our pack now, the luna. Elise needs to be included." Now Kleio had changed the subject on me.

I groaned, rubbing my hand over my face. "The rogues are dangerous and unpredictable. I don't want her anywhere near them."

"She'll be mad if she finds out about the rogues or the stone from anyone else but you. She'll lose the trust you've built."

Of course, Kleio was right. But it was too soon. Elise had just now decided to give her new life a chance, to give me a chance as her mate. I couldn't have her near the rogues. They were too dangerous. If anything else happened to Elise like it had in the woods...

There was a quiet knock on the door. If I didn't have my wolf senses, I would've missed the sound.

"Come in, Elise," Kleio called out.

My eyes shot to the door, my body standing straight up from the seated position it'd been in. *Mate.* My neck throbbed, wanting her touch.

The door opened slowly. Wide green eyes and brown hair peeked through the crack. I walked across the room toward her—getting close to my mate was an impulse I couldn't shake.

"Do you need something?" I asked as I wrapped her in my arms. She smelled earthy, a mix of dirt and wind locked into her hair as I buried my nose in the strands. I had an idea why she was here based on the way Kleio had welcomed her into the room without even turning around in her chair.

"Kleio mind-linked me to come. Is this a bad time?" Her green eyes met mine, searching my face trying to read my expression. Like there'd ever be a time I didn't want to see my mate.

"Never," I said, leading her into the room. There weren't any more chairs available, so I guided her around the side of the desk, sitting in mine before pulling her on top of me. I stuck my nose between her neck and shoulder, inhaling her scent. My body relaxed as I had her against me. I could feel her body relax too.

"Sorry I'm so dirty," Elise said, brushing her hands in front of her. "I came right from the garden."

"How's that going?" asked Jack. "I saw some yarrow growing in the planter beds."

Elise grinned. "It's been going really well. The soil here is so rich, everything is thriving. I've never seen selfheal grow so quickly—it'll be ready to harvest soon."

Jack nodded with appreciation.

"Oh, I brought some of the yarrow paste you asked for." She dug into the side pocket of her leggings, wiggling around on my lap and gently nudging my cock with her ass. "Sorry," she whispered, tucking her bottom lip beneath her top teeth. Her fang stuck out, and my neck throbbed at the sight.

"It's fresh. I made it out in the garden today." Elise held out a small jar of paste for Kleio. She started to stand up, to lean over the desk to where Kleio was sitting, but I grabbed her hip bones, keeping her securely on my lap where she belonged.

Kleio stood up from her seat, rolling her eyes in my direction before bending over the desk and grabbing the jar. "Thank you. I know someone who really needs this." She turned around, grabbing Gavrill's wrist from where he rested it on the arm of the chair and manipulated it so his palm was facing up.

She set the jar in his hand, taking the time to close each of his fingers around it. "For your arms," she said, winking.

Gavrill growled at her, causing Jack to growl back. I slapped my hand on top of the desk, ending the altercation. Kleio sat down next to Jack, a smirk on her face. Gavrill kept the jar tucked in his hand, slowly tucking it into the pocket of his pants.

"Do you think you could make more of the yarrow paste?" Kleio asked Elise. "There are some new...pack members that have arrived in less than perfect condition."

My body froze. *Don't you dare tell her, Kleio,* I growled in my head. Elise was a healer. I just knew she'd try to help the rogues if she knew where they were.

"Sure, I can get some more jars made," Elise said. She sat up a little straighter in my lap, her dirt-covered hands clenched together tightly. She was excited to help. I wanted her to, but not with the rogues. There was no helping those Lycans. She'd be crushed when she couldn't heal them—mentally and possibly physically. They were dangerous.

"That'd be great," Kleio said with a twinkle in her eye.

I glared at her, hoping to extinguish that twinkle that I knew meant trouble.

22

ELISE

THE SMALL WOLF SCULPTURE FELT HEAVY IN MY HAND. I was glad Everett hadn't asked me about it. It was strange enough that my mom had carved and sent me a wolf sculpture. She didn't know exactly who I was living with, just thought that I had a wealthy boyfriend with a giant house. Honestly, she probably thought nothing of it, off in her fairy cloud, overlooking reality.

The wolf reminded me of the house my dad had inherited and all the forest decorations that were on the walls when they'd moved in a few weeks ago. Maybe the charms of the new town and house were rubbing off on Mom, new inspiration.

I wondered what my mom had told my dad about her visit here. Soon, I needed to get back to the house and see my dad for myself. I could probably get there in my wolf's form in half the time, being able to run through the forest, not trapped in a car that could only drive on the winding roads. Being a shifter had its advantages.

I nestled the wolf sculpture between two sweatshirts in the

back of the armoire. Like usual, Everett had been gone when I'd woken up this morning, his side of the bed still warm. I'd rolled over to his side of the bed, absorbing his smell. I'd stopped when I'd realized what I was doing, becoming more wolf-like by the day. After marking Everett, my wolf had been a quiet silhouette in the back of my mind. Probably tired from all the excitement.

I got dressed in leggings and a T-shirt before opening the velvet shades covering the giant windows. At the last minute, I took out the wolf statue and put it in the pocket of my leggings. It was the reminder of home I needed right now.

A couple of girls who were sparring in the arena stopped to look up at the window before resuming their drills. My hand raised in an awkward wave that was unreturned. What did they think of me? There had to be so many rumors going around the pack house.

Rapid movement in my peripheral vision caught my attention. I squinted, looking out to the side of my garden, where Jenny was sitting on a blanket, waving at me. Her mouth was moving, but I couldn't hear what she was saying. I held up a finger, letting her know I'd be down in a minute. I wanted to hear how she'd escaped Gavrill's room this time.

I made my way through the pack house, silently nodding at the stray pack members who crossed my path. Everyone was still bending down to one knee when they saw me. They meant to be respectful, but I still found it uncomfortable. It felt strange that people had so much blind admiration for me, just because of who I was mated to. I'd done nothing to deserve their respect. Even the girls who I'd just seen through the window stopped hitting each other with what looked like sticks to kneel once I made it outside. They continued sparring after I nodded to them, the rhythmic noise of their sticks hitting each other like a melody.

"Elise!" Jenny called out to me, waving her arm at me as if I'd miss seeing her sitting next to the garden. I walked over to where she sat, leaning back on her hands, her legs extended in front of her. She wore an oversized sweatshirt and a pair of athletic shorts—still sporting bandages on her thighs. "You're like a queen, everyone kneeling for you."

I gathered my hair in my hands, pulling the strands off my neck. The sun was hot, beating down on us. "Yeah, that part of being luna is still super uncomfortable for me." I tied my hair up into a bun with the hair tie I had on my wrist.

Jenny brought her knees to her chest. "Should I kneel? I don't really want to get up."

"No, don't worry about it. Are your legs healing okay?" I mentally tallied what I was growing in the garden—maybe I could make a paste for her burns.

"Oh, they're fine, getting better every day. I'd remove the bandages, but Gavrill is making me keep them all medicated and covered up."

I nodded. "Does he know you're out here? Or am I going to witness an angry Gavrill come storming out of the pack house any second?"

"He can shove it," Jenny scoffed. "I need sun, fresh air. It's good for my healing."

So, he didn't know she was out here. I looked back at the pack house waiting for Gavrill to fly through the doors in search of her. Jenny lay back on her blanket, unperturbed, an arm draped over her face covering her eyes. Apparently she wasn't worried about him finding her.

Jenny looked relaxed, but I couldn't join her—I didn't do well sitting still. My fingers itched to dig in the dirt, check on the plants in my garden. "I'm going to work in the garden," I said.

She kept her eyes closed, her skin glowing beneath the sunshine. "Great—I'll be here."

The white-picket fence was still just as charming as it had been when I'd planted the seeds. The latch on the gate flipped open with a flick of my fingers, and I stepped into the dirt, sinking down into the rich soil. I should've asked about some rubber boots. The white sneakers I was wearing might be a lost cause.

Tiny green sprouts stuck out of the dirt in neat lines, just how I had planted them. That was quick. Usually seeds took a week to germinate. I crouched down next to the closest sprout, the start of a tomato plant. The soil around the green stem was darker than the soil between the rows.

I picked up a handful and let it fall between my fingers. It was moist. Someone had been watering my garden for me. The next raised garden had the selfheal I'd planted. Like I'd said in Everett's meeting, those were coming in nicely. Growing faster than I'd anticipated, they already had green leaves and the bud of the purple flowers that would soon bloom. The soil around these was a little dryer than I would like.

I checked out the watering can that had been given to me next to the crate of supplies. That would work for now, but not long term. Back at the pack house, there was a silver spigot sticking out from the house low to the ground. A green hose sat coiled next to it. Perfect.

I attached the hose to the spigot and dragged the hose to the garden. Luckily, it was a long one that had no trouble reaching. I pulled the hose up onto the raised bed that held the selfheal and laid it in the middle, along the space between the rows of plants, then I used the clippers I was given to poke a series of holes in the hose.

When I felt satisfied with the number of holes, I walked

back to the spigot and turned the water on. Back in the garden, I checked on the irrigation system I'd created. Water dripped out of the holes, dispersing the liquid throughout the plants. Now all I would have to do each day was turn on the hose and my plants would get water.

The rhythm of sticks hitting each other stopped, as did the bird calls around me.

I lifted my eyes from the ground, looking at the pack house where a scuffle had broken out in front of the doors to the dining room. A dilapidated red wolf broke free from two large men in their human forms, snarling and running aimlessly away from them. It ran into the arena, crashing into the carefully organized carts of weapons, causing a loud sound as metal hit the floor. It recovered from the crash, getting back on all four paws. The guards were right behind it, entering the arena with iron weapons and rope, ready to capture the escapee. The two girls who'd been sparring stood frozen in the center of the arena as Jenny's scream echoed off the pack house. As the guards closed in on it, the wolf looked for an escape.

"Don't let it get away!" Kleio's shrill voice cut through the chaos as she ran through the doors and toward the arena.

The wolf was looking more and more desperate by the second, its head whipping around, eyes wild with fear. Right before one guard released a looped rope to lasso the wolf, its blue eyes met mine. I probably looked like a sitting duck in the middle of the garden watching the commotion in front of me.

In a last-ditch effort to escape, the wolf jumped over the short wall of the arena, pushing once off the grass between the arena and garden before jumping into the dirt next to me, easily clearing the white-picket fence. I vaguely heard the guards yell orders as they tried to get over to the garden as quickly as possible. Now that it was standing a few feet away from me, there was no doubt this wolf was a rogue. I'd caught glimpses of them in the cages during the tournament, but seeing one unre-strained was frightening.

From a distance I had assumed it was a red wolf, but now I saw that its fur was more of a tan color—the red I saw came from the dried matted blood and open wounds that scarred its skin. I stood still, scared to make any movements that might cause the rogue to attack. When it looked at me, this close, I didn't see wickedness in its eyes. They resembled the eyes of a lost and scared child.

I took a step closer.

"No! Don't!" Kleio's voice cut through the trance I was in with the rogue. I broke eye contact to see the guards about to jump the picket fence into the garden.

"Stop," I said, raising my hand to the guards. They stopped their attempts to jump the fence. The two men stood there holding their weapons and breathing heavily, waiting for my next command. I didn't get the feeling that this rogue was as dangerous as the others I'd seen. It seemed more a victim than an aggressor.

"This is all my fault," Kleio said between breaths, panting just as heavily as the guards. "The rogue's dangerous, Elise. Let the guards handle it."

I ignored her pleas, looking back to the rogue who hadn't moved a muscle. I took another step forward. The rogue lay down on the dirt, giving up, exhausted. Its eyes almost closed as its chest moved up and down slowly. Too slowly. I reached out a hand to touch its side, crouching down next to it. I heard Kleio suck in air, nervous for me.

"Maybe I should get Gavrill..." Jenny, standing next to Kleio, turned to run to the pack house.

Kleio grabbed onto her arm, pulling her back. "Don't make

any sudden movements," she whispered through clenched teeth.

The fur was rough, matted with dried blood. The rogue didn't flinch when I touched it. I brought my other hand to its head, touching the soft fur between its ears. Maybe the only spot on its body that wasn't covered in blood or missing flesh.

Next to me, the selfheal grew, full of leaves and purple buds. Following my instincts, I picked a few of its leaves, pushing them into the rogue's mouth, careful not to puncture my fingers on its teeth.

A white shadow slid over my mind, like the black shadow that represented my wolf, but this time it was white, like steam from a teakettle. It clouded my mind and sent tingles down my arms to my hands. My fingertips grew warm against the rogue, and for a second, the white light blinded me. My eyelids snapped shut, a reflex attempting to shield them.

Beneath my fingers, the feeling of hard matted fur turned soft and warm. I opened my eyes, seeing the same eyes as before but set in an unfamiliar face. Her face was that of a young girl—a human girl with bright blue eyes and sandy blonde hair, no older than fifteen. She lay there in the dirt with her eyes open wide, glancing between me and the sky. Slowly, she lifted her hand to her face, examining it carefully. She flipped it back and forth as if she couldn't believe what was right in front of her.

"What the..." Kleio pushed past the guards and entered my garden, kicking up dirt as she walked toward us. "What did you just do?" She grabbed my shoulder, turning my body toward hers.

I lifted my hand from where they were still resting on the girl's forehead and stomach. "I don't know," I whispered. My hands were shaking now that they weren't against her body.

"It was a rogue, and now..." Kleio looked down at the girl in disbelief. "What's your name, sweetie?" She gestured to Jenny, who came forward, removing her sweatshirt and handing it to the girl.

"Molly," the girl said quietly, as if testing her vocal cords.

Kleio helped her put on the sweatshirt. "Well, Molly, you're a miracle. How do you feel?"

"I feel fine. Better now."

"Let's get you inside. Maybe some food?" Kleio looked down at her emaciated body. The wounds were gone, but she was still just skin and bones.

"My brother—where is my brother?" the girl asked anxiously, looking at us as lifelines. I knew what that felt like, everything hitting you at once.

"I'm not sure, sweetie, but we will help you find him. First, you need clothes that fit and some food." Kleio's reassurances seemed to placate the girl, and we both helped her to her feet.

She stood wobbly on her legs, not used to having just two feet. Jenny's sweatshirt was large and hung to her knees. With each of us taking an arm, we turned to the gate of the garden to exit.

The two guards that had been chasing the rogue kneeled on both knees with their heads bowed. "Luna, we didn't know you hold such power," one of them said. "You truly are the fated mate of our alpha."

I looked across from the girl to Kleio, confused.

She shrugged, addressing the guards. "Told you so." We passed them still on their knees, supporting the girl between us.

"Go get your boyfriend and have him meet us in the Vault," Kleio directed to Jenny, who looked at me for answers, but I was just as confused as she was. I couldn't put into words what had just happened.

Jenny let out a groan before turning around to find Gavrill, clearly annoyed that she'd have to admit she'd snuck out of his room again.

We walked to the dining room door, and I hoped Kleio had a plan.

"Let's drop Molly off with Bunny," she said, dictating the direction we would go in, and turned to me with excitement twinkling in her eyes. "Then let's see if you can do it again."

23

DAFNI, AGE EIGHTEEN

SOMETHING SCRATCHY BRUSHED AGAINST MY NOSE, coming and going. Just often enough to be irritating. My head hurt, throbbed. I rubbed at my nose. My movements felt slow, like I was moving through water.

There. The scratching was gone. But my head. *Frogfeet.*

I rolled slowly onto my back. I could hear the fluid inside my head sloshing as it turned. A breeze floated over my face. I held my head with my hands, trying to stop the pain. One eyelid lifted, the other following suit. It was sunny. They immediately slammed shut, leaving me in the dark with the memories of what had happened before I found myself lying on the ground in pain.

It was quiet except for the birds and the breeze making the leaves rustle in the trees. Mother wasn't around. If she were here, she'd be berating me for being knocked unconscious, even though it was of her own doing.

Grandmother.

My head pulsed.

Mother had killed her, thrown her into the fire like she was a log stacked along the side of the cottage. The cottage was gone as well, burned well to the ground by now.

My eyes opened again, this time prepared for the light that would flood them. It was bright, but not unbearable. I was alone, just as I'd thought. I was thankful for the solitude. It meant that my mother wasn't here. She was the only other individual that I knew who was alive, and she wanted me dead. Too chicken to kill me herself. She'd left me for the forest to finish off, as I felt sure it would.

What was I going to do? I had my air and water magic, yes, but what good did they do me out in the forest? I wouldn't be thirsty, but I would need food and shelter. Grandmother had never let me stray far from the cottage and had given me no instruction other than magic training and basic housekeeping. I was ill-prepared for a life alone in the woods.

I pushed myself up into a seated position, and my head retaliated. Even if my grandmother were here with me, she'd wouldn't have been able to help me much now. Still, I missed her presence, even though she was constantly pestering me to practice my magic and complete my chores. She'd been the only warmth I'd ever known, my mother too frigid to love me. Even an embrace with her musty-smelling dress, stained with splashes of potion from the cauldron, would be a comfort now.

There was little I could do right now except try to survive. I stood up slowly, keeping my legs far apart for balance. The ground was dry. There was nothing on my clothing except an errant dry leaf. The sun was warm and the temperature pleasant. Where had my mother dragged me? I'd never been farther than an earshot away from the cottage.

Which way should this witch go? I picked a direction and started walking, slowly at first, scanning my surroundings for any familiarity. I found none. Wandering aimlessly would get me nowhere. I stopped in a small clearing to think.

Branches snapped to my right. Something large was crashing through the forest. A bear? I crouched down behind a large tree, trying to hide myself.

A large man with brown hair and strange black markings on his body crashed through the trees and into the clearing where I'd just stood. His eyes scanned his surrounding, his nostrils flaring as he inhaled. He laughed loudly, throwing his head back. Hair grew from his face—a lot of hair.

This was the first man I'd ever seen. I'd only heard of them in the tales my grandmother would tell me as a little girl.

"I can smell you, witch. Come out, come out, wherever you are." The man looked around, still sniffing. He stopped when his eyes met the tree I was hiding behind. "This is too good," he spoke again. His voice was so low.

The man walked over to the tree. I held my breath. He poked his head around the tree and grabbed my upper arm. "Got you."

We locked eyes for a moment. His were wild and bounced around in his sockets. Sweat covered his face, dripping from his hairline. "They told me there were no witches, that they hadn't seen one in one hundred years. Liars—they're all liars." He spit when he spoke. Some fell and landed on my face.

I smeared it off with my free hand before he pulled me out from behind the tree. Were all men this unpleasant?

"If Elise doesn't have it, then you must know where it is. Your kind took it all those years ago. Where is it?" The man held me at arm's length, shaking me as he spoke.

"I don't know what you're looking for." I tried to make my voice strong.

"The Lifestone. The witches must have it." Another spray of spit hit my face. I closed my eyes. My mother had mentioned the Lifestone once or twice.

"I don't have it, but my mother knows where it is," I said.

Maybe if I was helpful, he would let me go. As much as meeting a man intrigued me, he was starting to scare me.

"Where is your mother?" The man stopped shaking me, suddenly still and focused.

"I-I-I don't know," I said. "She left me here."

"Does she have a name?"

"Matilda."

He stopped breathing for a second. "Your mother's Matilda?" he asked.

I nodded, hoping that my answer would satisfy him, and he would let me go.

He threw his head back again, laughing at the sky. "This can't be real! This can't be happening!"

The man let my arm go. I rubbed the spot where he had gripped me. Men were strong, their grip firm.

"Everyone will get what's coming for them when I have the stone." He was pacing in front of me, talking to himself. "I'll get my fangs and then payback." He stopped pacing abruptly, dirt flying from where his shoe struck the dirt. "You. You'll come with me. Your mother will look for you. I'll trade you for my fangs."

I watched him spout out his plan. Didn't villains usually keep their plans to themselves, only for them to be revealed later? This wasn't like any story Grandmother had told me. The world outside of the cottage was odd.

The man took my arm again. I winced at his tight hold. "You're staying with me until your mother comes to collect you."

"You're using me as ransom?" I asked.

"I suppose so," the man said, pulling me alongside him as he walked in the opposite direction from which he came. At least that meant he wouldn't kill me. His palms were sweaty against my arm, his grip constantly slipping.

I couldn't stay out in the woods alone without shelter or food. I would fall victim to the forest, just like my mother had planned. My mother wasn't coming for me. I knew that much. But this man didn't seem to understand that. Once I got my bearings and collected some supplies, I could escape, figure out a way to survive. Like a heroine in Grandmother's stories, I would endure.

I let him guide me over roots and dirt, through the woods. We walked until the sun met the horizon.

The farther we traveled, the more I noticed a change in the forest. The ground, usually green with foliage, turned brown.

At first, small clusters of brown caught my attention. They stuck out from the green surroundings. The patches of brown got larger the farther we walked. Our shoes became dirty with the dust that the brown plants made when we stepped on them. It was like the earth was dying.

Was this what it was like in the world outside the cottage? No wonder Grandmother had kept me there.

24

ELISE

It smelled terrible under the pack house. Maybe it was my heightened wolf's senses, but the smell was all-consuming, coating the back of my throat and tongue. After we dropped Molly off with Bunny, I'd run back to my garden to gather more selfheal leaves. Maybe they were what had caused the rogue to transition back to her human form?

Kleio led the way down two spiral staircases hidden by a door that was nothing special. I'd probably walked past it a dozen times while I had been here. I could tell we were underground by the damp walls and humidity in the air. And the smell. It was rancid.

"Just a little farther," she said over her shoulder. It didn't seem like we were walking anywhere pleasant, but I trusted my friend, otherwise I would have already turned around and climbed the spiral staircase two stairs at a time to escape.

We turned a sharp corner. I'd thought the smell couldn't get any worse, but it did. Behind the iron bars in front of me, rogues slithered over one another, fighting for a spot at the front of the cage. Their claws dug into flesh, not knowing or caring who was next to them. There wasn't enough air in the room for everyone to breathe. I found myself choking, trying to inhale.

"I know it's a lot." Kleio grabbed my arm to steady me. Blood had left my face and pooled deep in my gut, nausea bubbling up my throat. "Everett gave me a week to figure out what to do with the rogues. He wanted to dispose of them. I begged for a chance to figure out a solution." Her hands covered my cheeks, framing my face. "You're it. You're the answer."

I didn't have time to respond before Gavrill stomped down the stairs, with Jenny following behind. "Alpha isn't going to like this," he said, putting out his arm to keep Jenny behind him. She peeked around his body, her blonde hair poking out before her pale face. Her eyes widened when she saw what was behind the bars. "I don't like this."

"Yeah, yeah. Toughen up." Kleio took my hand and pulled me toward Gavrill. "It's her. She's the solution to the rogue situation." She looked back at me, smiling. "You should've seen it, Gavrill. She transitioned one back to their true form. A young girl, and she's alive and well, talking, communicating—she has full brain function."

"Prove it." He kept Jenny behind him as he stared down Kleio.

"I'm going to need help getting one out." She pulled a ring of keys off a nail driven into the dirt wall.

"I'll have to get Kostas if we're going to take one out. I can't handle it myself." Gavrill crossed his arms and spread his feet farther apart.

"I can help," Jenny squeaked. She ducked around his body, pulling a silver chain from under her shirt. "If these things are anything like the wolves I know, they'll be stunned by this." She held out the small whistle dangling from the silver chain.

"No, these aren't like the wolves you study." Gavrill tried to push her back behind his body, but Jenny dug her feet into the earthy ground.

"Oh, I know they aren't." She stepped closer to the cage, Gavrill following, keeping himself only a footstep away from her. "Let me show you."

She brought the silver whistle to her lips and blew a small burst of air into it. When she pulled it away from her lips, we all looked at her expectedly. The whistle hadn't made a sound. She smiled, keeping her eyes on the cage.

The rogues weren't fighting or clawing. They were lying on the ground, stunned, in a stupor.

We stared at them for a few seconds before they woke from their daze and continued clawing and fighting like nothing had happened.

"The whistle will stun them for about five seconds," she explained. "It should be enough time for Gavrill to grab one out of the cage and for Elise to do...whatever she does to it."

Everyone was silent for a moment before Kleio jumped into Jenny's arms, hugging her with wild abandon. "Oh, she's a clever one. I knew there was a reason Gavrill liked you so much." Jenny looked at me from behind Kleio's hair. Her look of confusion turned into a smile. Gavrill emitted a low growl that ended when Kleio let go of her. "Let's do it."

Kleio stood in front of the cage, key in hand, ready to unlock it. Gavrill stood in front of where the door would swing open, knees bent, arms out, ready to grab a rogue. We stood back a bit, Jenny with the whistle in her mouth and me with selfheal leaves in my hand.

"Three, two, one...go!" Jenny blew into her whistle, none of us hearing the noise.

Like magic, the rogues were stunned from the silent noise. Kleio unlocked the door of the cage with a twist of the key. The hinge didn't even squeak she moved so fast.

Gavrill met her speed, grabbing the first available rogue before she slammed the cage shut, locking it. He threw the cream-colored wolf onto the ground outside the cage, my cue to come forward.

With Gavrill holding down the rogue, I put my hand on its head like I had done in the garden, shoving a couple of selfheal leaves into its mouth. The white shadow returned; this time it didn't surprise me. I let it cover my mind, accepting the tingles that it sent down my arm into my hand. The bright white light came once again, and I shut my eyes. I let it all happen just as it did before.

Beneath my hand I felt warmth. Kleio, Gavrill, and Jenny all took a collective inhale, and I opened my eyes. My hand rested on the forehead of a man with age spots on his face and wrinkles in the corners of his eyes. He was staring right at me.

"What? What's going on?" His voice was a whisper.

Gavrill grabbed my arm, pulling me back from the rogue turned man. He pushed me behind his body next to Jenny, who stared at me with a mix of confusion and wonder.

Kleio knelt next to the man. "What's your name?"

The man turned his gaze from me to her. "Jonas."

"Well, Jonas, it's your lucky day. Welcome back." Kleio helped him into a standing position, helping him balance on two feet. "Your luna here was nice enough to save you."

"Luna! Let me give thanks to the one who saved me." The man used what little strength he had to fight her grasp, trying to kneel.

"We need to tell Alpha about this," Gavrill pleaded with Kleio.

"Let's do a few more before we get Everett." She walked away, pulling Jonas with her toward the hallway. "Give me a minute to put him somewhere and then I'll be back. Just a few more rogues!" Jonas's eyes never left me until she pulled him out of view.

———

When Kleio returned, we all went to work pulling rogues from the cage and transitioning them back to their true forms. Like an assembly line, we worked in tandem, each with their own station. It took ten rogues before I pulled an empty hand from my sweatshirt, out of selfheal leaves.

"I decided we aren't telling Everett about this," Kleio said. Gavrill opened his mouth to argue. "Just think of what his face will look like when we tell him that Elise healed *all* the rogues!"

That was a lot of rogues they expected me to heal. I opened my mouth to speak, but Kleio beat me to it.

"It'll be like a surprise, a good surprise. His birthday is coming up, you know."

His birthday? I really knew nothing about him. What kind of mate was I that I didn't know about his birthday?

"Even if we kept this from Everett, where are we going to keep them all?" Gavrill said. "There are...eighty-eight more to heal. And once we heal them, that's a lot of malnourished and sickly Lycans roaming the pack house. He'll get suspicious." I watched them argue like a Ping-Pong match.

"There are shifters from his father's pack arriving every day. He won't even notice."

"I'm trying to reason with you, Kleio. We can't keep this from him."

"You *will* keep it from him—you know why?" she said. "Because he would kill you if he knew you were down here with his mate, next to the dangerous rogues."

"I could say the same about you," he said.

"Unlike you, I'm not afraid to take that chance. I'm not a

wimp." Kleio punctuated the *p*. She played the part of the inner circle's annoying little sister exceedingly well.

Gavrill exhaled loudly. "Fine. We'll keep it from him for now." He looked back at Jenny. She'd watched the sparring match between the two next to me. "Let's go. You shouldn't have even been down here." He herded Jenny to the staircase, keeping her in front of him.

"I'm practically healed! I'm not some dumb girl you can hide in your room, keeping me there to fu..." Jenny's voice trailed off as they climbed higher up the spiral staircase.

"Oh, he's in trouble," Kleio said to herself, giggling. She turned to me. "You really are something, Elise. I don't know what kind of plant magic you have in you, but it's something special." She made sure the door to the rogue cage locked, giving it a couple of pulls. "The Magical Luna—it has a certain ring to it, doesn't it?"

She pushed my shoulder playfully, and I pushed her back, rolling my eyes at her. We left the rest of the rogues in the cage, ascending the spiral stairs that led above ground. Before I lost sight of the rogues, I looked back quickly. Seeing them writhe and fight, trying to escape their bodies, made me queasy.

Soon I could help them. I sent a silent promise down to the cage. I would be back. I could save them all. Finally, I could do something for the pack that would make me worthy of the luna title bestowed on me.

Kleio left me to find Jack and tell him the good news about the rogues. I climbed the grand staircase, skipping every other stair. There was a new weightlessness about me. I'd done *something*. Something that made a difference to this pack. I wasn't the freeloading human turned Lycan mated to the alpha, hated by Bethany, a weird gardening girl. I was a healer. My research had led to something good. I'd transitioned twelve rogues back to their human forms today. All of them healed and unscathed.

Kleio might've had Gavrill under her thumb, but *I* didn't have to follow Kleio's commands. I was the luna. Everett needed to hear the good news from my lips. Prove that he'd chosen the right mate. I would get a different present for his upcoming birthday.

Speaking of...that was really something I should've known about. When was his birthday? I felt his pull from our room.

Our room. Was that what I was calling it now? It sounded good.

The smell of evergreen hit my nose when the air from our room rushed over me as I opened the door. I looked around for Everett and noticed the bathroom door was closed. He was probably in there.

The closed curtains in the room provided privacy from the darkness outside. A fire was crackling in the fireplace, casting a glow around the room.

I threw myself onto the massive bed, my body facing the bathroom, ready for him to come out. I tingled with excitement. The look on his face when I told him the news was going to be something. I could imagine the smile that would grace his lips and how the corners of his eyes would wrinkle with pride. Would we spend the rest of the night here, on this bed, him thanking me with his fingers and maybe his tongue?

I smoothed the white duvet in front of me, pushing out the lumps my body had made when I'd thrown myself down. A few strands of straight blonde hair tangled around my fingers. I stopped the smoothing motion and sat up on the bed, holding the hairs between my fingers. They were long and very blonde. Bunny had gray hair, mine was dark brown, and Kleio's was strawberry blonde. Jenny was a blonde—but her hair was curly. Whose hair was this?

It hit me. A certain bleach blonde jealous shifter did. Why

was Bethany's hair in our room? Had she been in here? With Everett?

My mind raced with different scenarios that would've put Bethany in our room. Bunny, a diligent cleaner, would have swept up hairs from whenever she and Everett had been together long ago.

All the anticipation of telling Everett what I had accomplished whooshed out of me like air leaving a balloon. The whole time I'd been in the smelly dungeons, saving rogues, he had been up here with...her? That couldn't be right. We were mates. Made for each other.

The door to the bathroom opened, revealing Everett. "Where have you been, Lyka?" His voice had a certain purr to it that made it sound like he had missed me. His eyes looked at me like they always had, devoted and intense, like I was the only girl in the room.

But I hadn't been the only girl in our room.

"Who have you been with?" My voice was sharp.

Everett paused, stopping his slow saunter to the bed. I held up the long blonde hair between my fingers, letting it hang. In the light of the fire, it glimmered.

He walked over to the bed and took the strand of hair. Slowly, he wrapped it around his finger, examining it. "I've been here, alone, all night...waiting for you."

"It looks to me like you had someone over to keep you company while you waited." My insides bubbled. Where was his outright denial? He knew whose hair it was.

"I don't know why this hair was on the bed. I cut things off with Bethany weeks ago. This shouldn't be in here."

"Damn right it shouldn't be."

"I promise you, Elise, nothing happened. This must be some sort of joke. I'm going to figure out who did this."

"You do that," I said. "Until then, you'll stay away from me. I don't want any part of you right now."

My chest hurt at those words. Like my body knew the words were untrue. Of course, I would always want him. He was my mate; the attraction was too primal to deny. But I could fight it, keep as much distance between us as possible. Everett didn't get to have a side piece. I wasn't about that.

He walked over to the fire and dangled the hair in the flames, letting it burn.

Like the fire, my chest was hot, boiling. "Screw you, Everett! My whole life has changed since I met you. I'm a new...person" —I still didn't feel completely comfortable calling myself a Lycan —"you introduced me to the entire pack as your luna, and this is what you do when I'm not around? Find your old bed buddy? Am I not enough for you? Have I not given you enough?"

Forget the rogues, forget the good news. This was such a betrayal. I didn't know if I should believe him or the evidence he'd just destroyed. I wanted to believe him. It would make everything so much simpler. I shouldn't have followed Kleio into the Vault.

Maybe Bethany had been in our room, and they'd just talked. No, that wouldn't have been acceptable either. Everett had never heard about what Bethany had done to me at the Deca Party because I hadn't wanted to seem petty. I should have told him. Maybe then he wouldn't have entertained her.

I laid my head on the pillow by the headboard and curled into a ball. If I held myself tight enough, maybe I wouldn't fall apart.

"I'm not leaving you." Everett's voice was imposing. "I can't leave you; our bond needs us to be together." He paused for a moment. "That sounded bad. I don't want to leave you. I love you, Elise. I want to be with you and only you."

Air caught in my chest. He'd never said those words—we'd never exchanged them between us. Was he sharing them now that he'd gotten caught? Maybe just to placate me?

"We've been apart too long today," he said.

I wanted to argue. I wanted to fight with him. But the boiling in my chest had come to a simmer, and I was left with sorrow that blew over me like a cloud of steam. I wanted to share those words back, but now I couldn't. Not after this betrayal. I still felt them, though. I loved Everett, and that made this hurt even worse.

Tears found their way down my cheeks, soaking into the pillow beneath my head. They felt cold, like my heart.

"I won't hold you; I know you need space." Everett climbed into bed next to me. "I promise I didn't do anything with anyone else. I'll figure out what happened, why her hair was in here." He had remained calm this whole time. Was it because he was guilty and didn't want to implicate himself further? Or was it because he was innocent and truly didn't have an explanation?

"I'm going to touch you here," Everett said, putting his hand on my back between my shoulder blades. "Just enough contact so our bonds can restore."

The warm energy from the bond flowed into my body. It felt good and right. I tried not to relax too much, so he wouldn't think I was falling for his assurances. I wasn't. I needed time to recharge our bond so I could get space away from him. In the morning. Yes, in the morning.

My eyes felt heavy. The process of healing a rogue took more of my energy than I'd imagined. Maybe that was why I was so upset. I was exhausted. No, Everett needed to give me a plausible explanation for the hair. The salty tears pasted my eyelids shut, and I felt my breathing even out.

Everett's words were the last thing I heard before I fell asleep. "I'll fix this, Lyka."

25

EVERETT

Last night had been horrible. I'd hardly slept between listening to Elise's cries and racking my brain about how that hair had ended up in our bedroom. Things were over between Bethany and me. They had been for a long while. She'd been mad when I'd broken things off and I probably hadn't been nice about it, but there hadn't been any feelings there, at least not on my end.

It had taken so much willpower not to pull Elise close last night and tuck her back into my chest, letting her body shake against mine. I wanted her to punch me, to curse me out, anything but the quiet crying that made my heart ache. I'd said I loved her—and I did. It hurt that she hadn't said it back. Although I didn't blame her. She'd thought I betrayed her. My wolf was on edge, pacing in my head. He was anxious to make those who wronged my mate pay.

The door to my office creaked open, and my inner circle filed in. They all took seats on the opposite side of the desk.

"You look like shit," Gavrill said. He was probably right. I hadn't even looked in the mirror this morning. I didn't want to see what a shifter who'd spent his entire night trying to comfort his mate without touching her looked like.

"I had a rough night." I took a breath before I corrected myself. "Elise had a hard night."

"What did you do, Everett?" Kleio's tone was that of a scolding mother.

"That's the thing—I didn't do anything. Elise found blonde hair in our bed and assumed that I've been seeing Bethany on the side."

"That little bitch." Kleio was never one to mince words. "We should've gotten rid of her after you cut her loose. She's been scheming to get you back ever since."

"She's flirted a few times, but nothing sinister. This is the first time she crossed the line."

Kleio tried to hold back a laugh. I knew that look. She was hiding something. "What aren't you telling me?"

"Elise is going to be mad if I tell you."

"*I'm* going to be mad if you don't tell me."

She let out a breath and adjusted herself in her seat, sitting up straighter. "Fine. At the Deca Party, Bethany cut off the bottom of Elise's dress."

"She what?" I tried to remember back to the party. Elise had been wearing a long green knit dress. After the last flag had raised, it had suddenly been shorter. I had assumed it was a cool fashion trick that Kleio had devised to impress the pack.

"Bethany attached Elise's dress to one of the flags, and when the flag was raised the dress unraveled."

"So, you're telling me that Bethany tried to embarrass her luna on purpose in front of the entire pack?"

Elise had never said a word. It was impressive that she'd kept her composure throughout the incident. My heart fluttered at the thought.

"Yeah, that's exactly what she did," Kleio said. "Bethany's trouble, Everett. I don't think she's going to stop."

The alpha part of me stood poised, ready to attack, to take retribution for my mate. Another part of me felt my heart dropping in my chest. "I've lost her trust."

"No, you haven't, Everett." She leaned forward in her seat. "You need to get a confession out of Bethany and make sure she doesn't do anything to sabotage your relationship ever again. A mate is too precious to lose."

I couldn't have pack members assaulting Elise. Bethany must've thought she'd gotten away with it. Kleio was right—she wasn't going to stop. Elise would always be in a constant state of anxiety around the pack, especially when Bethany was around. Elise needed to feel safe here, loved. It was her home, and we were her family. Bethany needed to be made an example of. One bad apple could rot the whole bunch.

"Then it looks like we'll be welcoming a special guest to our meeting." I watched my inner circle look at each other, contemplating what I was going to do. Good—they were on their toes. I mind-linked Bethany to meet me in my office.

"She's going to come in here thinking you want her bent over your desk," Kleio said.

"Watch it," I responded.

The door latch clicked open, and Bethany slinked through the doorframe, suddenly stopping to eye up Kleio, Gavrill, Jack, and Kostas. Clearly she *had* thought she was coming here for something other than a reprimand.

"Come in, Bethany."

She walked in slowly, clutching her hands together in front of her. Her blonde hair was down in waves, and a new set of bangs graced her forehead. There were no more chairs in my office and none of my inner circle made a move to stand so she could sit. Good. She deserved to stand there wondering what was going on, what I was going to do.

"Something funny happened today. I thought you'd want to hear about it," I said, walking from around my desk toward her.

"Sure, I like a funny story." Bethany looked at me directly in the eyes. She didn't know that I knew.

"The luna found some blonde hair in our bed."

"Really? That's weird." She was being quite the actress, enunciating the word *really*.

Kleio scoffed. I gave her a look before I continued.

"I brought it up to my inner circle here today, and to my surprise, Kleio had another funny story for me."

Bethany glanced at her before quickly looking away. Kleio was shooting daggers with her eyes. Even I could feel them.

"She told me you did something to the luna's dress the night of the Deca Party." I stared at Bethany's face, looking for any sign of guilt. Her eyes widened, and she glanced to the side before righting herself and staring back at me.

"I can't help that Elise's dress ended up being poorly made," she said. "Or that it got snagged on the flag rope."

"Funny you know what happened to her dress, because I didn't know, nor did anyone except the luna and Kleio."

Bethany took a small step back. I could feel fur sprouting from my shoulders, pushing against the confines of the shirt I was wearing. My wolf in my head charged at her, jaws dripping with saliva, snapping at her.

"No one makes my mate cry. No one comes between me and my mate." Spit flew from my mouth, landing on the floor between Bethany and me. They wanted a strong alpha? Here I was.

"I, the True Alpha, reject your membership to the Cedar Moon Pack."

Bethany looked panicked, gathering her hair into one hand

on the side of her head. "No. I'm sorry. You don't have to do this." She backed up until she hit the wall.

"Kostas will chaperone you to your family's home, where you will be able to gather your belongings. I expect you to be absent from my pack's lands by sunset."

"Your pack lands are...everywhere," Bethany said, her voice wavering. The rejection from my pack had already taken affect. To be a Lycan without a pack was unpleasant. We were pack animals, needing one another to survive. A Lycan outside a pack was vulnerable—a target.

I didn't take my decision lightly. I could no longer trust her to be a part of my pack—even if she didn't live at the pack house. She'd made Elise a target, made her uncomfortable in her own home, tried to put distance between me and my mate. It was unacceptable.

"You're wrong. I have to do this," I said. "You can't seem to get it through your head that we're over, that you need to leave the luna and me alone."

"What will I do? Where will I go?" she asked.

"Wherever you want—as long as it's not on my pack's land."

"Everett, you aren't thinking straight," she said, her eyes growing desperate. "She's messed with your head. Remember what we had together? How good it was?"

"*This!*" I yelled. Kleio sucked in a breath, and Jack tucked her close to his side. "This is why you are leaving. I've found my mate. You've already targeted her twice now, and I can't trust that you won't do it again."

Bethany shrunk down, her shoulders collapsing, her head hanging low. "You'll regret this."

"I'm sure I won't. Now please, leave without a hassle. You've caused enough trouble." I gestured to the door and Kostas swooped in, corralling Bethany toward the door. She looked back at me one time before leaving, her eyes narrowing at me.

The door clicked closed behind them, and I sat down in my chair, rubbing my chin. That hadn't felt great, casting out a pack member, but it'd been the right thing to do. For me. For Elise. For us.

"Remind me never to piss you off," Jack said.

"That was the right thing to do," Gavrill said. "I couldn't imagine if someone was targeting my..."

"What's that?" Kleio asked.

He rubbed his lips with his hand shaking his head.

"Finish your thought, Gavrill. I know I'd love to hear the end of *that* sentence."

My beta shook his head, slinking out of the room before she pressed any further.

We all knew he'd been about to say, *my mate*. Was he referring to the curly blonde he kept—no, tried to keep—in his room?

Mate. That reminded me that I needed to find mine.

26

ELISE

"*Luna.*" Everyone kneeled before me as I walked through the pack house. The news of my healing was spreading. It was one thing to hear the lone whisper when I crossed paths with a pack member, but it was another to have them stop mid-step to kneel before me. The first time it had happened, I hadn't known how to react. I'd frozen mid-step, watching an older female shifter gingerly lower herself onto one knee, her face grimacing as her joints had bent. I'd reached out to stop her, but she'd swatted me away, insisting on bending the knee. The attention was too much.

With everyone living in such close quarters, it shouldn't have been surprising that everyone knew about the rogue healing. Despite the fact that Kleio had wanted to keep this from Everett, clearly the guards who'd seen me help Molly had taken it upon themselves to spread the word. It wouldn't be a secret from him for long.

Everett's little secret wouldn't be quiet for long either. Bethany would talk soon. She probably already was bragging about bedding the alpha again. My heart didn't believe he'd do something like that to me, but it was hard to ignore the evidence I'd found in our bed.

I shivered as I recalled her hair twisting around my fingers, followed by the smell of burnt hair that had filled our bedroom that night.

"Have we located the Lifestone?"

My body immediately detected my mate's voice. It was low and quiet, like he was trying to keep his voice from carrying.

"No, Alpha. Our trackers sense it's near, but they haven't been able to find it. Something keeps throwing them off the scent." That was Gavrill.

I pressed my back against the wall to my right. They were right around the corner, and I hoped Everett couldn't sense me. I held my breath.

"My father said something about smelling it on Elise that day in the forest." A long pause followed Everett's words.

"Don't go back there, Everett. She's here with us now, safe," Gavrill said.

"I know she is, but he smelled it on her. She has something to do with this."

"We'll figure it out. The answer is probably right under our noses."

I let Gavrill's voice be the last I heard of the conversation between them. Everett thought I had something to do with the Lifestone? That I was hiding something? Well, maybe I was. Before Everett had come to my rescue at the cabin, Professor Robinson had said the witches had the Lifestone. I hadn't even remembered to bring it up after he had brought me to No Bars and all the trouble we had gotten into there. Why would I share that with him now? Especially when he was hiding the rogues from me.

I walked past the opening to the hallway where Everett and Gavrill were standing, not caring if they saw me—though

I hoped they didn't. I didn't want to talk with them right now.

Pack members scattered around the dining room, finishing up a late breakfast. Everyone's eyes bored holes in me as I walked through the room, trying to keep my head up, my eyes forward and my feet moving underneath me. I tried to look busy or maybe lost in thought as I weaved through the tables, making a beeline for the doors to the back. My fingers turned the wolf statue around inside my pocket, the only part of me that revealed how uncomfortable I was. Those at the tables closest to where I walked left their chairs and fell to one knee, bowing their heads.

No one was training in the arena as I opened the doors of the dining room. Good. A few less people to wave off from worshipping me.

I took a minute to let the sunshine warm my face. My wolf pulled toward the surrounding forest, ready for a run, but I focused on the garden ahead of me. It was flourishing. The rich soil nourished the plants and ample sunlight pulled them toward the sky. The irrigation system I'd installed didn't hurt either. I bent down to turn on the spigot, straining my muscles to turn the sticky wheel to the on position.

"Aahh!" A man with short brown hair shot up from where he hid behind the white-picket fence, ducked down among the plants. He turned and looked at me.

It was Kostas. I laughed, throwing my head back at the sight of water dripping from the tip of his nose. I reached for the spigot again to slow the flow of water.

"Sorry about that, Kostas," I said as I made my way to the garden fence, unlatching the gate and stepping inside.

"You upgraded." He held up the hose irrigation tubing that was slowly dripping water.

"Yeah, it's a little easier than lugging cans of water back and forth." I cocked my head to the side as I looked at him. "Wait. How'd you know the irrigation system's new?"

He smiled, looking at his feet.

"It was you, wasn't it? You were the one who was watering my garden!"

"Guilty," he said.

"You're so sweet!" I walked over to give him a hug.

He backed up, waving me off. "The boss would kill me if I touched you. Plus, his stink is all over you." Kostas made a fake gagging sound, looking at me, expecting a laugh.

My face dropped at the mention of Everett. "I'm surprised you can even smell him. We've been...distant."

"He didn't do it, Elise." Kostas took a few steps closer to me.

"How do you know...?"

"Everett called us together this morning and told us about what Bethany did. Kleio told us about the dress."

"Everyone knows?" Of course everyone knew. There were no secrets in this pack house.

"Just the inner circle."

"Just like the inner circle knows all about the Lifestone?"

Kostas got a nervous look on his face.

"I overheard Gavrill and Everett talking earlier. Does Everett think I'm too weak to be included? Does he remember it was me who saved him in the forest during the tournament? Did he not make me luna?"

"Do you think Everett is hiding things from you?" Kostas asked.

"Of course he is! Bethany, the Lifestone, the rogues? He keeps it all from me."

"The rogues... Aren't you hiding things from him, too?"

"Kleio?" My question was rhetorical. She must have told him.

"No, Gavrill."

"Ugh, does anyone keep their mouths shut around here?"

Kostas chuckled. "Give Everett some slack, Luna. He's dealing with a lot."

"A lot of which he could let me help him with."

"Give him some time," he said.

I rolled my eyes. Men and the time they needed.

"In the meantime, you won't need to worry about Bethany. Everett sent a clear message to her this morning." Kostas dragged his thumb across his throat.

I looked at him, confused. *Did he kill her?*

"He kicked her out of the pack," Kostas said. "She'll be gone by sunset."

My mouth fell open. Damn.

"He loves you, Elise. I don't have a doubt in my mind. The lengths he would go to prove it to you..." Kostas shook his head. "He's letting his wolf take over more and more. He's trying his best to be a good True Alpha."

Walking toward the gate, he paused, turning around to face me. "Talk to him. Let him explain. I think you also have some explaining to do." Kostas walked out of the garden and into the pack house.

Everett had kicked Bethany out of the pack? That didn't seem like something Everett would do if he cared for her. However, he was good at hiding things from me. He probably thought he was protecting me. I'd proven myself more than capable of protecting myself. I'd survived multiple weekends in the Deca Tournament, survived his father's attempt to murder me, survived attacks by his ex-girlfriend. What more did I need to prove?

A deep breath filled my lungs before I forcefully exhaled it, pushing out all the air. I took in a new, clean breath, filling my lungs with the air of determination.

Where the fuck was Everett Silas? I needed to talk to him.

27

ELISE

I didn't notice the stares or words of admiration as I weaved through the dining room once again. Maybe I was being rude? Probably. I pushed those thoughts out of my head. I had bigger things to worry about right now.

There were only so many places I knew Everett to be. Hopefully he was in one of those places and I could have a serious conversation with him. I kept to the first floor, guessing he was probably in his office holding meetings, discussing things he didn't trust me with. Too bad. If he wanted me to stick around, then he needed to be more open, share more with the one he chose to be his luna. Kostas had reminded me I needed to be more forthright, too. It was the only way we were going to make this work. No more secrets, no more hiding from one another.

The hallway turned sharply; I was too busy watching my feet to notice Gavrill on the other side of the corner.

"Oof." We both bounced off one another, stepping back a few steps.

"Have you seen Everett?" I asked. He had to know where

he'd gone—he had just been talking with him in the hallway a couple minutes ago.

"He's busy right now, Elise." Gavrill crossed his arms in front of himself, letting me know I couldn't go any further without saying the words.

"Too busy to speak with his luna?" I said, wanting to see what would happen if I pulled out the luna card. Maybe my rank would persuade him to let me pass.

Gavrill looked away from me, shifting his weight back and forth on his feet. "He doesn't want to be bothered."

Anger bubbled deep in my stomach. "So now I'm a bother?" Did Everett really not want to see me? Was this about the Lifestone and how he thought somehow I was associated with it?

"I didn't mean it like that. He's busy with..." Gavrill motioned haphazardly in the air. "Everything."

"Are you keeping me from him, so I won't tell him about the rogues?" Maybe he was trying to save his own hide.

"No, he's just busy—"

"Fine." I cut him off. "If Everett doesn't want to see me, then I don't need to see him either. Why don't you tell him when he has a break from dealing with 'everything' that I'm here *right under his nose.*"

Gavrill's eyes widened as he stared at me. I stared right back at him, daring him to call me out for eavesdropping. He didn't. I turned away, my hands clenched in tight fists at my sides.

Mind-link. I was always forgetting I had that ability.

"Everett?" I waited a few seconds before I reached out a second time. *"Everett? I need to talk with you."*

No response. Ugh. I still hadn't mastered the mind-linking thing. My wolf leaped around in my head; all this frustration made her jumpy.

I glared at where Gavrill stood, still blocking my way. Whether Everett was busy or Gavrill was protecting his own hide, I didn't know. I stomped my foot once, crossing my arms in front of my chest. Gavrill didn't move.

Fine. If Everett didn't want to be *bothered,* then I'd find something better to do with my time. I found the nearest exit and pushed the door open, letting it fly open and hit the wall of the pack house. Maybe that would bother him too.

The grass pressed beneath my feet as I headed to the forest that surrounded the pack house. I looked behind me to see if anyone had followed me or was watching. I wouldn't put it past one of the pack members to follow me. The last time I'd left, to go check out the cabin, the gate had been open and the guards distracted. This time I needed to find another way out.

Giant oaks with large sturdy branches grew along the perimeter of the property, sandwiched between the trees was a tall stone fence that kept unwanted guests out, but it wasn't enough to keep me in. I lifted my foot, finding a knob in the tree to use as a step. I put some weight on the knob, testing if it would hold my weight. After I felt satisfied it would hold me, I stepped onto it, reaching up for the large branch that was now right above me. My arms shook as they pulled my body up onto the branch, my stomach rubbing against the bark. I swung my leg over and pulled myself up, straddling the branch between my legs.

About six feet off the ground, I looked up at the wall next to me. Six more feet to go. I hugged the trunk of the oak as I stood up, balancing. The next branch wasn't that much higher, and I easily stepped onto it, still keeping my arms around the trunk for support. Almost like stairs, I climbed up three more branches before I saw the top of the wall.

Giant oaks grew on the other side of the wall, their branches intertangled with the oak branches on the pack house side. I simply stepped onto the oak tree on the other side of the wall and made my way down the tree, using the branches like steps. It was easier than climbing up. I let myself hang from the lowest branch before I let go, falling about six feet to the ground. My knees bent as I absorbed the impact.

The forest surrounding the pack house was dense. Probably made that way to deter any hikers or enthusiastic explorers like me. This would have been a problem for pre-Lycan Elise. There was no trail for human feet to run without twisting an ankle.

I started taking off my clothing, letting the humid air touch my skin. My wolf leaped around; she knew what was coming. I folded my clothes as neatly as possible, setting them on top of an exposed root from the oak tree I'd just descended. I patted my sweatshirt, making sure the wolf statue was still safely in my pocket.

With my back toward the pack house, I shifted, letting my wolf take over. It was easier than the last time I'd shifted. Less concentration was required.

Now lower to the ground in my wolf form, my senses heightened. I could smell every drop of dew and hear every bird hopping around in the canopy of the trees. Rustling of leaves caught my wolf's attention. Two brown ears popped up from behind a log. A rabbit. My wolf crouched down, keeping her hindquarters in the air, ready to pounce. She waited for my go ahead. I let her loose, enjoying the chase.

The rabbit bounded through the woods in a zigzag pattern, trying to outrun us. Its white cotton tail was a beacon for my wolf's eyes among the surrounding green of the forest. The rabbit's tail got farther and farther away even though my wolf pushed, trying to run faster and faster. Fatigue came over my muscles—maybe from disuse? I hadn't been this tired during my run with Everett.

My wolf stopped, panting loudly, whining with displeasure. We watched the rabbit disappear into the woods, its tail flashing white a few times before it was gone. Was I that out of shape? I hadn't run more than a half mile and I felt drained.

Leaves rustled again to our left. A flash of orange stuck out from the green leaves on the forest floor. A tiny orange kitten tumbled out of the foliage, rolling before stopping just before it hit my white paws.

The kitten found its footing quickly and stood, looking up at my wolf. Its short fur stood up straight on its back, its tail puffing out like a scrub brush. Tiny orange ears folded back onto its head as it let out the cutest hiss I'd ever heard. It was trying to be so fierce in the face of danger, just like I'd been at the beginning of the summer.

I pushed my wolf to the back of my mind, allowing myself to shift back into my human form. A chilly breeze blew my hair off my face. Goosebumps pebbled my skin. I didn't want to scare the kitten too badly. What was it doing all alone deep in the forest? It looked to be about ten weeks old—old enough to be away from its mother but not old enough to where it would choose the separation.

Crouching down, I tried to make myself smaller, less intimidating. The fur on the kitten's back lay back down slowly, and its ears popped back up into little triangles on top of its head. Curiosity took over as I held out my hand for the kitten to smell. After the first whiff, the kitten's back arched and its ears pushed back. I probably smelled like a dog. It didn't hiss, though. It took another smell, looking up at me with orange eyes before it rubbed the side of its face against my fingers, asking for attention.

I picked up the kitten, surprised by how light it was. I felt its ribs easily beneath the skin and fur. Poor thing. I held it up and saw that it was a girl. So sweet.

"Do you want to come home with me?" I asked the kitten, knowing I wouldn't get a response. The orange fur ball purred against my chest as I cradled it with both hands.

I couldn't just leave her out here. Without food or shelter, she'd surely die. Something cold landed on my nose. I brushed it off with my finger, holding the kitten in a cradle hold with my other hand. A drop of water. From where?

Glancing up at the forest canopy, I spotted tiny snowflakes fluttering down from the sky, landing on me and the kitten. Snow? In the middle of summer? What was going on?

"Okay, you're definitely coming with me."

I navigated my way back to the stone wall and my clothes, holding the kitten close to me. Her purrs against my chest made me smile. At least someone liked having me around. The snow shower ended as abruptly as it had started. Warm air enclosed us as we walked, ridding my body of the goose bumps.

Back at the tree, I set the kitten down briefly to get dressed. She continued purring and weaving herself around my legs. I couldn't help but laugh as I tripped over her and myself, trying to pull on my leggings. The kitten was small enough to fit inside my sweatshirt pocket, next to the wolf statue.

That gave me pause. I was bringing a kitten into a houseful of wolves. She'd have to be another secret I kept from Everett. Maybe now we would be closer to even in our secret keeping—no, he still had more than I did.

I patted the pocket, making sure she settled. I needed both hands to climb back over the wall. She let out a small chirp, and I felt her relax in the hammock of my pocket. It was easier to traverse the trees and wall this time now that I had located my route up over and down the oaks.

The kitten stayed in my pocket as I walked into the pack house, now very aware of my surroundings. I didn't want a shifter to smell the orange furball I kept in my pocket. I put my hands inside my pocket, cradling the kitten, who was sleeping. The few pack members I walked by nodded to me, whispering "Luna" as acknowledgment. I tried to walk as quickly as possible so they wouldn't catch the scent of a feline.

Our room was empty when I poked my head into it. The bed was made, and the nightstands dusted. Good. Bunny had already done her morning routine and she wouldn't be around.

I pulled the kitten from my pocket and set her on the bed. She looked even more tiny lying on the giant bed, like a little orange puff ball, all curled up.

Food. Water. The kitten would need those things.

I pulled my gaze away from her and looked around the room. A shallow decorative dish holding some weird twine balls was on the side table next to the couch. I dumped the twine balls into the drawer of the table and took the dish to the bathroom, filling it with water. I set it on the nightstand next to the bed and moved the kitten up by my pillow. She probably wouldn't be able to jump down from the bed. It was too high. When she woke, hopefully she would find the water. I would have to find some chicken or something from the kitchen later for food. She needed to put some meat on her bones.

As she slept, I took time to inspect her closer. Her fur was soft and completely orange. There wasn't any white on her paws or face like our family cat, Bessie.

I stroked her, starting at her head, making the way down her back to her fluffy tail. She was orange like a pumpkin—a cute little tabletop pumpkin people used to decorate in the fall.

"*Lyka?*" Everett's voice entered my head.

I scoffed. Now he was ready to talk? Maybe now *I* wasn't available. I ignored him.

"*Elise, I know you're there. Come see me in my office.*" That seemed like an order. He didn't get to order me around like he did his minions—like Gavrill.

A moment later, another mind-link came through. *"Please."* His tone was different this time. More desperate, pleading.

"You sleep, Pumpkin. I'm going to see what your father wants," I said to the sleeping kitten, who wasn't listening.

Had I just called Everett her father? Stupid bond muddling up my thoughts. "Just kidding—not your father. The True Alpha."

She must've been exhausted. Who knew how long she had been in the woods before I'd found her. I kissed the top of her head, right between her ears, before I left the room, ready to knock some sense into Everett.

28

DAFNI

MEN WERE DISGUSTING. NOTHING LIKE THE FAIRYTALES. They weren't clean, and they didn't smell nice. They also ate nothing except bread with spicy red sauce and melted cheese. It came in a paper box that opened like a treasure box. The first time Wilder had brought it home, I'd thought it was a treasure. It was warm and filled my hungry stomach. But now that I'd eaten it for every meal for the last seven days, I'd decided it wasn't a treasure—it was trash that made my gut rot. I missed Grandmother's cooking.

"Why hasn't she come to get you yet, Dafni?"

We'd started to use each other's first names. The name *Wilder* was adequate for him. He was constantly moving, pacing, and ranting when he was in the house. Although he often wasn't here.

I was also on a first-name basis with his two roommates. Matt and Lucas kept mostly to themselves, coming out of their rooms only to use the toilet or grab another piece of the bread with sauce and cheese. They never answered the door when there was knocking, which happened every day. Knocking, followed by an angry man's voice demanding to see Wilder. I didn't dare answer the door.

I spent a lot of time alone, on the stained couch that sat in the middle of the living room. I slept there too, using a crusty blanket to cover myself at night. It wasn't great, but it was better than dying alone in the forest.

"She isn't coming," I answered. It was the same thing I told him every day when he asked me the same question.

"You're her daughter. She'll come," he said.

I shook my head like I always did. He didn't know my mother. She wouldn't be coming. "Can you witches mind-link?"

I looked at him, clueless.

"Well, if you can, you'd better let her know her time is running out to come and get you," he sneered. "My kindness is fleeting."

I used my time alone in the house finding what minimal food they had and searching every corner of the house for a map or something that would give me an idea of where I was and where I could escape to. Not that I had any place in mind. But I couldn't stay here forever. Soon Wilder would finally get the hint that my mother wasn't coming and either kick me out of the house—or worse.

He was a terrible kidnapper. He did nothing to keep me in the house. But I was always there when he returned from wherever he had been, smelling of mud and sweat, cursing about a guy named Everett. I wondered what he would do when he came home and I wasn't there. Would he try to find me again? Or just curse and kick a piece of furniture like he always did? Hopefully, the latter.

Wilder stomped to his room and slammed the door.

I waited a few minutes before I pulled out the backpack I

had squirreled under the couch. It had some packaged food I'd found. Some sort of noodles in an orange bag, and a blue package of black cookies with white fluff in the middle. They were delicious. I'd tried one already.

It wasn't enough to sustain me for a long time, but hopefully it would be enough to get me to a location where I could find more food. Or a place to stay. There were a few other random things I had found around the house that I'd had shoved into the backpack. A coil of rope that I'd found hanging on a hook by the front door, a wool blanket tucked in the back of a closet, and a comb. I don't really know why I'd grabbed it; it was there, and maybe I would need to untangle my hair at some point?

I heard a doorknob twisting. Quickly, I tucked the backpack and its contents under the couch, and pulled the crusty blanket over my lap, trying to act casual.

Wilder appeared in the doorway of his room in a new outfit. "I'm going out. You stay here," he said.

I nodded like I always did, although this time I was lying.

After Wilder left, I waited for what seemed like the longest time, listening to the snores and mutterings of Matt and Lucas. It was time.

Checking out the lone window by the front door, I saw nothing. No Wilder, no movement. Now was as good a time as any. I pulled out the backpack from under the couch, checking the contents one last time. Shrugging on the backpack, I inhaled and exhaled. My lips lifted in disgust. Hopefully this was the last time I would have to smell days-old bread with spicy sauce and cheese.

The front door opened quietly. Outside, the familiar sounds of birds chirping in the sky and frogs croaking in nearby bodies of water filled my ears.

Why had I waited so long? I couldn't help the smile that

pulled my lips upward as I walked down the steps to the side-walk, making my way into the woods surrounding the house. It didn't matter where I was going as long as I got somewhere. Anywhere was better than here.

———

I held my last chocolate sandwich cookie in my hands. They were shaking from either the lack of food or sleep or just plain exhaustion. I'd tried to ration the food I had, scavenge for berries when I could, but it wasn't enough to sustain me. I lived in constant fear of being hunted by animals in the woods and freezing to death at night. Some nights, even the wool blanket wasn't enough to keep away the chill. The forest was killing me, just as my mother had predicted it would.

I'd counted the sunsets. Seven. My body was falling apart under the conditions I had put it in. Seven days with minimal food and rest were taking its toll. My ribs protruded more than they ever had. Soon, I would have little choice but to transform to save myself. In my other form, I was smaller, could stay warmer with the fur on my body. Even at my age, I still took the form of a kitten. My lack of poison had stunted my transformation growth, keeping me from maturing into a full-grown cat. Being small meant I could also survive on smaller amounts of food. But that also meant leaving my backpack and other supplies behind. They weren't much, but they were the only comfort I had.

I bit into the cookie, my taste buds exploding. I closed my eyes while I chewed, savoring the last bit of food I had. When it was gone, I knew it was time. I had to transform while I still had the energy to.

I tucked my backpack behind a large tree, covering it with

leaves, giving it one last pat goodbye. My eyes closed as I willed myself to transform.

In an instant, I felt the dirt under my paw pads, my claws extending. I sat as I opened my eyes, now much lower to the ground. I picked up my paw to lick my orange fur. *Frogfeet*. It was going to be hard to keep clean in these woods.

<hr>

The backward spines on my tongue kept the worm in place as it slithered down my throat. As much as I despised the taste of insects and other slimy creatures, it was necessary for survival. Water wasn't an issue. I easily drank from streams and the small amount of dew that collected on leaves. It was enough water for my small form.

I hadn't traveled much, only as far as my small legs could take me each day. Every night before I curled up and fell asleep, I practiced my water and air magic, as my grandmother would have insisted. It was good to keep up some sense of normalcy. I drew breezes that made the leaves flutter from the trees, raining down on me. I made a game of trying to pounce on them as they hit the ground. As for water magic, I froze dew on the leaves or the random mud puddle in the dirt. It wasn't much, but it was enough.

It was in the middle of practicing my magic when I heard footfalls fast approaching me. I tucked myself behind some grasses right before a wolf burst through the brush, running. What was it running from?

It stopped, sniffing the air close to where I was hiding. My paws were still clumsy things, bigger than my body. I tripped, tumbling into the fluffy paw of the wolf.

The next instant, it transformed into a naked human woman, who looked just a couple years older than me. She had long brown hair and a kind face. She crouched down next to where I was hiding and let me smell her hand.

It smelled gross. I hissed, and then she let me sniff her again. Her hand smelled a little better this time.

The woman smiled at me.

"Do you want to come home with me?" she asked.

29

EVERETT

The door to my office slammed against the wall, leaving a mark. It surprised me she'd come so quickly. I'd been ready to get her myself if she didn't.

I couldn't help but smile at my mate as she walked into my office. The smell of her always made my lips turn upward, though her face didn't mimic my own. She looked...mad. The corners of my lips fell.

Elise's hair was wild, with pieces of tree bark stuck here and there. What had she been up to?

I walked from behind my desk to greet her. Even when she was angry, she looked adorable. It had been torture not to touch her, to hold her last night in bed. I'd given her space, and now it was time to eliminate the space between us.

"I have a lot to explain to you, Elise," I said.

"You've been hiding things from me—everyone has."

I felt my cock twitch in my pants. "I love it when you're feisty."

"Save it, Everett." Her quick glance at the buttons of my pants made me smirk.

Elise bypassed me and settled herself in my chair behind my desk. She made a spectacle of putting her dirty running shoes on the top of it before crossing her ankles and leaning back in the chair.

"I didn't sleep with Bethany—she planted that hair in my room," I explained. "She was trying to come between us."

"I know," Elise said.

She knows?

"I might've run into Kostas earlier. At least *he* tells me what's going on around here."

My inner circle could never keep their mouths closed.

Elise uncrossed then recrossed her ankles, putting the opposite foot on top.

"You look good there, Luna," I said.

"Do I?" she asked, tilting her head to the side. "Do I look good doing this?"

Elise swept her arm across the surface of my desk, pushing all my papers, books, and knickknacks onto the floor, then looked at me for a reaction. She was mad at me for something else.

I kept my face expressionless. I thought my desk would be cleared off for other reasons than her anger.

"How about this?" She pulled a drawer from my desk, removing it before tipping it upside down, dumping the contents on the ground.

"You can do anything you want. What's mine is yours."

Elise glared in my direction. "You're hiding things from me, Everett, hiding things *right under my nose.*"

Those words. I racked my brain over for where I had heard those words. My conversation with Gavrill earlier in the hall. The Lifestone. Had she been listening?

"Where are you hiding things, Everett. In here?" Elise took out a second drawer and dumped its contents onto the ground.

Okay, that was enough. Before she could protest or wreck my office further, I walked behind my desk and snatched her up around the waist. She kicked and bucked under my arms. It was cute but useless.

I set her down on a chair on the other side of my desk and kept her caged in with both of my arms on the armrests. Elise knew she was caught. She sunk back into the chair, crossing her arms. I reached over to pick a piece of bark out of her hair, and she swatted at my hand. Like I said, feisty.

"So, now I know you overheard Gavrill and me talking about the Lifestone," I said.

"Sorry to ruin your plan to hide it from me."

I rubbed my hand across my face. She *had* been eavesdropping.

This was going to be hard to explain. "I'm never trying to hide things from you. I'm trying to protect you—we all are trying to protect you."

"Protect me from what?"

"From me."

Elise's lips snapped shut, and she looked at me funny.

"I'm the True Alpha now," I said. "There are dangerous rogues to deal with, pack members that challenge me, and witches on the loose. I have to be ruthless with my pack, or they won't respect me." I felt myself soften. "I don't want you to see me like that. I want to keep that part of me from you."

I watched her, trying to gauge her reaction. She was surprisingly quiet, her face not giving me clues to how she was feeling. I reached my hand out to touch her face, slowly, not wanting to get swatted again. She let me touch her cheek, run my thumb down her jaw to her chin. The bond between us hummed.

"I like when you're soft with me," Elise whispered.

"Funny, as I'm only hard with you,"

My hand got swatted, this time not as sharp.

"I mean it, Everett. You can be open with me. Tell me things," she said. "I can handle it. You don't need to be mean or harsh to be a good alpha. Compassion can be just as powerful." Elise put her hand on my arm. "Please let me help you."

Those were the words I had spoken to her not so long ago, when I'd begged her to let me in. Hearing those words recited back to me brought up those desperate feelings. Elise shouldn't be feeling like that. I needed to let her into my heart, as she had bravely let me into hers.

"The Lifestone...I think you have something to do with its disappearance," I said.

"I don't know how many times I can say it," she said softly. "I don't have the Lifestone, and I don't know where it is."

Elise paused. "Actually, I might have some information I forgot to tell you."

She glanced back up at me, and I waited for her to continue.

"Professor Robinson might have said something about the witches having the Lifestone."

I stood up, running my hand through my hair as I walked behind my desk, sitting in my chair. That was something that I would have liked to know that day, that instant, with Professor Robinson. He was now long gone to who knew where, creating who knew what with the stone.

"I'm sorry I forgot to tell you," Elise said, her voice quivering. "I had just shifted for the first time, and seeing the cabin like that..."

"Thank you for telling me. That's good to know."

She relaxed, seeming relieved by my words. I put my elbows on my desk, leaning over the tabletop. "I still think you're tied to it somehow," I said. "All the growing you do in the garden, how you healed my arm during the Deca Tournament."

"I've always had a green thumb," she said.

"But how plants grow under your care, it isn't normal, Elise. They thrive when they shouldn't. My arm healed within one night after you took care of it. Something irregular is going on."

She looked away, deep in thought.

"I think we should visit your parents," I said. "Maybe they've been keeping something from you—protecting you, like I've been doing."

Elise turned back to face me. "Let's make a deal." She didn't respond to my mention of visiting her parents. There was some sort of tension there that I didn't understand.

"What sort of deal?" I asked.

"The kind where you show me something you have been hiding and I'll show you something I've been hiding."

"You're hiding things from me?"

She smirked. "What little you know, Alpha."

30

———

ELISE

HE SAID HE'D SHOW ME WHAT HE'D BEEN HIDING FROM ME first.

After a pit stop to the garden to collect some selfheal (for my surprise, I told him), Everett led me down the spiral staircases underground to the Vault. Right—he didn't know that I knew about the rogues hidden down there.

"I don't want to scare you," he said, turning around to grab my hand.

"I don't scare easily," I said.

"I know. I've been keeping the rogues down here until we decide what to do with them."

Snarls interrupted the silence. Everett kept his back to the cage, opening his arms, displaying his secret.

He watched me, expecting a bigger reaction than the one I was giving him. "Elise, say something. Kleio told me I should've told you sooner, but I didn't listen. I didn't want you to think of me as a monster, locking them up."

I looked around him at the cage where only a few dozen

rogues were left. Kleio, Gavrill, Jenny, and I had been hard at work healing the rogues. It was slow work logistically. Removing each rogue and individually healing them took time, and because I didn't have an unlimited source of healing energy, I became fatigued after healing ten to fifteen rogues.

Everett followed my gaze. "What the hell?" He looked back at me, confused. "Where did they all go? I need to get the others. Your secret will have to wait."

"Wait!" I grabbed onto Everett's arm before he had time to mind-link his inner circle. "That's what I've been hiding from you."

"That the rogues have been escaping? Elise, this is serious..."

"No, just watch." I grabbed the key to the cage from the dirt wall and walked over to the gate.

"What are you doing?" Everett came over and grabbed my wrist, stopping me from pushing the key into the lock.

"Just trust me," I said, grabbing his wrist with my free hand and looking at his golden eyes. They were swirling with doubt. I needed him to trust me. That was what this was all about— letting each other in completely.

Everett kept eye contact with me for another moment before letting go of my wrist.

"What can I do?" he asked.

"Catch one when I open the gate."

He looked at me like I'd grown an extra head, but he nodded, agreeing. Jenny wasn't there with her whistle, but there were so few now in the cage and they were moving slowly, like bumblebees on a cold fall day.

When I opened the gate, the rogues noticed the movement and started crawling toward the door. The first to make it was a tan wolf who looked like it had been through the gauntlet, missing chunks of fur and skin. Its ears lay limp on the sides of its head, its eyes droopy.

Everett easily grabbed it and brought it out of the cage, laying it down on the dirt floor. I closed the cage behind us and locked it before any of the other rogues could amble their way to the gate.

The rogue wiggled under his grasp, but Everett barely had to use his muscle to hold it down. He looked at me for direction. After hanging the key back up, I walked back to the rogue, its droopy eyes now open and frantic. It was scared but too weak to put up a fight.

I crouched down next to its head and placed my hand between its ears. After putting a few leaves of selfheal in its mouth, I closed my eyes and let the warmth travel down my arm and into the rogue.

Everett sucked in a breath. When I opened my eyes, a young girl's forehead lay under my hand, her eyes the same frantic ones from the rogue.

"Thank you," the girl said between gasps of air. She looked around the dingy room, curling up to cover herself when she saw Everett. He removed his shirt and handed it to her. She snatched it out of his hands and pulled it over her body. It fit like a dress on her boney frame. I stood next to him, watching her.

"How did you..." Everett looked at me in awe.

"I don't know how," I said. "I just did it one day in the garden. Kleio saw me, and we've been healing them slowly ever since."

"Kleio knows?" he asked.

"Yes, well, Gavrill does too...and Kostas."

"So, everyone except me," Everett grumbled. I nodded. "I don't know if I should punish you all or thank you."

"I was going to tell you, but then we had our argument..."

He put his finger over my lips, quieting me. "I think you had the best secret."

"Especially since yours wasn't a secret at all. I already knew," I said, smirking. If I had the upper hand with Everett, I needed to rub it in.

"You're a wonder, Elise." Everett took a step closer to me, grabbing my waist and pulling me against him.

"Luna," I reminded him. I was a luna, and he needed to remember that. I was capable and strong. He couldn't hide things from me ever again.

"Don't ever let me forget," he said as he bent down and brushed his lips against mine. "I know you don't have your research anymore, but you're a healer, Elise. The pack needs you. I need you."

He leaned in for another kiss. At first soft and gentle, and then harder, with more intensity. His hand snaked behind my head, cradling my skull, keeping me from pulling away. His tongue pushed into my mouth, rubbing on my own, teasing. The bond between us hummed, pulling us together, twisting and tightening, distorting anything around us.

"Um, excuse me?" A quiet feminine voice broke us out of our daze. "Can I get out of here? Maybe get something to eat?"

We had completely forgotten about the girl.

"Oh my gosh, yes. I'm so sorry," I said, breaking away from Everett, my face as red as a tomato. She had just watched us kiss rather intensely.

"Can you make it down the hallway?" Everett asked her. She nodded. "I'll meet you at the stairs. We'll find you some food."

She nodded again and began her slow accent to the ground level.

Everett found me again, pulling me close. "I want you to come to a meeting. One with my inner circle."

I gave him a stern look, trying to repress my amusement. "Am I finally worthy?"

He shook his head and looked at the ground. "You've always been worthy. I've been too stupid to realize it."

The smile I was holding broke free. "I'm glad we agree on something."

31

ELISE

Everett mind-linked his inner circle, commanding them to meet him in his office. From the face he was making, he was also reprimanding them for not telling him about the rogue-healing situation.

He brought the girl to Bunny, while I went to our room to check on the other secret I'd been keeping. I could hear yowling from outside the thick wooden doors of our chambers. I looked around to see if anyone was hearing the noise before I ducked into the room, rapidly opening and closing the door to hide the noise.

The kitten paced along the perimeter of the bed with her mouth in the air, letting out the highest-pitched yowling noises I'd ever heard. It was like a child screaming.

I rushed over to the bed and picked up the orange fluff ball and snuggled her into my chest. Purrs replaced the screams as the kitten calmed itself against me. Her little body shook from the apparent trauma of being left alone. It must've been frightening to wake up in a strange place all alone.

I sat on the bed with her still tucked against my chest. She was probably hungry. I looked at the water dish I'd left on the nightstand. The water looked opaque, as if it was... It couldn't be.

Leaning over, I felt the water with my finger, only to discover it was cold and hard. Frozen. What in the world?

Holding the kitten under my arm, I brought the bowl to the sink and hit it against the basin to loosen the ice. It fell into the sink, breaking into several pieces. I refilled the water dish and placed it back on the nightstand for later. It wasn't that cold in our room, was it? The shifter blood made me run warm. Maybe I hadn't noticed the chill.

I looked down at the kitten in my arms and sighed. I couldn't leave her again. She'd been traumatized enough. She'd have to come with me to my first inner-circle meeting.

I exited our rooms and made my way to Everett's office. It felt good to have the kitten in my hand, even though she was helpless. It was like having a sidekick.

The door to Everett's office was cracked open. I pushed it the rest of the way and walked into the room. His inner circle was already there, sitting around his desk. By the redness in Everett's face and the annoyed look on Kleio's, he was laying into them. Everything from earlier had been cleaned up. The room was once again spotless.

"What the hell's that?" Gavrill asked, his eyes trained on the orange fur in my hand. Kleio stood up, her nostrils flaring. "Is that a...cat?"

"We're a bunch of wolves, Elise. We don't like cats," Kostas said from his chair.

I looked down at the kitten. She was shaking in my hand.

"I found her in the forest, all alone. I couldn't leave her there," I said, staring at Everett. I knew he was soft with me right now.

He sighed and glanced down at his feet, while his inner circle turned to look at him in shock.

"You can't be serious," Kostas said to him. "A cat? In the pack house?"

"Sorry, Elise, even I don't think you should keep it," Kleio said.

"I promise Pumpkin won't be a problem. Look, she's so sweet." I held up the kitten for the shifters to see. The poor thing was still shaking.

"Oh man, she already named it." Kostas looked to Everett for the final decision.

"You can keep it," Everett said.

I smiled and tried not to act too excited. Tucking Pumpkin into my chest, I found the empty seat in front of his desk and slid into it, putting Pumpkin on my lap. Next to me, Kleio growled at the kitten.

"Kleio!" I said, covering Pumpkin's ears.

"I'm sorry. I can't help it. They have that...smell."

I rolled my eyes and faced forward toward Everett. I was officially part of the inner circle. Time to get serious.

He cleared his throat. "Elise showed me what she can do today down in the Vault." Everyone looked away from Everett except for me. "I don't appreciate everyone hiding it from me," he said. "Or that you put your luna in danger like that."

I opened my mouth to speak up. It hadn't felt that dangerous. We had taken precautions.

Everett gave me a look that made me close my mouth. He paused for a second, letting everyone heed his words. "But what's done is done, and I'm glad it solves the rogue problem."

Everyone let out a collective sigh of relief.

"From now on, I will be present when Elise is healing the rogues," he said. "You will not do it without me there." He looked pointedly at Kleio and Gavrill, who nodded their heads in agreement. "Let's move on."

Everett sat casually on the corner of his desk with his arms crossed. He looked good up there, his biceps bulging, being all in charge. I couldn't tell if he was tempting me on purpose. He must've known how he looked up there on the desk. "Elise and I discussed the Lifestone. She agreed we should go visit her parents to see if they have any knowledge about it."

"I never agreed to that!" Pumpkin dug her nails into my thighs, startled by my outburst.

"It's a good idea," Jack said. "The True Alpha smelled something on her; Wilder did too. Maybe they know something that they haven't told her yet."

The others nodded in agreement, looking to me to agree as well. Everett smiled at me. He was well-versed at this alpha stuff, turning the inner circle against me so I'd agree to the visit.

I felt my face flush. Was it hot in here? The windows were closed and covered with thick curtains.

When I looked back at Everett, I noticed he was tilting his head staring at me with those golden eyes, amusement swirling in his irises.

Ugh. I did need to visit my dad, see how he was doing. It had been a while.

"Fine," I agreed.

"Speaking of Wilder, any word on his whereabouts?" Gavrill asked. As Wilder's brother, I was sure he was concerned about him. Everyone looked at each other, shaking their heads. "Can you all keep an ear out for any information?" He looked worried.

"Do you think he went looking for the witches?" Kleio asked.

"I hope not," Gavrill said.

"About the witches. What news have we heard?" Everett looked at us for a response.

The witches, Robinson, the burned cabin. I shivered at the memories. Everett stared at me, his muscles tensing at my movement.

Kleio squirmed in her seat. "I've heard rumblings from the new pack members—the ones from your father's pack. The witches are...multiplying, their Coven growing."

"I heard that too, from Elise's professor," Everett said. "Well, her bogus professor. He's a male witch."

The air in here felt thick. I could smell the outdoors coming off Everett's skin. Pheromones. My nostrils flared.

Everyone looked at me. I stroked Pumpkin for comfort, centering myself. "Yeah, he claimed he was using the Lifestone to...impregnate female witches."

"Gross," Kleio said. I nodded my head in agreement.

"If they have the stone, then why did your father smell it on Elise?" Gavrill asked.

"I'm not sure. I think that's a question for your parents, Luna." Everett stood up, accidentally knocking over a cup of pens that sat near the edge of his desk.

My breathing stopped for a moment, remembering earlier —me throwing things off his desk, the look in his eyes as I'd done it. His eyes had held a look of excitement, like he'd been turned on by me clearing his desk. Was that why he hadn't been angrier at my outburst? Maybe he had imagined me on top of the desk in a precarious position. It was a large desk, large enough for me to lie on or drape myself across while he...

Everett cleared his throat. The intense look he gave froze me in my chair.

"Everyone out. My luna and I need to talk...alone." He used his commanding alpha voice.

The others stood up without a word and exited his office,

sneaking glances behind their shoulders. A breeze from the doorway brushed my hair away from my face. The cool air felt good against my hot skin. Papers from Everett's desk blew off and landed against the wall on the floor on the other side of the room.

Pumpkin jumped from my lap, following the alpha's orders as well. She trotted out of the room, sneaking through the door before Kleio closed it.

"The cat..." I said.

Everett stalked over to me, gripping both arms of the chair I sat frozen on. His pupils dilated. Only a thin ring of gold remained. He closed his eyes for a second, mind-linking.

"Kleio's got her," he said when they opened. "I can smell your desire. The room's filled with it."

Him and his nose. I had smelled him too. Was that his desire? The outdoor smell that had drifted to my nose?

"You up there, acting all alpha...I couldn't help it," I said. "You didn't have to end the meeting. I could've waited."

"*I* couldn't wait," Everett said, leaning in closer to me. I melted into the chair, my body limp with need. My head fell to the side, displaying my mark. He growled as he nuzzled my neck with his nose and lips, letting his fangs graze my skin.

"Everett," I whispered against his ear.

He picked me up under my arms, and I immediately locked my legs around his waist, taking my turn to nuzzle his mark. The outdoor scent I had caught during the meeting was even more potent. Fresh spring air mixed with the smell of rain? Yes, please.

I put my lips over his mark, sucking it into my mouth. He tensed and groaned, letting me fall a little in his grasp.

"I need to tell you something," I whispered into his neck.

Everett paused, grasping the underside of my thighs tighter. "I love you too."

His fingertips pushed into my thighs as a silence came over the room.

Shit. I'd messed up. He'd only said those three words to me to placate me—when I thought I'd caught him cheating.

Everett cleared his throat. "Elise..."

"Never mind!" I buried my face deeper into his neck. I couldn't look at him.

"Look at me, Elise." *The alpha voice.* I pulled my face out of his neck, leaning back to meet his eyes. "I've loved you always." My stomach dropped low into my body. "The moment I saw you heal that baby tree—I knew I loved you."

A smile tugged at my lips. "So, the fated-mate bond means nothing to you?"

He smirked. "Well that certainly helped. But that doesn't take away the fact that I love you for *who* you are, not just *what* we are to each other. You are compassionate, smart, and will cut down on the pack's produce bill." I playfully smacked Everett on the chest. "The pack's lucky to have you as their luna, and I'm even luckier to have you as my mate."

I shut him up with my lips before he could say any more sweet things that might cause happy tears to roll down my face.

When our lips separated, there was that look in his eyes— the one that set my body aflame.

"Let me finish what you started." Everett set me on top of his desk and let go of me. He used his long arms to push all the papers, pencils, and books off his desk, clearing the wooden surface. "That better?"

I looked around the empty desk and nodded.

"Good, because I'm going to take you on my desk like I'd imagined earlier, when you were so...angry."

Everett stared at me, and I could tell he was remembering me throwing things and dumping out his desk. Maybe I should make a mess more often. He pulled me off the desk so I was standing with my chest against his.

Using his thumbs, he pulled down my leggings, practically purring like a cat at my lack of underwear. I braced myself with my hands, my arms behind me on the desk as he knelt, helping pull my ankles out of the pants, carefully removing each one from the tight fabric.

I looked down at the top of his head as he paused, eyes level with my soft folds. He glanced up at me before he opened his mouth and stuck out his tongue, inserting it between my folds, licking me from bottom to top. I fell back onto my elbows as my head fell back and my mouth opened, trying to suck in air.

"You're so potent." Everett licked his lips, tasting me on his tongue. He stood up, towering over me. My knees felt weak. "Turn around," he said.

I followed my alpha's instructions willingly, turning to face the desk. Now that I couldn't see him, anticipation was building. Behind me, a zipper opened and clothing hit the ground. I felt the warmth of his body, even though his skin wasn't touching mine. He was radiating with need. His warmth traveled through my skin and deep into my body, making my already warm center hot. I squeezed my thighs together, trying to quell the need between them.

Everett laid his warm, rough hand on the center of my back between my shoulders and pushed me down, folding me at the waist over his desk. I felt cool air rush over my warm backside, which was now completely exposed to him. The wooden desk was cold against my cheek, centering me a little.

"So pretty, all bent over my desk," he said. Everett kept one hand on my back and used the other to tease me, rubbing the wetness I had already created all over my folds. "And already so wet for me."

I trembled under his hand as he caressed the pink skin

between my legs, finding the sensitive nub at the top and rubbing it in tight circles. The pressure of his fingers and the hand on my back increased the more I moved beneath him, moaning and gasping for air. The tension in my center grew tighter and tighter the more Everett rubbed. I squeezed my thighs together, only to have one of his thick thighs wedged between my knees, keeping my legs apart.

"Let go, Lyka." Everett put more pressure on my chest as he leaned in, whispering into my ear. His fingers never stopped moving, even when I came undone, writhing beneath his hand and coming on his fingers. He slowed his movements, tucking his face against my neck as I came down from the climax, breathing deeply through each aftershock.

"You've made such a mess," Everett whispered into my neck. "Let me help you clean it up."

I tensed, trying to stand up as his body left mine. He kept his hand on the small of my back, holding me in place. I twitched as he licked my most sensitive parts with his warm tongue, cleaning the mess with his mouth.

Once he was quenched, Everett stood back up, keeping his hand on my back. "Sweet."

I turned my head so I could see him. The veins in his neck swelled, as did the veins in his arms. He breathed deeply through his nose, his nostrils flaring. Using his free hand, he palmed his shaft, giving it a couple pumps before pushing it through my folds and to my entrance.

"Hold on tight," Everett said, giving me a second to extend my arms and wrap my fingers around the far edge of the desk, bracing myself for what was coming. He pushed his head into me slowly, taking his time, letting me fully consume him inch by inch. We both let out a groan once his tip hit the deepest part of me.

With my stomach pressed against a hard surface, there was

nowhere for me to expand to take him. The full feeling over-whelmed my senses. With each thrust, Everett's balls swung forward, slapping my clit. The feeling was intense, but I didn't want it to stop. Every plunge into me was amplified, hitting both the sensitive spot inside me and the one already engorged outside of me.

I choked on my moans, trying to inhale oxygen fast enough to keep up with the demand he was putting on my body. My upper thighs hanging over the edge of the desk slammed into the edge each time he pumped into me. I started seeing black dots in my vision. I closed my eyes and opened them, but they didn't disappear.

With one hand, I let go of the desk to grab onto him. I found his hand braced on the edge of the desk next to my exposed ass and wrapped my fingers around his wrist, the motion causing Everett to pause.

"Is something wrong, Lyka?"

"No, it's just so...intense," I whispered.

Without speaking, Everett pushed me farther onto the desk. Keeping himself inside of me, he slowly turned me over, lifting my leg as I twisted, pulling it out from between his thighs and straightening it, letting the back of my calf brush his chest. I rotated around his shaft, letting him feel every groove inside of me. He groaned as I found my way onto my back, Everett still holding my leg straight in the air. He looked down at me, fully open and exposed to him, his cock hidden inside of me.

"I can't last much longer," he said as he grabbed my other leg by the ankle, lifting it parallel to the leg that was already in the air. Using one hand, he grabbed onto both of my ankles, keeping them tightly together. With my legs straight and my knees locked, Everett held them slightly to the side of his body so he could see my face. Slowly, he pulled out of me before he slammed back in, my back sliding across the desk.

"Hold on." With his free hand, Everett wrapped my fingers around the edge of the desk closest to him. After he had me positioned, he continued his tireless drive, making me moan with each fast thrust. My fingers became fatigued from keeping my body stationary on the desk. He was pumping so hard and fast, my fingers slipping.

"Fuck, you feel so good, Luna," his said, his voice strained and breathy.

My walls tightened around him as my fingers slipped from the desk. I yelled his name over and over as I climaxed, him following quickly after me, shooting his come inside of me.

I lay there, catching my breath, beads of perspiration running down my back. I could feel the sharp edge of the desk on the back of my head. He'd almost fucked me off the desk.

Everett took my breath away literally as he found my mouth and deeply kissed me.

"I missed that," he said, looking into my eyes. "I love you."

32

ELISE

Pumpkin slept soundly in my lap, curled up into a ball like her namesake. Her belly was rounder now that she'd been eating frequent meals—mostly chicken that Kleio snuck into our room for her. It still made me smile whenever I thought about how, after being forced to take care of her while Everett and I had been occupied in his office that day, Kleio had developed a soft spot for the little fur ball. Pumpkin might have spent more time in her lap than my lap the past few days.

Between healing the rest of the rogues and all the meetings Everett had about the witches and the Lifestone, Pumpkin had become my constant companion, giving me a sense of security in a world I was still getting used to.

Rain hit the windshield of the car and the windshield wipers swiped back and forth against the glass. It was our soundtrack for the drive to my parents'. Everett manned the wheel, and I sat in the passenger seat. We held hands on top of the center console, like I had imagined we would weeks ago. Everything felt so right with him. I finally felt like I was where I needed to be.

At the beginning of the summer, I'd made myself a straight and narrow path to follow. Deviation had been unacceptable. It had taken me being turned into a shifter to make me see that the offshoots of some paths could be just as alluring as the original. Now I was here, a luna, a healer, with Everett. Not where I'd thought I would end up, but where I needed to be.

My backpack sat on the floor resting against my legs. Before we'd left, I taken out the research and tucked it away in my armoire. I couldn't find it in myself to throw it away—I'd worked hard on it. There were still valuable findings that any university would be interested in. But turning in my research now felt like I was exposing the Lycans and the forest, opening it up to others who might have different intentions than me. It didn't feel right.

It was too wet to shift and run in our wolf forms. We probably would've gotten there sooner, cutting through the forest, bypassing all the curvy roads. But it was raining, and I had Pumpkin with me. Beneath her sleeping body, my wolf statue remained in my sweatshirt pocket. I kept it with me, transferring it from one sweatshirt to the next, and I could feel the rock push into my stomach with Pumpkin's every exhale.

"I hope everything is okay with my parents," I said, mostly talking to myself. I didn't expect an answer from Everett. "I haven't talked to them since my mom came to visit."

I grimaced, remembering her awkward visit and how pushy she had been about Everett and my relationship. Well, she had gotten what she had wanted. I was still with "the attractive man."

"They're fine," Everett said, his eyes still on the road.

I looked at him confused. "I mean, they haven't said otherwise, right?" he asked.

Right. I nodded.

Signs for *America's Best Small Town* started popping up

along the highway, getting bigger and bigger as we approached. Everyone looked so happy in the signs. I hoped their smiles were genuine. I wanted my parents to be as happy as those people featured on the billboards.

Soon enough, we reached the supposed best small town, and we were on their street within minutes. Their house number was easy to remember—1120. It was my birthday, after all. I pointed that out to Everett, who joked his house number would be 726, reminding me what Kleio had said. His birthday was only a few days away, on July twenty-sixth.

Our black SUV pulled up the driveway of my parents' house. Everett threw the car into Park before he pulled out a large black umbrella tucked between his seat by the door—always prepared. I made sure Pumpkin was tucked inside my sweatshirt pocket before I grabbed my backpack. He walked around the front of the car, umbrella opened, and opened my door, helping me out of the car. I let him. It was sweet.

"Welcome, Everett! Welcome, Elise!"

I rolled my eyes. Of course she'd welcome Everett first. I hadn't missed that I was already rolling my eyes and we weren't even in the house yet.

With his arm around my waist, Everett guided me to the covered porch my mom was standing on, waving like we were celebrities. I kept my eyes straight ahead, letting Everett guide me. The street was quiet, most likely because it was raining. The only other car out on the street was the next-door neighbor's—a black Range Rover parked in the driveway despite the rain.

"Aren't you such a gentleman?" My mom tucked her arm through the bend in Everett's elbow on the arm that held the umbrella, "guiding" him to the front door. "Come in, come in! Your dad will be out in a minute."

Everett let go of my waist and took a minute to shake out

the umbrella before entering the house. I walked ahead of him, letting the smell of my childhood hit me in the nose. The earthy scent of wet clay brought me back to the times of mom's chalky hands and the whirl of the throwing wheel.

The living room looked different from what I'd remembered. The furniture that had come with my uncle's house when they'd inherited it was gone, and in its place was brand new, *nice* furniture. That was not in their budget. In her letters, Mom had mentioned a few neighbors buying some of her work but not so many customers that they could purchase all new furniture like this.

"It looks...nice in here," I said, walking toward the suede couches, running my hand along the top of the backrest. I put my backpack on the floor, leaning it against the couch.

"Thank you, Elise! I need to be thanking your man. Is that what they call them nowadays?" Mom laughed at her own joke. "He put in a good word for me with our neighbor, and the guy loves my work! He's been buying my sculptures left and right."

I looked at Everett, staring at his face, suddenly suspicious. Everett kept his face emotionless.

"He's so nice. His garage is full of my stuff. He said he has a place abroad he's going to ship it to!" Mom kept talking as she went into the kitchen, unaware we could no longer hear her.

Such a *nice* neighbor that he let Mom, someone he could've only just met, borrow his expensive black Range Rover to come visit me. A wealthy buyer living in a small house in a town in the middle of nowhere who kept all her sculptures in their garage?

I turned to Everett, getting close enough to him that he had to pay attention to me. "It's you, isn't it? The wealthy neighbor?" I whispered.

He smirked. I'd caught him. There could be no more secrets between us.

"Not me exactly," he said.

I tilted my head at him and arched a brow.

"An acquaintance of mine."

I tilted my head the other way, giving him an icy glare now.

"Someone I hired from the pack house to keep an eye on your parents and help them out as necessary."

Letting out a sigh, I looked down at my feet. That was sweet but over the top.

"'As necessary'?" I said. "Buying everything she makes isn't necessary."

"I needed to make sure they were taken care of, so you didn't have to worry," Everett said as he reached out and wrapped his arm around my lower back, pulling me close to him.

Okay, that was worth swooning over. I stood on my tiptoes and wrapped my arms around his neck. He leaned down to touch his lips to mine.

"Oh, here we go!" Mom walked back into the living room carrying a tray of crackers and cheese.

Who was this domesticated hostess? The most I'd ever gotten coming home from college to visit was clean sheets on a twin bed.

Everett and I pulled apart.

"Don't stop on my account!" Mom called.

I purposefully put some space between Everett and me. Mom didn't need to be egged on further.

"What's with all the sculptures?" Her art was all over the room. Some were so large, they stood on the floor. A lot of her work looked inspired by nature, with a lot less nudity.

I picked up a smaller piece from the end table next to the couch. It was two rabbits, one on top of the other, connected at the—ugh. I put it down. Okay, same amount of sex, just in a different form.

"I have a new buyer coming in a bit," she said. "Word must be getting around!"

I looked at Everett. Was this another one of his "acquaintances"? He shrugged his shoulders. Must not have been. Well, that was good—a fresh stream of income that didn't involve Everett.

"I moved stuff around." Mom motioned to the kiln sitting by the bay window of the living room. "It got too stuffy in the garage working. We don't even need to use the fireplace at night! I just start up the kiln and it warms the place right up."

That wasn't safe at all. She could burn the whole place down. Even the fumes from the clay firing... I should have visited sooner.

"I don't think that's the best idea, Mom. Everett can move it back to the garage before we leave," I said.

"Don't be silly. I open a window. It works just fine. I even have a bucket of water here, just in case." She motioned to the five-gallon bucket next to the kiln. "Sit down, try the new couches."

Mom sat down, patting the couch cushion. It was no use telling her what to do. I never won arguments with her.

Everett and I sat on the couch, sinking into the plush cushions.

"Nice, right?"

I nodded.

"We also upgraded the windows. They were so drafty before! These windows are rated for hurricane-force winds!"

I looked over at the bay window. They didn't look any different from the old ones. Pumpkin chirped, stretching her legs, her orange paw sticking out of my pocket. I pulled her out, careful to keep the wolf statue in my pocket, and set her on my lap. She looked disoriented. Last time she was awake we had been in the car.

"Who's this new baby?" Mom got up from her seat and picked up Pumpkin from my lap. "Isn't this the most precious kitten I've ever seen!" She cradled the kitten against her chest, showering it with kisses.

Pumpkin looked at me with *save me* eyes, but I only shrugged. She'd have to get used to my mother's smothering—that was her grandma now.

"Did I hear something about a kitten?" My dad emerged from the bedroom, dressed in his usual slacks and button-down plaid shirt. He held Bessie in his arms, as orange and as fluffy as ever.

I stood up to hug him, or what was left of him. His clothing hung from his thin frame. He'd lost weight since the beginning of the summer. I really should've visited sooner.

Before I could walk a step toward him, Bessie jumped out of his arms, her paws pushing off his chest in her race to the ground. With an oomph, my dad fell back into the bedroom he'd emerged from, landing on his behind.

"Dad!" I yelled, taking long strides to reach him.

Bessie stared up at Pumpkin in my mother's arms with an arched back, her ears flat against her head. I grabbed my dad's arm and helped him to his feet.

"I'm fine, I'm fine," Dad said, trying to brush me off. "She doesn't usually act like that."

Bessie continued to stare at Pumpkin, her orange fur spiked along her back. Mom yelped as Pumpkin wiggled out of her grasp, jumping to the floor, landing on her feet. She mirrored Bessie, flattening her ears and arching her back. The tiniest hiss left her mouth. Everyone watched for a minute while the cats stalked one another, keeping their distance while still acting fierce.

"Cats don't always get along right away," Mom said, watching the two felines.

A low unnatural yowl came from Bessie, a sound I'd never heard a cat make before.

It was quick, the way Bessie went from arched-back stalking to attacking. She launched herself at Pumpkin, claws out with her jaws open, ready to rip into her. I tried to grab her, to keep her from getting Pumpkin, but my fingers only grazed the tips of her fur. Bessie was airborne, headed straight toward my kitten.

Everett stood from the couch and dived for Pumpkin, trying to get her out of the way of the family's crazed elderly cat. Mom screamed. He landed on the wood floor at the feet of a girl.

A girl who hadn't been there a second ago and now stood where my kitten had been.

—

33

ELISE

The girl caught Bessie midair and threw her to the ground next to the kitchen.

"You will not hurt these people!" Her voice was quiet but strong.

We all froze, even Everett on the floor, looking back and forth between Bessie and the girl in the living room. She was young, with long bright red hair. She had clothes on, a faded green sundress that looked like it could use a wash.

I'd never seen someone keep their clothes after shifting before. And that was what she had to be, right? A shifter?

Her eyes kept to Bessie, who had recovered from being thrown and stood on all four paws with her back arched aggressively. Everett pulled himself up from the floor and removed himself from where he was between the two.

"Fucking witches!" he bellowed. "There was one right under our noses!" He calmed for a moment and apologized to my mom for his language.

"I think it was warranted, dear," she said. Her eyes

remained fixed on the red-haired girl who had once been a kitten.

Was Everett saying Pumpkin was a witch? She had just been in my pocket, had slept next to me. I had scooped her litter...

"Why are you yelling at my cat?" My dad was the only one with enough wherewithal to ask the right questions.

A knock at the front door interrupted whatever was happening in the living room. The girl kept her eyes on Bessie, the knock not interfering with her stare. I couldn't look away from either of them.

Mom rushed over to the door, opening it just a crack. "Something's come up," she said quickly. "We're going to have to reschedule...wait a minute. What are you—"

The front door was yanked out of Mom's grip, and the person barged in right past her, revealing a tall man with brown hair, thick-rimmed glasses, and a bushy beard. Everett immediately growled, his black claws poking through his fingertips.

"I see I've arrived fashionably late to the party," Wilder said, walking into the living room.

Everett walked over to where I was standing and stood in front of me, blocking me from Wilder's view.

"Be careful," I whispered. "My parents...they don't know about the shifters."

He growled again, this time showing his teeth.

"This is my buyer I was telling you about," Mom said when she realized he wasn't leaving anytime soon. Then she paused. "Do you two know each other?" She looked between Everett and Wilder, confused.

"Unfortunately, this isn't a buyer. I would imagine he's here for reasons other than your art," Everett said.

"Oh, dear," Mom said.

"It's good you're already here." Wilder broke eye contact

with Everett and walked over to Bessie, seemingly talking to her. "Funny how things just all seem to fall into place." Then he sneered at the girl who used to be Pumpkin. She looked down at her feet.

Bessie lowered her arched back and sat on her haunches, studying Wilder. He turned back to the cat. "I know it's here, Matilda."

Matilda... Where had I heard that name before?

At the cabin—I'd heard it out of Robinson's mouth at the cabin. Matilda was a witch.

Everyone was silent as Bessie—Matilda—lost her orange fur and tail, transforming into an older woman with the same fiery red hair as the first girl who'd shifted. She didn't have smooth skin like Pumpkin. Her skin was bumpy and discolored, her nose hooked at the tip.

The only one in the room who wasn't surprised by the shift was Wilder. He stood there waiting. For what, I didn't know.

"Bessie?" my dad asked of the woman standing in the place of his beloved cat. She ignored my father, instead turning to the girl, who resembled her. They not only shared the same hair color but had the same face shape.

"Where have you been, Dafni?" the older woman asked of the younger. "I see you found shelter with the Lycans, of all the beings, in the woods. I knew you were weak without your poison, but I didn't realize you were pathetic."

"Mother," Dafni said, glaring at Matilda, "I won't let you hurt these people. They took care of me when you wouldn't."

She leaned in close to Dafni, smelling her. "You even smell like them. Like dirty dogs."

A hiss left Dafni's lips, and Matilda cackled.

"So fierce, even without your poison. No one could ever tell that you didn't have it. But we all know that you lack it, don't we, Dafni? Lack what makes a witch a witch." Matilda opened her mouth. Green liquid dripped from her gums and down her white teeth. "You may as well stay with the dogs; you no longer have a place among the Coven. More of your replacements are being born every day, ones that aren't broken."

I watched Dafni become more and more defeated with every word her mother uttered. Her powerful gaze faltered, leaving her staring at the ground. Clearly this was not the first time Matilda had cut her down and left her in pieces.

"Pumpk—I mean, Dafni," I said. "Why did you stay in your kitten form all this time?" Dafni's eyes met mine. The same eyes I'd stared into as I petted her orange fur snuggling in my bed.

"We could've helped you back at the pack house." I heard Matilda scoff at my words.

Dafni continued looking at her feet, not making eye contact with me. "I heard you talking about the witches, how you hated them. I couldn't risk you kicking me out—I couldn't survive in the woods alone."

"We would've never kicked you—"

Everett interrupted me with a snarl. I grimaced back at Dafni. *Everett probably would've kicked her out.*

"I felt safe with you at the pack house." She played with the hem of her worn dress. "As long as I stayed a kitten, I knew I'd be safe."

My heart shattered into a million pieces. I complained about my mother, but to have Matilda as a mother—I couldn't imagine.

"It's here, Matilda," Wilder repeated himself. "I've found it."

She turned to him. "You're a good tracker, Wilder. I didn't think you'd find it. Too bad I already knew where it was. It's been here all along."

With her index and middle finger, Matilda pointed toward

my parents' bedroom. Shuffling noises came from the room before my dad's wooden box appeared, floating out of the room and toward Matilda's outstretched hands. Wilder dived for the box and snatched it from the air. She let out a screech, pulling her hands back like someone had snapped them with a rubber band.

"You said once I found the Lifestone for you, you would give me fangs. I want my fangs." He gripped the wooden box, his eyes wildly bouncing between Matilda and the rest of us in the room.

"You don't need fangs to be a wolf, Wilder." Everett's voice was calm, although I could tell how tense his body was from where I was standing behind him. He was thinking of Gavrill, trying to protect his brother.

"Stop saying that!" Wilder yelled. Everyone was quiet. "I want my fangs." He turned to Matilda, who smiled with her poisonous teeth.

"Don't let your fate be determined by what you think you're lacking," Everett said. "There's a place for you, even without your fangs." The guy had kidnapped me and given me to Everett's father to kill. I knew Everett wanted vengeance, but he was holding himself back.

"I want my fangs," Wilder repeated.

"If the boy wants fangs so bad, I'll give him some," Matilda said.

"Wait!" Everett stepped toward him. "She's going to trick you, Wilder. That's what witches do."

"Give me my fangs," Wilder commanded, his voice low.

Everett shook his head, and I held my breath.

"Very well," Matilda said. She put her index and middle finger together and pointed them at him. His eyes grew wide, his lips pursed together, his cheeks expanded like he was holding his breath. All at once, he opened his lips, revealing two fangs in the space where his canine teeth were. They were large, larger than mine or Everett's.

Wilder's bottom lip flipped down as his fangs grew past his lips. As much as he tried to close his mouth, he couldn't. His fangs kept growing. They were now past his chin.

I grabbed onto Everett's arm, squeezing it, still holding my breath. Wilder's eyes got even wider as he realized what was happening and that he couldn't stop it. He dropped the wooden box he had grabbed from the air. It fell to the ground with a loud bang, the wood of the box and the wood from the floor hitting each other. His fangs were past his chest when he really panicked, looking around the room for help.

Everyone in the room froze, watching in horror. It was like watching a car wreck. We couldn't look away. His feet shuffled as he tried to save himself. The white fangs were now past his torso and continuing to lengthen. Eyeing the door, he waddled toward it, taking careful footsteps as he was now top heavy with the weight of the teeth. A few paces from the door, his teeth scraped the floor, leaving two parallel scratch marks along the wood. He halted, his body pitching backward. His fangs had punctured the floor, rendering him unable to move. He screamed, incapable of moving his head.

"Shut up." Matilda flicked her fingers toward Wilder's back. The next instant, he was silent and still, but the up-and-down movement of his shoulders told me he was still alive.

My stomach recoiled, my hearing as static as a lost radio station. *Witches can do that?*

"I'm going to have to sit down," my mother said from where she was standing near one of her larger sculptures of an evergreen tree. Mom's knees gave out on her, and she hit the floor, thankfully missing the hard sculptures surrounding her.

"*Mom—*" I lunged toward Mom, but Everett held me back, keeping me behind him.

"Where were we? Yes, the box that was so rudely snatched from me." Matilda walked over to where the box was lying on the ground, the lid still closed. She picked it up, rubbing the lid like it was a magical genie lamp.

With careful fingers, she opened the lid, looking inside the box. She picked out some photos and let them flutter to the floor. The bag that held my baby teeth hit the floor next. Her eyes focused on the inside of the box, her hand searching, her breath growing heavier. Turning the box upside down, she screeched, letting a few baseball cards join the other miscellaneous rubbish on the floor. My ears rang from the pitch of the scream.

"Where is it?" Matilda shrieked at everyone in the house, glancing at everyone's faces. We all gave her blank stares except Dafni. She stood where she had been standing since she'd transitioned to a witch, her eyes still on her feet.

"The stone," Matilda said. "It was here. Where is it?"

I looked at the back of Everett's head, his muscles in his neck tensed, then to my father, still standing there watching everything that was unfolding inside his home.

"The rock that my great-grandfather gave me?" my dad asked.

"No, the other sizeable stone you kept in this box," Matilda mocked.

"Bessie, let's talk this through," he said.

"I'm not Bessie, you fool!" she yelled. I saw her physically calm herself, breathing deeply in and out, but as she squinted her eyes and looked into each of our faces, I knew she wasn't calm inside. She was piping hot.

"I'll have some fun with each of you one by one until someone tells me where the stone is. I'm feeling especially inspired after that one." Matilda motioned to Wilder, who still stood there imprisoned by his fangs. "Who shall I start with?"

She extended her index and middle finger, taking turns pointing at each of us.

"I sent it to Elise! It's not here!" Mom yelled right before Matilda's fingers pointed at me.

"What are you talking about, Mom?" I asked.

"The wolf sculpture. I was going through your father's things and found the rock. I didn't think it was anything special. Some inspiration hit me, and I carved it into the wolf for you."

I'd had no idea. So, they'd been right—I'd had it all along. But it wasn't back at the pack house. I rolled the wolf in my pocket. It felt warm in my fingers.

Matilda turned to face me. She walked toward me slowly, an eerie smile on her face, her fingers still extended. Everett used his arms to tuck me further behind him.

"So, the luna has been keeping the Lifestone." Her pointed words sounded like nails on a chalkboard. "It's taken a liking to you, hasn't it? I can feel it pulsing for you from here."

Now that she mentioned it, I could feel a slight flutter, like a heartbeat inside the stone.

"Give it here like a good girl, and we won't have any problems."

Everett growled. "Don't you dare lay a finger on her."

"Or I can get it myself." Before Matilda completed the flick of her wrist, I pulled the wolf from my pocket and tossed it to the ground, away from me.

It clattered along the wooden floor, stopping at my dad's feet. He slowly bent down to pick it up, his eyes wide. It hummed for him as he held it in his hand. His knees hit the floor, and he grunted at the impact. His eyes were wide as they looked over at me. I could see the color leaving his face. He looked ashen, his cheeks hollowed out.

"Dad?"

He didn't respond. He just kneeled on the ground, looking at me, scared.

"It's pulling the last of your energy. Just let it. It'll be over soon," Matilda said, watching the stone leech life from my father.

"Give it to me, Dad." I crouched down next to him and tried to pry the wolf out of his hands. It wouldn't budge. "Let go."

"I can't. I can feel it pulling. It won't let go of me."

"It's pulling your energy." Matilda cackled. "The last generation of your family has been feeding it. It knows you, recognizes your likeness. When your idiot great-grandfather removed it from the tree, from the earth, the stone needed an alternative power source," she said. "You've been a good conduit, Roger. You let the stone drain you slowly, feeding it just enough of your energy that it stayed viable. It helped me create so many new witches. But now you have nothing left to give. Let it take what's left of you. You already gave it everything else."

"I didn't know, Elise. I'm so sorry." My dad trembled, struggling to speak.

I crouched there frozen, struggling to move. The skin on his hands sunk in, draping tightly over his bones and tendons. The stone was sucking him dry.

"Just let go of the stone," I begged, staring into his eyes.

Dad shook as he tried to unfurl his fingers. "It...it won't let me." Our eyes met, mirroring panic to one another.

Mom came over and wrapped her arms around Dad's back, holding him as he shuddered against her. "I'm here, Roger. Let go of the stone." She tried to peel his fingers back, but they were clenched tightly, immoveable.

Dad sunk to the ground, like he was melting. The Lifestone was taking the last of his energy. In front of me, my dad's body flashed to that of a wolf, a white one. I blinked, shaking my head before I reopened my eyes. He was back to his human form, lying there in my mother's arms, his eyes closed. My mouth hung open. *Did anyone else see that?*

"No, Roger, don't do this." Mom had given up trying to retrieve the stone, instead shaking him back and forth, his head flopping on his shoulders. "No!" My mother wailed, lying my father back on the floor, her head against his chest as she lay on top of him.

He couldn't be...he wasn't. There was no way my cheerful, patient, supportive father was dead. He couldn't die like this. That was never part of the plan. He was supposed to enjoy retirement with my mother—with Bessie.

No, not with Bessie. She'd caused this entire situation.

Angry tears streamed down my face. I shuffled my knees even closer to my father, wrapping my arms around him and resting my head on his chest. Then I noticed it. His breathing was shallow, the strength of his breath weak, but he was with us.

"He's still breathing," I whispered to my mother. She nodded, tears still flowing down her cheeks. "Don't let her know he's still alive." Mom stayed on top of my dad, blocking his moving chest from Matilda's view.

"It's over, ladies. Time to hand over the stone." With a flick of her wrist, Matilda sent my mom flying back toward the chiseled evergreen sculpture. There was a popping noise followed by a squishing sound as the pointy tips of the tree pushed through mom's skin and into her back. I screamed, frozen in place next to my father. Everything was happening so quickly.

Matilda laughed. "Maybe some blood will improve these ugly stone creations."

I stood up, taking a few steps toward my mom.

She waved me off as she sat on the floor with the stone tree impaled in her back. "I'm...fine."

I paused, standing between my injured mother and unconscious father. There wasn't a right answer of who I should go to, who I should protect. My father lay there, pale, but still breathing. My mother was wounded, blood dripping from the sculpture onto the floor. I stood there stuck in the middle—in limbo.

"You're not fine!" I cried.

"I'll be fine. I can still breathe."

She *was* still breathing and speaking, which was a good sign.

Everett appeared by my mother's side, looking behind her, assessing the damage to her back. "I think the stone has stopped the bleeding. She's stable—for now."

Movement behind me caught my eye. I looked away from my mom to see Matilda, moving my father's body trying to pry the Lifestone from his hand. Without thinking I lifted my foot and kicked her right in the side of the head. Tremors from the impact traveled up my leg and into my hip. I got her good. She fell over on her side, cursing, holding her head in the spot where my foot hit it.

"Don't touch my dad!" My throat burned from the yelling and ragged breaths I kept inhaling.

It was unnatural how fast Matilda recovered, standing quickly, facing me with vengeance in her eyes. Everett emerged behind me, grabbing my arms, pulling me back against him.

"You little harpy." Matilda separated her feet and put her hands in front of her, a stance that certainly meant attack. She snarled, green poison dripping from her teeth. In the next second she lunged, fiery red hair flowing behind her, her mouth open, ready to take a chunk of flesh out of me.

Time slowed. Everett flung me aside, into the hallway, leaving himself in her path. My back hit the wall with a thud, and I watched as Matilda flew straight for him. He growled, crouching with his hands in front of him, ready to fight her.

Without warning, a gale force wind hit Everett's body, pushing him into me, his massive body smashing me against the wall he'd just tossed me against. Matilda landed in the open space where Everett had been standing, missing her target. She twisted around, looking for where the wind had come from, and her eyes landed on her daughter.

Matilda was shaking, her body filled with anger. "You have air magic?"

Dafni raised her head and looked at her mother. "Yes, Mother, I do. You would have known that had you spent any time with me when I was growing up."

"It doesn't matter. A witch without poison is worthless," she spat. "I would've wasted any time I spent with you."

Dafni cleared her throat. "Just because I don't have poison doesn't mean I'm less than or not worthy." Her voice was stronger than before, her eyes focused. She stood a bit taller too, drawing her shoulders back.

"I should've killed you when I ended your grandmother," Matilda sneered.

Hissing, Dafni extended her index and middle finger slowly, like a cowboy would draw his gun in a duel. "Don't talk about my grandmother."

Matilda paused, tilting her head to the side as she stared at Dafni, almost as if she was perplexed by her daughter's words. Taking advantage of her mother's pause, Dafni flicked her wrist, sending a gust of wind at her mother, but Matilda jumped out of the way just in time. The wind hit a painting behind her, causing it to fall off the wall, the glass shattering when it hit the ground.

"You'll have to be faster than that, witchling," Matilda

taunted, jumping out of the way as Dafni's wind blasted several times in a row.

Dafni snarled in frustration before picking up the speed of her strikes. Her mother was jumping around the room quickly, dodging wind gusts that hit the walls, chipping paint and blowing down frames. Mid-jump, Matilda transitioned back into Bessie, making herself a smaller target, harder for Dafni to hit.

The girl was focused and better with her magic than her mother assumed her to be. With cat agility, Matilda leaped along the furniture and landed on the sill of the bay window by the kiln. She stood there, claws digging into the wood of the sill, tail erect, and her ears pinned back.

Dafni took a quick glance at the kiln and then at the bucket of water next to it. She took a breath, before she sent a powerful gust of wind flying across the room to where Matilda was standing, her tail to the window. The wind whistled through the air before it hit the glass of the window.

With nowhere to go, the wind ricocheted off the window, pushing Matilda off the windowsill and into the bucket of water headfirst. Orange fur hit the water, splashing drops out of the top of the bucket and onto the floor. Her orange tail was the last thing to be submerged in the water. Everett and I were quiet, our eyes on the bucket.

Creaking and groaning sounds came from the bucket. It almost sounded like...ice.

"I also have water magic," Dafni said, panting with the amount of effort she'd just exercised.

Everett released some of the pressure against my body by pulling away from me slightly. I let my lungs fully expand as I took a breath.

"Is she..." I looked back and forth between Dafni and the bucket.

"She isn't dead. It takes a lot more than ice to kill a witch," Dafni said. Everett grunted in agreement. "I'll just have to keep her in an icebox."

She sent a gust of wind over to the frozen bucket, and it fell over on its side. The large ice cube in the shape of the bucket slid out and skimmed across the floor before stopping. In the middle of the cylinder of ice was Bessie, or Matilda, suspended in the ice, her claws extended, her tail fluffed from the shock of hitting the water. Although frozen, her eyes were open, her diamond cat pupils dilated. *Can she still see?* I wondered.

Dafni walked over to the ice cylinder and crouched down next to it. "Don't worry, Mother, I'll put you next to the frozen frogs I keep in the icebox."

Time resumed at a normal speed, and what had just happened suddenly flooded back to me, overwhelming me.

"Mom!" I pulled away from Everett to check on my mother. Her chest moved up and down, she was still breathing. Blood covered the back of her shirt, seeping into the fabric along the sides of her body.

"I'm fine. I just need a little help to get up," she said. She spoke like she was in pain. I looked back at where my dad lay, still unconscious on the ground. From where I was crouching next to my mom, I could see his chest rising and falling. He was still alive.

I can only do one thing at a time.

I put one of my hands on her shoulder and the other on her elbow. Everett was by my side in an instant, grabbing the same places on the other side of her body. The stone tree had luckily only impaled her along the top of her back, missing many vital organs. The wounds didn't seem terribly deep. On the count of three, Everett and I slid my mother's body from the sharp spikes of the tree. She groaned, clenching her teeth together.

We carefully laid her on her stomach on the wood floor. It

wasn't the comfiest spot, but we didn't want to move her more than necessary.

Fresh blood bubbled from her wounds, staining her shirt further. I grabbed my backpack from beside the door and dug through it to find the herbal supplies I needed. There was a container of yarrow paste and some gauze. It seemed so long ago that I'd been researching the rot. My time with the university might've been over, but I had a new use for my knowledge and research. The shifters needed me, as did my mother right now.

Everett whispered into my mother's ear, and she nodded before he used two hands to rip my mother's shirt open, revealing the puncture wounds along her upper back.

"I never imagined you would ever rip off *my* clothes." My mother's words were muffled, her cheek pressed against the floor, but everyone heard them. Everett chuckled in disbelief while I rolled my eyes. She was fine, still making uncomfortable jokes.

I pulled out a bit of yarrow paste and packed it in her wounds, stopping the bleeding. Unrolling the gauze, I wrapped it around her body, carefully lifting her head and chest to not cause her pain. All this time, Everett held her hand, comforting her.

We pulled her into a seated position, with Everett's chest acting as a back rest behind her.

Mom shooed me away. "Go check on Dad. I'm fine."

I ran over to where he lay. His skin was still pale, but some color had returned to his lips. His hand was limp when I picked it up, holding it between my own, although his fingers were warm. *A good sign.*

"Dad..." I whispered, giving his hand a squeeze. "It's over; Matilda's contained."

His lips parted, and his eyelids twitched before they

opened, his lungs drawing in a large breath of air. As quickly as his eyes opened, they closed, his body falling limp again.

I could hear my heartbeat in my ears.

No.

He'd made it this far—it wasn't going to end like this. I didn't know what I was supposed to do. I twisted my head around, looking over at my mom and Everett and then at Dafni, where she stood next to the ice block that held her mother. Dafni had her head cocked to the side, staring. Her eyes met mine and she instantly snapped out of the daze, and in a few quick steps she was crouching down on the other side of my dad.

Delicately, Dafni unfurled each of his fingers, revealing the wolf statue, the Lifestone, in his palm. She picked it up, rolling it around in her fingers. My father visibly breathed easier, color returning to his skin as soon as the stone lost contact with his body.

"Roger!" my mother cried out. Everett picked her up effortlessly, carrying her in a cradle hold over to Dad.

Dafni flitted out of the way as he placed Mom gently on the floor next to Dad. She reached out and grabbed ahold of his other hand, the one that'd held the stone.

My father opened his eyes, looking around the room, then at me and my mom holding his hands. Color flowed into his face, the hollows beneath his eyes filling back in. "It's over?" he asked.

Mom nodded, squeezing his hand. "It's over, Roger. It was that damn cat and that damn stone the entire time."

"I feel better," he said.

She brought his hand to her lips, kissing the inside of his palm. "You're looking better."

There were footsteps behind us. I turned around, finding Dafni standing close. I held my breath as she glanced down at me and flinched as she extended her arm, opening her hand. There, in her palm, was the Lifestone. "I think this is better off with you than it is with me."

I looked back at Everett before I picked it up out of her hand. As soon as the stone touched my skin, I could feel it pull, draining energy from my body. Immediately I felt fatigued. Why hadn't I noticed this feeling in the past weeks? I'd had the stone in my pocket often. Thinking back, I had felt more tired, especially on my run when I'd found Pumpkin—or, should I say, Dafni. Maybe the pull was like inertia. It had been draining me at such a steady pace that I hadn't felt it consistently pull from me.

My dad cleared his throat. "Promise me you won't hold onto the stone. It'll drain you, just like it drained me."

I nodded my head. The stone was going back into the woods—where it belonged.

He closed his eyes, and I squeezed his hand. "Don't worry about me," he said. "I'm just going to rest my eyes." I squeezed his hand one more time before letting go.

Everett was by my side, his hand rubbing my back before scooping my father into his arms, turning to carry him to the bedroom. Dad had gotten so small since the last time I'd seen him.

I looked down at the Lifestone in my hand. This stone was dangerous if held in the wrong hands. It could destroy a body, a life, someone's loved one. It was potent. I shivered as I felt it pulse.

"That stone's powerful," Dafni said. "Its influence shouldn't be underestimated."

I nodded in agreement. "It'll be returned to where it belongs."

Dafni bent her head down, her lips pursed. She turned around, walking away.

"What will you do now?" I asked. I'd found her in the woods as a kitten, had fed her and cared for her. I felt some obligation to make sure she was okay, even in her current form.

Dafni stopped, turning her head to answer me. "I will not let my fate be determined by the circumstances I was born into. I might not have poison, but I'm still a witch." She glanced down at the ice that contained her mother. "A damn good one." Dafni looked back up at me, a new confidence gleaming in her eyes, making her seem older and wiser than the scared young girl she'd been when this had all started. "My mother's Coven is suddenly without a leader."

With a few twists of her wrist, Dafni tied her curly red hair back, pulling it tight before she lowered her arms, clenching her fists at her side. "I will take back what is rightfully mine."

I wanted to hug her, but she wouldn't be that soft fluffy poof ball I was used to. This kitten had claws. She would be okay.

Dafni slid her mother back into the five-gallon bucket and picked up the bucket by the handle. With a flick of her wrist, she sent a gust of wind that opened the front door. Wilder made a shrieking sound as Dafni got close. I'd forgotten he was there.

She paused for a moment and looked down to the floor where Wilder's fangs were still stuck. "I'd leave you here, stuck in the floor, but I'm not my mother." She pointed two fingers at the frozen bucket, a stream of liquid water drawing up into the air. When the stream was six inches long, her eyes narrowed, and she bit her lip as she flicked her fingers again, sending the water spinning.

The house filled with a kind of white noise, the rushing twister of water moving toward Wilder. His eyes grew large, and snot dripped out of his nose as he cried out—his mouth opening wide—although no one could hear him over the sound of the water. With a final flick of her wrist, Dafni sent the twister barreling at Wilder. It sliced through his fangs, cutting them below his bottom lip.

The twister stopped spinning the moment it cut through the second fang, the water falling to the floor with a loud *splat*. Wilder tripped backward, away from where the fangs still jutted from the floor. His hand slapped against his mouth, feeling the rough edge of the cut fangs.

Dafni brushed a curl from the sweat along her brow. "My kindness is *also* fleeting." She took a step toward Wilder. "The next time I see you, I'll end you."

He stumbled back, away from Dafni, only stopping when his back hit Everett's chest. "You won't be seeing Wilder around here anytime soon." Everett grabbed hold of his triceps, leaning in close to his ear. "I, the True Alpha, reject your membership to the Cedar Moon Pack."

Wilder let out a gasp, his knees buckling. Everett guided him past Dafni and out the front door, giving him a push. Wilder toppled down the stairs and began running as soon as his feet hit the ground. He didn't look back once before he disappeared into the trees.

Everett reentered the house, his eyes bouncing between Dafni and me.

She nodded at him and then looked back at me, a slight smile on her lips. It was the first time I'd seen something resemble happiness on her face. Happiness and hope looked good on her.

Holding the bucket in one hand, Dafni walked through the open front door without stopping. I rushed out to the porch and held my hand up in a wave.

Halfway down the driveway, she turned and looked at me, her eyes glowing with the same orange Pumpkin's had been. With a flick of her wrist, she took some ice from the bucket and sent it my way. Cold flakes fluttered down from above me, collecting in my hair and landing on my nose. I looked up to see a personal cloud of flurries above me, just like from the day I'd found her. Dafni smiled and nodded her head as if to thank me.

I looked down at the Lifestone in my hand, still humming, draining me. With what was in my hand, we could finally rid the forest of the rot. I'd return it to the tree as soon as possible and heal the forest.

At the beginning of the summer, I never thought I'd be here. Saying goodbye to a witch, one frozen and one...not frozen. Having a shifter as a mate—heck, becoming a shifter myself. Holding the key to solving the mysterious rot in the forest in the palm of my hand.

I'd always imagined myself at a university—working in a lab, going on expeditions to gather samples. But that wasn't what happened. Instead, I'd made my way into these woods, finding not only the plant life I'd dreamed of discovering but friends who'd turned into family. And that was enough. I didn't need the fame or the glory of becoming published or presenting at a big conference. I had everything I needed right here—in these woods.

I closed my eyes and tilted my face toward the sky, letting the cold snowflakes fall onto my face. This was right where I needed to be.

EPILOGUE 1

Elise

Kleio had conveniently reminded me this morning that it was Everett's birthday. I reprimanded myself for not remembering or getting him some sort of gift, although I wouldn't even know where to shop for a shifter. Maybe Kleio had an idea. Belated gifts were still good, right?

He was busy doing alpha things this morning, so we'd made plans to meet at the tree later this afternoon. Now I held the stone in my hand, letting it hum and pull energy from me for the last time. Soon it would be back in the dirt, back where it belonged. Hopefully, the forest would heal when it was returned, bringing life back to the woods. The rot had only gotten worse since I'd been here. The ground was brown as far as I could see, no new sprouts poked up from the soil, no crisp green leaves. Just brown.

Everett walked through the trees with a huge smile on his face. I wasn't sure if the smile was because he saw me or that we were finally returning the stone to the tree. I'd take either.

"Are you ready?" he asked, framing my face with his hands. His golden eyes swirled with hope. I nodded my head. He kissed my forehead before walking with me up to the tree. It was just how I remembered it, the empty hole that had been filled with my blood. I shuddered, remembering how Everett's father had drained me.

"Let's fix the imbalance, Lyka." Everett stood behind me, rubbing my arms in support.

Slowly, I kneeled, holding the stone with both hands. It vibrated in my palms, like it anticipated its return to the earth. Dust puffed up from where I kneeled, the brown matter floating down slowly to the ground. I looked back up at Everett. He nodded. He was ready.

Like a magnet, the stone snapped back into its place in the earth as soon as I set it down. The earth around me moved, a wave emanated from the tree, lifting me up and back down as it radiated from around the tree out into the forest. My hands fell to the ground as I braced myself. Everett stood with his feet farther apart and his arms out, having almost lost his balance from the wave.

Behind me the earth continued to ripple, the movement traveling out into the woods. The skin between my fingers tickled, like a feather had brushed against them. Tiny green shoots pushed up from between my fingers, opening their leaves to the sunshine. More shoots sprouted around my knees, their leaves tickling my skin.

I stood up on my knees and turned around. Green appeared around Everett's feet. We looked out into the forest, following the wave of green that was covering the forest floor. Our eyes met, smiles on our faces.

"Happy birthday, Everett."

If this wasn't the best birthday gift I could give him, I didn't know what would be.

EPILOGUE 2

Gideon

OUR FOOTSTEPS ECHOED DOWN THE HALLS OF THE COVEN. Robinson walked faster than me, his shiny black boots hitting the floor in a rhythmic pattern.

My steps were more muffled, less assured. Like my feet didn't want to follow him down the hallway, into his room for our weekly *male meeting*.

Robinson looked forward to our weekly time together. He enjoyed lecturing me, giving me "advice," preparing me for my approaching new role in the Coven.

I had no choice but to follow him. Listen to him. Sit there once a week for our two-hour meetings while he prepared me to be the newest procreating male witch in the Coven. Although he used words like *breeding* and *impregnate*. There really wasn't an appealing word for it—for what I'd be expected to do after the Autumn Equinox.

I was already twenty years old. A full-grown male witch, but witches loved ceremonies and traditions. I wouldn't be expected to...participate until after my "coming out" ceremony on Autumnal Equinox.

So, I still had time.

I was going to get out of here before any of what Robinson had lectured me about could occur.

"Gideon!" His voice startled me, and I looked around. We were already in his room. He pulled out two chairs from the small table in the corner. He had a bigger room in the Coven, and that came with certain amenities.

Where will I live after the Equinox? I wondered. I'd be out of the dorms—where I lived in the Academy.

No. There was no use in even thinking about it. I was going to escape this underground prison—soon.

Did I have a plan? No. They kept the witches at the Academy underground. I'd only been outside once in my life, as an infant when I'd been brought to the Academy. Male witches were rare. So rare that my own mother wasn't allowed to raise me—the witches at the Academy did instead.

I sat down in the chair Robinson had offered me, trying to get comfortable in this entirely uncomfortable situation.

"Matilda still hasn't returned," Robinson said after he'd lowered himself into his chair, letting out a "Humph" as his knees bent to sit. She had been gone for a while now. Longer than usual, but it still wasn't entirely unusual for her. She was known for disappearing—doing outside work for the Coven. "Everyone in the Coven is getting nervous. Some are saying she won't return."

I scoffed, kicking at the laces of one of my boots that'd become untied on my long walk from the Academy.

"Do you think it's funny, Gideon, that our leader's missing?"

Here we go. Robinson was beginning his patronizing lectures early this time.

"She'll be back," I said. "She always comes back."

"This time could be different. Matilda could really be gone." Robinson swung one of his ankles over the top of his bent knee, the fibers in his khaki pants stretching to their limits. He grabbed onto the hem of his pants, pulling his ankle up farther onto his thigh. I could almost hear his pants groaning in protest. "I think it's time we talk about the future, Gideon."

"We always talk about the future," I said.

"This time we need to talk about a future where Matilda doesn't return. A future where you and me, the two male witches, take over control of the Coven."

"What if I don't want that?" I asked. Being a male witch in a female-dominated Coven, had its advantages—don't get me wrong, but I didn't feel that pull, that need for power.

"Why *wouldn't* you want that?" Robinson asked. Now satisfied with the placement of his ankle, he used his fingers to smooth his mustache. "The power, the dominance, the control? We could do great things, you and me. With the two of us, we could grow the Coven to numbers never seen before."

I kept quiet. I'd learned from a young age there was no use in arguing with him.

"I think it's time we start making some moves," Robinson said, "assert our control."

I needed to get out.

THANK YOU

Did you enjoy *Shadows in the Woods?*

If you did, please leave a quick review on Amazon. Reviews are crucial to independent authors like me. Your review also helps other readers find books they love!

Thank you,

Evi James

ALSO BY EVI JAMES

The North Woods Series

Entangled in the Woods

Magic in the Woods

ACKNOWLEDGMENTS

The second book should be easier, right? In some ways it was easier to write, and in other ways it was more challenging. I wanted to give readers a satisfying sequel to *Entangled in the Woods* while still leaving the door open—giving readers a glimpse into the last two books in the series. I hope I accomplished both.

To my fairy godmother editor Mandi: Thank you, thank you! Without you, Everett would've gone down a dark path and the Subaru would've been lost forever. (Among many other things...)

I can't tell you how much I enjoy working with you—this shifter romance series would be a mess without you! Here's to the final two books in this series...and maybe a new era of Evi James romance books in the future.

To my readers: Your support and excitement over this series has meant the world to me. It makes my day, every day, when someone reaches out to me about these books.

ABOUT THE AUTHOR

This is Evi's second novel. Her first, *Entangled in the Woods*, was published in October 2024.

Evi lives with her husband, two daughters, and a clingy cat in Minnesota.

Website: www.evijamesauthor.com

9 798991 198837